THE NINTH DISTRICT

FBI THRILLER - BOOK 1

DOUGLAS DOROW

D1301998

The Ninth District

An FBI Thriller

© 2011 Douglas Dorow

ISBN 978-0-9994862-0-7

ABOUT THE NINTH DISTRICT

The Federal Reserve has never been robbed.

FBI Special Agent Jack Miller, pulled into a high-profile case to mentor a new agent, finds himself in a clash with the toughest opponent of his career.

The chase culminates in the bowels of the city; the storm sewers and tunnels beneath The Ninth District Federal Reserve of Minneapolis.

What others are saying about THE NINTH DISTRICT:

ThrillersRockTwitter declares THE NINTH DISTRICT is one of the top 3 Indie Thrillers of 2011!

Douglas Dorow debuts with a fantastic new FBI thriller! ... Fans of Crime Drama will be happy to welcome Douglas Dorow into the fold! -- *NovelOpinion.org*

Suspense, intrigue and dazzling plot twists power this tale

of an FBI special agent and rookie investigator racing through the darkest layers of Minneapolis to chase a sinister Federal Reserve robber. -- *Book Bub*

For updates on new releases, exclusive promotions and other information, sign up for <u>Douglas Dorow's Thriller Reader list</u>

1

The woman stood in the middle of the bank atrium. She stood there with a look of anguish on her face, staring at the gun pointed at her, and moved her hands to her mouth and to her stomach and ended up with one hand over each. She was in her early thirties, dressed in black pants and a striped top with sleeves to the elbows. She had dark, shoulder-length hair held back by a white headband and she was pregnant. She looked close to term the way her stomach stretched the shirt. She shook her head back and forth, her eyes never leaving the gun.

A man in a long, black trench coat stood in front of her and motioned with the gun for her to move towards the rear of the bank. She didn't move. He finally pointed the gun at her stomach and motioned with his head for her to move. The woman wrapped her arms around her belly to protect her unborn child before moving in the direction he'd indicated. The man followed and reached out and pushed her shoulder with his gloved left hand to move her along. His right hand held the gun, pointed at her back. The woman stumbled, and shook her head back and forth; her shoulders hitched up and down as she struggled against the tears. She trudged ahead. They disappeared as they turned left around the corner into a hallway, first the woman, and then the man.

Later, they came back around the corner, the woman again in the lead. The man had a black computer bag slung over his shoulder. The woman walked to the desks in the middle of the bank lobby atrium and turned towards the man. She was crying and repeating "I don't know" as she stared at the gun pointed at her unborn child. The man's right arm raised and pointed at her head. She repeated the words.

The man took a step forward and pressed the muzzle of the gun against her forehead to emphasize his point.

The woman stepped back and raised her hands up. "I don't know," she shouted in three deliberate words. There was a puff of smoke and the woman's head rocked back before she fell, her hair billowing up and following her down to the floor.

The man stood with the gun pointed out for a couple of seconds before lowering it. He looked down at the woman, then walked over and nudged her with his foot. The smoke from the shot hung in the air of the lobby and swirled over the spot where the woman had fallen. He knelt and put his hand on her belly, held it there for a count of three. Then he stood. He turned towards the exit without looking back at the pregnant woman lying dead on the floor with blood pooling around her head. As he approached the door, he looked up at the camera posted over it and gave a little salute.

"FREEZE IT!" Staring out from the television was the face of a bank robber, a killer, in a mock salute. "What the hell? Is that who I think it is? Rewind it and play it again."

"Jack, I've watched this ten times and there's nothing there, nothing but that salute."

"Rewind it. I want to see it again." Jack pointed at the flat screen television on the wall and worked his thumb up and down against the imaginary remote in his hand. "Come on, let's go, Junior. I want to see it again."

"It's Ross."

Jack glanced back at Ross and then stared at the screen, waiting for him to play it again. "Listen. The SAC asked me to help you. I'm here to help. Let's watch it again."

Jack Miller was in no mood for a pissing match with a new agent who had four months in the Minneapolis FBI office after graduating from Quantico. The Special Agent in Charge assigned Jack to help with this case so he could tell the media he had his most experienced agent looking into solving the string of bank robberies, especially the last one that had resulted in a murder.

Ross pointed the remote at the television and the video started again. "These bank videos suck. We're bringing in video from the other cameras at the bank, the ATM, the highway traffic cameras, and gas stations within a two-mile radius. I know it's the same guy."

"OK, so what do we know about him?"

"He's on a schedule. March, he hit a Wells Fargo branch in Duluth. April, he was at the Stillwater branch. I was looking for a May job and found one in Wisconsin after talking to the Milwaukee field office. This morning, as you see him here, he was at the TCF Bank in Wayzata. That's the June robbery." Ross paused, inhaled, and audibly exhaled. "And no, that's not who you think it is. It's a guy, or a person, wearing a mask that kind of resembles a former Governor of the State of Minnesota."

"OK, so we know what he's done, but what do we know about him?"

"We don't know anything about him other than he's been robbing banks and wears a mask," Ross said.

"Let's call him the Governor. He hasn't killed anybody before, has he?" Jack asked.

"Nobody has even been hurt, until now."

"Play the video." Jack Miller stared at the screen and watched the scene unfold a second time; he rested his chin in his hands, elbows on the table. He looked for details as he watched it again.

When it was over, Jack was talking softly to himself as much as to his new partner. "Why did he kill her? He hasn't done that before. There was no reason to kill her. And what's he asking her that she doesn't know?" He shifted in his chair, raised his arms, and locked his fingers together behind his head. "Rewind it. Let's see it again."

Jack got up from his chair and paced the room while he continued mumbling to himself. "For the money?" He looked at Ross. "How much has he been getting?"

Ross reflexively patted his pockets for his notebook.

"Junior, just give me a rough idea."

Ross stared at Jack without answering.

"Agent Fruen?" Jack asked.

Ross nodded and answered. "He's grabbed between five hundred and five thousand and a couple of laptops."

Jack returned to his monologue and paced around the table. "So, he's not getting rich doing this." He stopped and sat down in his chair. "What's with the mask? And why's he robbing these banks? A drug user would still be sleeping." Jack looked up at the ceiling and raised his voice so Ross could hear him. "Did you check out the casinos or the card room at the Canterbury race track?"

"That's one theory for the mask. He doesn't want us comparing videos. I'm working on it, checking on casinos in the area."

"Don't forget Wisconsin. OK, Junior, so why did he kill her?"

Ross didn't answer until Jack stared at him. "I don't know."

"Well, what's your guess?"

"I'd guess he killed her either because she knew something, who he was or what he was doing there, or she was at the wrong place at the wrong time, or just to do it."

"Tell me about her."

Ross pulled his notes out and paged back to the information. "Her name is, was Lisa Humphrey. She's worked at the bank for eight years and had experience in different areas. She was there this morning to open up, get things ready for the day."

"Did she have a family?"

Ross flipped forward a page. "She was married. The husband's devastated. There's a two-year-old girl at home and," Ross paused.

"And what?"

"You saw she was pregnant. It was a boy. Due in about two weeks."

Jack shoved himself back from the table and stood up. As he made his way to Ross at the back of the room, he pushed a chair out of the way, sending it rolling across the floor until it struck the wall and fell over on its side. Ross didn't move. Jack stuck out his hand.

"Give me your notes." Ross handed the notes over and

Jack walked to the window and leaned against the wall as he reviewed what Ross had written.

As he looked over the pages, Jack thought of his own kids, a girl and a boy, a couple of years apart. He looked at his reflection in the window and then out at the world a few floors below. "Damn it."

Jack walked back over and sat at the table. He closed up the notebook. "We don't know much, do we? Get the files from the other three robberies up here." He slid Ross' notes back across the table to him and rocked back in his chair. "And we need some analysis done. You're on the right track getting all of those other videos from cameras around the area. I want to know all I can about this guy. I want to know for sure it's the same guy. Get the geeks on it. We need to know how he got to and from the bank, his height, weight, color of his eyes, type of clothes, shoe size, how big his hands are, and the length of his stride, anything to help ID this guy. Tell them I want to know everything. What he had for lunch, if he prefers boxers or briefs. And make sure those lab guys check her forehead. He had his gun pushed up against her forehead."

Jack rocked forward and worked the imaginary remote in his hand again. "OK, let's see it again."

Ross hit play on the remote control and the video started for the third viewing. His thumb hovered over the pause button, ready for when Jack wanted to stop it again. He fumbled for the phone with his other hand, not taking his eyes off the picture in front of him.

Cradling the receiver between his ear and shoulder, he dialed an extension with his free hand. "Hello, Barb? Yeah, it's Ross. Jack and I are in the back conference room. We need the files from the Duluth and Stillwater robberies we were talking about earlier. Bring them in as soon as..."

"Freeze it!"

"...you're ready."

"You missed it."

Ross exhaled heavily in frustration, hung up the phone and hit pause, and then rewound the video frame by frame.

"There," Jack said.

Ross paused the video. "What?"

Jack got up from his chair and approached the screen. He looked at it straight on, squinting, and traced the face on the screen with his finger. The killer was saluting him, the eyes staring right at him. Jack stepped back trying to take in more of the picture.

"Get some stills made of the mask that show it from different sides and figure out who made it, where it's sold, how long it's been around, etcetera, etcetera. He didn't just go pick this mask up at the mall off the rack. This one's too good. Send a photo to the costume department at the Guthrie Theater and the U of M theater department. Maybe they'll have some ideas. And print one off for me, the one where he's saluting. Make yourself one too if you want one." He rubbed his hands over his face and stretched. "I'm going to go take a leak and get some other work done. Call me when you've got everything ready. It's almost July. We better get busy and solve your case before the next robbery."

2

J ack sat in his cubicle and looked at the pile of case folders in front of him. It was time to catch up on his active cases while he waited for Ross to pull the other videos together for the next viewing. He grabbed the top folder, laid it on an open spot amid the clutter on his desk, and started to flip through it. He made it two pages into the details, refreshing himself on the follow-up issues, before his mind drifted to the images on the video. It was hard to watch somebody being killed and not be able to stop it. That was the tough part of the job. As FBI agents, they were brought in as a reaction to something bad having happened. This was no different. Learning that this victim had a family, Jack thought of the father with a daughter at home, his world turned upside down. The killer had pulled the trigger and gone about his business. Jack wanted to get ahead of this guy and stop him before something else like this happened again.

He looked at the framed pictures on his desk. They had been there long enough that he almost forgot they were there. Jack picked up the one that had both kids in it, brushed off the dust from the edges of the frame and the glass, and smiled. He could remember Julie taking the picture last summer. The kids went from running through the sprinkler to starting a water fight, with him as the target as he sat in the Adirondack chair in the shade working on the crossword puzzle. Julie snapped the picture just after he had grabbed the kids and pulled them onto his lap. They'd squealed and laughed. The newspaper was soaked and water dripped from his chin. The trio then went after Julie, but she'd claimed immunity as she held the camera in front of her like a shield, knowing they wouldn't dare get it wet.

With the picture in one hand, he grabbed the phone and called Julie. His thumb caressed the kids' faces in the picture as he waited for her to answer. On the fourth ring, Jack was ready for it to go to voicemail. He cleared his throat, preparing to speak, but then he heard a voice.

"Hello?"

Jack cleared his throat again and then spoke in the hushed, hoarse voice used in cubes when the conversation was of a personal nature. "Hey, Jules. It's me, Jack. Just thought I'd call, see what's going on. I wanted to talk birthday plans for tomorrow and about the Fourth, where we all might go to see the fireworks."

"Jack." She paused and continued in a soft tone matching his. "The Fourth, I don't know."

"Come on, Jules. I thought we were still going to try."

"I'm not ready for a big family thing yet, Jack. I know the kids would love to see you. But all of us together. I think it's just too confusing right now."

"Confusing for who? You? Or the kids?"

"Them, me, us. Why don't you plan a birthday outing with them? Let's start with that."

"Sure, Jules. One step at a time. I want to keep things

normal. I'll pick them up tomorrow afternoon about one? I took the afternoon off."

"They'd love it, Jack."

"What about the Fourth? Should we make our annual trip to Nicollet Island? I'm sure they'll have the same family activities and the fireworks display."

"Jack, quit pushing. Let me think about it."

"OK. Think about it." Jack looked at the framed photo in his hand. She said she'd think about it. "Tell the kids I'll see them soon and I want some ideas for where we're going." He looked up and saw Ross standing in the doorway of his cube. "I have to run. Give them a hug for me."

Jack hung up the phone and put the picture back in its spot.

"Birthday, huh?" Ross asked. "How old are you going to be?"

"Older than you."

Ross picked up the picture frame. "These your kids?"

Jack reached up and took the frame from Ross. He blew off the dust clinging to the photo and put it gently back in its spot. "Yeah."

"They have names?"

"Yeah." He looked at Ross and stood up. He'd learned long ago that the secret to getting somebody out of your cube was to get up and walk out. The intruder wasn't going to hang out in your cube without you. Jack walked by Ross and turned down the aisle towards the conference room. "So, everything ready for review?"

Ross took a couple of quick steps to catch up with Jack. "I've got the videos from the other bank robberies ready for us to look at. The surveillance video from this morning is still being picked apart by the boys in the lab. They've started on the stats we talked about to learn more about the guy."

Jack said "Hmm," and kept walking towards the conference room.

Ross kept at his heels. "I'll show you them in order. They aren't much different from the others. A guy in the mask, with a salute to the camera on the way out the door."

They got to the conference room and Jack took a seat. "OK, let's see what we've got."

They watched each of the videos through from beginning to end. Ross pointed out items he thought were of interest from his previous viewings. Jack stayed silent, intently watching each of the scenes unfold in front of him.

"Get these videos to the lab, too," Jack said. "I want to make sure it's the same guy. Same mask. See if they can find anything we didn't see. I know it's not like CSI on TV, but they might be able to find something for us."

Ross pulled the USB drive from the computer and grabbed the file folders. "All right. I'll get them down there. We'll see what results we get from these."

"What's next?" Jack looked at his watch.

"I should look through my notes, finish some interviews, check on the crime scene, touch base with the Wayzata police."

"Are you hungry?"

"I could eat. I skipped breakfast after I got the call this morning."

"Let's go touch base with the SAC and then we'll take a little drive and I'll buy lunch."

Jack led the way down the hall with Ross at his heels. Jack heard a folder hit the floor, but just kept going. He heard Ross swearing behind him after the other folders fell.

"Hey, is he free?" Jack asked the Special Agent in

Charge's administrative assistant who was sitting at her desk. Her name was Barb and she was the gatekeeper for the SAC. Nobody got in to see the SAC without her approval.

Ross joined Jack in front of Barb's desk. "Junior, put everything here on the desk; we'll grab them on the way out."

Barb cleared her throat and stared at Jack.

"I mean, put them on the credenza here behind Barb. Have you two met?"

Ross piled the folders onto the credenza and stuck out his hand. "Special Agent Ross Fruen, nice to meet you, ma'am."

Jack chuckled. "Can we go in, ma'am?"

Barb quickly flipped him off and then waved them through. "Let's go, Junior. Don't be nervous." Jack rapped his knuckles on the open door of the Special Agent in Charge and walked in.

The SAC, Timothy Spilman, just over fifty, had a full head of close-cropped gray hair, reading glasses perched on the end of his nose, and wore a starched white shirt. He looked up as Jack and Ross entered his office.

"Gentlemen, what have you put together so far?" He looked at Jack.

They stood in front of the SAC's desk. Jack was loose, with his hands in his pockets. Ross stood stiffly, almost at full attention, arms hanging straight down at his sides.

"Junior has a good start on this. I'll let him fill you in on the Governor." Jack walked over to the window and took in the view of the neighboring downtown buildings and Mississippi beyond them.

"The Governor?" the SAC asked.

"That's what we're calling him. Go ahead, Agent Fruen."

Ross opened his notebook and cleared his throat. "Well, sir, we've linked four bank robberies together over the past four months. We're pretty sure all four have been committed by the same person wearing the same mask, which appears to be custom made. It's a very good likeness of the governor from a few years back." Ross paused, cleared his throat, and continued.

"The MO is very similar, other than the murder this morning. And he's exhibited the same habit leaving each of the banks."

"What's that?"

"Well, sir, he salutes the security camera as he leaves the building."

"Salutes?"

"Yes, sir. Like this." Ross imitated touching the first two fingers of his right hand to his eyebrow. "Every time."

"Don't publicize that detail. What's next, Jack?"

"It's his case."

Ross glared at Jack, and thought for a second. "I have a couple of interviews I want to follow up on. I'd like to revisit the crime scene and we have the videos from the banks and the surrounding area from the bank this morning being looked at by the lab."

The SAC took off his glasses, leaned back, and looked at Ross. "Sounds like you have a mask, a salute, and nothing else. We're not too close to nailing this guy, are we?"

Ross kept his head up, but his voice gave away his lack of confidence. "No, sir."

"Well, I told you how the media's all over this one. Keep digging. Follow procedure. It's your case, but use Jack's help and experience, don't be afraid to ask questions and bounce things off him." He nodded towards the door. "Why don't you give Jack and me a minute?"

"I'll meet you at the parking lot door," Jack said to Ross.

Once Ross had left, the SAC asked Jack to sit. "Is he up to this?"

Sitting in the comfortable chair, Jack thought of his first field office assignment. He was Junior once; a fresh agent full of confidence, wanting to prove himself, looking for that case that would make a difference and help accelerate your career. This was one of those.

"Sure. He's full of energy, smart, wants to do well. He'll nail it, but it's going to take some time." Jack leaned forward. "This guy in the mask is smart, but he's cocky. That's how we'll catch him."

"Jack, I know you'll support Ross and help him out. But, if he's not up to it, you have to step in. This one is going to get noisy. Nobody likes multiple bank robberies; throw in the murder in Wayzata, politicians will start talking, and Washington will call me. We don't need that. You need to catch this guy before he robs another bank or kills somebody else. It's starting this afternoon with a news conference in Wayzata. I want this to be an FBI case; don't let the police take it. Our spokesperson will be there, but keep this one on our side. The bank robberies are ours and we'll help with the murder investigation too." He turned and looked out the window. "Are you doing OK, Jack?"

"I'm doing OK."

"This case can be a springboard, Jack. Things are good here, not that I want to lose you, but this case can do something for your career."

Jack was surrounded by the SAC's hall of fame; pictures on the wall with politicians and celebrities. He had comfortable chairs, four walls, and a door. Jack thought about his cube and his call with Julie.

"I know it'll be under the microscope. I'll work with Junior and we'll get this guy."

"OK." The SAC leaned forward on his desk. "You and Julie OK? This job can be hell on relationships."

"We're working on it." Jack stared at the SAC. "Why, did somebody say something?"

"Just noise."

"We're fine."

The SAC waited a couple of beats for Jack to go on. Jack stayed quiet and they stared at each other. The SAC blinked first and turned to some papers on his desk.

"All right, go see if you can help Ross and let me know if you need anything. Anything needs to go public, you work it through our spokesperson. I don't think Ross is ready for the media circus without your guidance, yet. Stay ahead of this one."

Jack got up to leave. When he reached the door, the SAC called out, "Hey, Jack."

"Yeah?" Jack was halfway out the door and turned around.

"Please don't call him Junior in public. And happy birthday."

Jack smiled and gave him a little salute.

3

The heat rippled across the parking lot. Jack stood with his hands in his pockets and looked out the glass door at the parking lot. He reminded himself to check the weather for tomorrow so he could figure out what to do with the kids.

Ross was doing OK with the case so far, but Jack knew he had the experience to teach the new agent something. He could get used to having a junior partner, somebody with energy to do the grunt work. Leave the heavy-duty thinking, theorizing, to him while his assistant ran the errands. He pulled his left hand out of his pocket to check the time. His right hand jingled the change in his pocket. What could be keeping Junior? He thought about the morning, the videotapes, the man in the mask, and the murder. Solving a case was like putting a jigsaw puzzle together. Today they had a few pieces, but a lot were missing. They weren't even sure yet what picture they were trying to create.

The sound of a door opening behind him jarred Jack from his thoughts. Looking back, he expected to see Ross, but it was another agent with a gym bag slung over his shoulder.

"Hey, Jack. No run today over lunch?"

"Not today. I'm following up on a case. You're going to run in this heat? You're nuts."

"That's me. Stay cool."

"Don't forget to drink some water."

The door closed behind the agent and a blast of hot air enveloped Jack in the small entryway. As he watched the agent walk through the waves of hot air rising off of the black pavement, a picture of Clint Eastwood riding off into the desert popped into his head and he whistled the ditty from *The Good, The Bad and The Ugly*. He leaned back against the wall trying to catch the breeze from the overhead vent as he let his mind drift to his kids and plans for the next afternoon. The birthday outing was his tradition and he wanted to make it one they would enjoy, another birthday to remember, a special time with Dad. With this heat, they had two choices, the water-park outside or go somewhere indoors, out of the heat. The kids would probably pick the water park. The door behind him banged open again. Ross interrupted his thoughts as he bounded through the door.

"Afraid to go outside, Jack? Thank God for air-conditioning."

"Just waiting for you. Let's go. I'm hungry."

Ross pushed open the door, the blast of heat greeting them when he opened it. They both audibly exhaled. Out in the parking lot Ross stopped, waiting for Jack to lead the way to his car.

"What's wrong, Junior? Forget where you parked?"

Ross glared at Jack. "Can you quit calling me Junior? It's Ross."

"It slipped out." Jack took a step forward. "Let's go."

"Are we taking your car?" Ross asked. "It has to be newer than mine."

"Exactly why we're taking yours." Jack pointed across the lot. "See that silver spec there?"

Ross walked over to the car and circled it. "This Mercury Cougar? Looks nice. Nice and fairly new." He bent over and peered into the window. "And clean. I bet it still smells new."

"They told me I was getting a new car. The advantages of being a senior agent. What do I get? This. It's newer, but it's small. Look at me." Jack raised his arms up and swept them down like a model showing off clothes. "I need something a little bigger. I feel like a Shriner driving a go-cart when I drive that thing. All I need is the fez."

Ross laughed.

"And try doing a stake-out in that thing. There's no room to move. It's like a space capsule. A couple of hours in that thing and my legs go numb." Jack looked around. The sweat started to trickle down his back. He reached up, loosened his tie, and unbuttoned the top button of his shirt. "No, we're taking your car. Where is it? It has to be bigger than mine." He ran his palm over his forehead, rubbing the sweat back through his hair. "I hope the AC works."

"Bigger's not always better." Ross pulled the keys from his pocket. "It's over here. You can leave your fez behind. There's plenty of room in the blue barge." Jack followed Ross to an older, dark blue, Ford Crown Victoria. "She's not pretty, but she's comfortable. And the AC works."

A small smile broke out on Jack's face. He raised his left hand to his face, kissed his fingers, and gently patted the hot roof of the car. "La Reina," he whispered.

"What did you say?" Ross asked as he unlocked the driver's door. "La what?"

"La Ray Eee Na," Jack said. "It's Spanish for the queen. This is my old car. I called her The Queen, La Reina. I guess it came from Crown Victoria." Jack opened the passenger door to let some of the heat escape. He took off his suit coat, got in the car, and settled into the seat. "I'm not used to sitting on this side in this car."

"You can drive if you want," Ross said as he started the car.

"No, you drive. I've always wanted a driver." Jack threw his coat onto the back seat, reached over to the familiar controls, and turned up the fan for the air-conditioning. He held a hand over the vent, feeling for the cooler air that should be coming out.

"Come on Princess, it's me. I need some cool air here." He looked over at Ross in the driver's seat. "I hope you're taking good care of her." Then he leaned over and peered closely at Ross' face. "Don't you sweat?"

"No. I grew up on the east coast, DC area. This is a normal day for me. I think I'm acclimated. Thin blood."

"Well, I'm hot and sweaty and on top of that, I'm hungry. Let's go get some lunch and some cold ice tea."

"Where to?"

"Drive by your bank, the TCF in Wayzata. We'll get something out there."

Leaving downtown Minneapolis, they headed west on Highway 394. Ross reached into his pocket and put on his sunglasses. Jack sighed.

"What's wrong, Jack?"

"That's what I get for not taking my car. My sunglasses are in the spec."

Ross reached under the seat. "Here, take these. I have an extra pair."

Jack held them up and examined them. They were

runner's glasses, silver wrap-arounds with mirrored lenses. "Thanks, not really my style, but I'll wear them." He slid them on. "How do I look?"

"You're right. They don't really go with the suit."

After driving on in silence, Ross spoke. "I'm Junior and I'm driving La Reina. Does everything have a nickname?"

Jack stared out at the world going by while the passenger-side vent and one of the center vents blew cool air over his face and upper-body. He arched his back to try to get some of the air to circulate behind him to dry his shirt before he answered.

"In the field office, just about everybody has a nickname; some we call them to their face and some are used behind their backs. And some people have names for other things...their cars, their guns."

"What do they call you?" Ross asked.

"You can call me Jack and refer to me as Special Agent Miller," Jack replied. "Others may refer to me with other names of respect." He looked at Ross. "You'll have to find out for yourself."

Ross rolled his eyes and drove on another mile in silence. As they passed under Highway 100, he decided to take another stab at conversation. "Any theories on these bank robberies yet? Anything you want to share? Something pushed your button with the last one. Was it the little girl left behind and the unborn baby brother?"

"Theories? None. None other than this guy is smart. He doesn't think we'll catch him. His little salute tells me that. He's taunting us. And he's got some sort of plan. The mask, the early morning robberies. He isn't some gambler or junkie looking for the quick snatch and run during the day."

"OK, so what's he after? He's hitting banks, but he's not getting a lot of money."

"I don't know. That's what we need to figure out."

Jack reached over and turned on the radio. Heavy metal music assaulted him. He quickly pushed a preset button, looking for his jazz station. Some more testosterone music filled the car. He tried another station, looking for something to match the pace of the drive west as La Reina glided along through traffic. He needed something to think to, music without words.

"Doesn't the driver get control of the radio?"

"Not when I'm in this car." Jack punched another button. "Did you mess with the settings for these buttons?"

"It's my car. I may have changed a few of them. What are you looking for? AM, there's KFAN for sports and fifteen-hundred for talk radio. FM, it's mostly rock with a country station thrown in."

"I'm looking for jazz. Do you know jazz?"

Ross reached over to help but Jack just slapped his hand away. "Keep your eyes on the road."

"Just trying to help. Try button five and then push seek."

Jack pushed the buttons and the sound of a saxophone filled the interior of the car. Jack smiled and closed his eyes.

"I know what jazz is, but not who plays what. Who's this?"

Jack cocked his head and held up a finger, indicating that Ross would have to wait for an answer. His head rolled and bobbed on his shoulders as the sax sailed through another riff building to the climax at the end of the song. "Man, that was good, wasn't it?"

"It sounded good, I guess."

"I guess? Oh, Grasshopper, I have so much to teach you. Not only about bank robbery investigations, but music as well. What else? Women? Sports? You know about sex, don't you?"

Ross laughed. "Let's start with your ideas on this investigation and you can throw in some jazz knowledge. I think I can figure most of the other stuff out on my own." He reached over and turned down the radio.

"I need to learn a little more about my teacher. Tell me about Special Agent Miller. Today, I learned you have a couple of kids. Somebody has a birthday coming up. How long have you been doing this? Take your pick."

At the mention of his kids, Jack started thinking about them again. It tore him up that he couldn't go home and see them at the end of the day. He was really looking forward to spending time with them tomorrow. He loved being with them. They had an outlook on life that made some of the stuff he dealt with day to day seem insignificant, while at the same time helped him understand why what he did was so important. He was glad he had them to help him escape into the other world. Tomorrow was going to be fun.

"Jack?"

"Sorry, I drifted there for a minute."

"So, are you going to tell me something about yourself?"

"I've got two kids. You saw their pictures. They keep me honest. I like to run to keep in shape so I can keep up with them." He looked at Ross. "Your turn."

"Me, hmm. No kids. I'm pretty new to town. Haven't met many people. You know how it goes with this job. Working weird hours. Plus, some people are put off when they find out you're an FBI agent. When I'm not working I like to work out. I'm into triathlons. There's a big one here in Minneapolis as part of the Aquatennial in a few weeks. I'm hoping to find enough time to stay in good enough shape to compete in that one. I'm ready for it. Maybe we could run together."

"When it gets a little cooler."

Jack asked another question to keep Ross talking about himself and added the appropriate nod or grunt when it was required. The jazz playing in the background and Ross' monologue engaged one part of Jack's brain while the other part worked on the case.

"Jack, I've been running at the mouth. Your turn."

"Isn't this our exit?"

"Right." Ross swerved to the right into the ramp that led off the highway, the wheels of the Crown Vic spitting loose stones.

Jack braced himself and leaned into the door. "Geez, Junior."

"Sorry, I guess I wasn't paying attention." Ross stopped the car at the stop sign at the bottom of the ramp. "You had someplace in mind for lunch?"

"Head over to the lake."

Ross drove the car through the streets of Wayzata making his way towards the main street of downtown that ran along a bay on the east end of Lake Minnetonka. Wayzata was a small village about twenty minutes west of downtown Minneapolis. It was a community of upper middle class and above that prided itself on its relationship to the lake and summer. It was a popular spot with its views and docks and was one of the easier communities around the lake to get to from Minneapolis.

"I'd like to show you the site first hand."

"OK," Jack said. "The bank and then lunch."

Ross drove into an open parking spot, put the car in park.

"Wait. When you were here before you concentrated on the bank. Let's sit here for a couple of minutes, look around, then tell me what you see."

Jack left the jazz playing. Ahead of them was Lake

Minnetonka. The afternoon sun reflected off the lake and the small waves that rolled across its surface. The hot weather brought out the recreational users. Speedboats and jet skis cut across the waves leaving behind their wakes. Sailboats were farther out criss-crossing the lake, driven by the breeze.

Between them and the lake were railroad tracks that ran parallel to the shore between the lake and the bank building. The bank building itself looked like it had been by the railroad tracks for a long time, but it was relatively new. It was brick with a steep, pitched roof and old style windows.

Ross was looking off to the left towards the rows of storefronts along the main street of downtown Wayzata.

Jack opened his door and got out of the car. He got his coat out of the back and threw it on to cover his holster. "Ready, Junior? Let's go."

Ross hurried out of the car, locked the door, and ran a few steps to catch up with Jack.

They walked to the entrance of the bank, Ross quickly making his way to the door, all business. Jack meandered, looked at the ground, across the street, stared at the roof, and finally got to the door, hands jammed into the pockets of his pants. They flashed their credentials at the Wayzata police officer waiting at the door and he let them in.

The interior of the bank was dark and eerily quiet. No personal bankers sat at the desks, no tellers were behind the counter, and there wasn't anybody at the information desk. The bank was closed for business until they were through with their initial investigation.

Jack stood silently inside the entrance with Ross a half step back and to his right. Ross turned on the lights and Jack had a strange sense of déjà vu as he looked over the scene, the same scene he had seen in the video many times, from a slightly different angle. "Look familiar?" Jack asked.

Ross answered in the same library voice that Jack was using. "This is weird. We watched that video so many times I'm able to see this with my eyes closed. I'm just waiting for the Governor to walk out from around the corner."

"Well, we're here because there are things we can see here we couldn't see on the tape. Where should we start?"

"Jack, let's go see what's behind door number one," Ross answered in his *Let's Make a Deal* announcer voice. "I want to go see what's down that hallway."

"OK, that's a start. But, here's how I want to do it." Jack grabbed Ross from behind by the shoulders and maneuvered him to the spot they had seen the Governor and Ms. Humphrey on the video. Jack looked back over his shoulder at the camera above the door to make sure they were standing in the right spot.

"I'm the Governor, you're Ms. Humphrey. How much time elapsed from the time they disappeared from view until they came back?"

"Five minutes and forty-six seconds."

"OK, Junior," Jack looked at his watch and pushed Ross in the back like the Governor had pushed Ms. Humphrey. "Let's go see what's down that hallway."

They walked around the corner. "Slow down. You're scared, pregnant, and crying, and don't know where you're supposed to go." The first doorway on their right led to a room with a fax machine, copier, and a supply storage cabinet. Jack glanced in and they kept moving towards the end of the hall. "It was just a few steps from the corner to here. Where do you think they were going?" Jack asked.

"The vault?"

"Walk down to the end of the hall and we'll see how we're doing time-wise."

Standing at the end of the hallway outside of a VP's office, Jack looked at his watch. "OK, twenty-two seconds from the corner to here. Let's say thirty, a minute round trip. Can you do the math, Junior?"

"That leaves four minutes and forty-six seconds for something."

"There's the fax room and a couple of offices. Everything's been processed?"

"Yeah. Her prints are everywhere, but we think she was in this office at the end of the hallway." Ross walked in. "Her prints are all over the arms of the chair in front of the desk, like she was sitting there, and that wouldn't be normal for her."

"Who pushed the chair back in?" Jack stood behind the dark, wooden desk and looked it over. The family pictures sat on one corner. The phone, with a headset, was within easy reach on the left side of the desk. The high-back, leather office chair was pushed into its spot at the desk.

"I'll check and make sure this is how it was found, but it was probably either the victim or the Governor," Ross answered.

"The PC is missing. This one was taken?" Jack asked.

"Yes."

Jack walked to the door. "Let's run through it again, make sure we're not missing something."

4

The deli wasn't crowded so they had their pick of wrought iron tables covered with plastic, blue and white checked tablecloths. Jack picked a table by the window looking out over the street. The plastic utensils and the paper napkins sat at the center of the table in a mason jar with paper menus propped against it.

"Whoever invented air conditioning was a genius," Jack said. He settled into his seat and looked over the menu.

"Have you eaten here?" Ross asked.

"No, but it has to be good. Main street of Wayzata, facing the lake. It wouldn't survive if it wasn't good."

"Hi guys. Can I get you something to drink? Or are you ready to order?" The waitress had her blonde hair tied up in a ponytail and her blue eyes stood out against her tanned skin.

Jack ordered a sandwich and an unsweetened iced tea. Ross ordered a salad and a lemonade. Jack watched the waitress walk back to the kitchen and then turned to Ross.

"What about her? You're new in town and could use a

date. Want me to find out if she's available? Nice tan and looks like she works out."

"Too young and GUD."

"GUD?"

"Geographically Undesirable. I don't date anybody over ten miles away. I may drive this far to take a date out to dinner or for drinks, but I don't drive over twenty minutes on a regular basis to pick up my dates. I don't have the time."

"Picky, picky." Jack looked back towards the kitchen. "Your loss." He settled into his chair, which wobbled as he shifted his weight, and then crossed his arms and directed his gaze at Ross. "So, we know what happened in the bank. We learned a little this morning. What's your theory? How did he leave the bank?"

"What do you mean, how did he leave the bank?"

"By land or by sea?"

Ross thought for a second before answering. "I assumed he drove. It was early morning, nobody around. No reason not to drive."

"You didn't even check the lake?"

"I assumed he drove so we're concentrating on that. But, we're checking the lake. Looking at rentals, reports of stolen watercraft. It's a big lake."

"There are a lot of roads."

Ross replied, "We're checking the videos from the convenience stores, highway traffic cameras, the other banks, and ATMs. They should be done with the analysis in the next day or two." Ross glanced outside. Jack remained quiet.

Ross spoke, facing the window. "I'll get some people to walk the tracks in both directions twice as far as we went yesterday, see if they find anything." He looked back at Jack. "And I'll contact the Sheriff's office to see if any of their boats reported finding anything strange on the lake.

I'll coordinate pulling tapes from stores around the lake and interviewing store owners near the landings and marinas."

"You're learning." Jack looked towards the kitchen at the waitress carrying two plastic baskets with their lunches. "Now observe."

The waitress placed their lunches in front of them on the table. "Anything else you gentlemen need?"

Jack answered. "Well, miss, my friend here is new to town and is trying to figure out where he should live. Do you know this area very well? Have any ideas where he might look?"

"I know there's a realty office down the street here. My mom works there. Ask for Mrs. Whalen. Tell her I sent you. My name's Beth."

"Thanks, Beth. We'll do that right after lunch."

Jack watched the young woman walk away and picked up his sandwich. "You were right, she's too young."

As they ate lunch, they talked about the heat and the lake. They talked about how Ross was going to deal with both in the triathlon after the Fourth. They weren't in a rush, so they ate slowly and motioned to Beth to refill their drinks. Ross was watching the jet skis fly across the lake.

"What do you think is going on over there?" he asked.

Some trucks pulled into the park across the street and stopped under the trees. A van with a satellite dish on top and a logo of a local television news station pulled to a stop at the curb.

Jack leaned back in his chair and watched the activity as the drivers and crews got out of their vehicles.

"Oh, didn't I tell you? There's a press conference this afternoon. I thought we'd observe. Another learning experience for you. We'll hear what questions the press has. See how the Wayzata police chief responds. You can see an FBI spokesperson in action."

Ross glared at Jack. "No, you didn't tell me. What, you forgot? I thought this was my case. I need to know what's going on." Ross pushed his chair back from the table.

Jack stayed seated. "Whoa. What's the hurry? It's ninety-two degrees in the shade." Jack looked at the watch on his wrist. "The press conference starts at three o'clock. Sit down. Have some more iced tea. Observe from this sanctuary and stay out of the heat. We'll go out in thirty minutes."

Ross looked out the window, but didn't move.

"Come on Junior, sit."

Ross remained still. Only his eyes moved as they tracked something as he looked through the window. "It's Ross."

"Come on. Sit down. Let's talk." Jack turned and looked out the window to see what had Ross' attention. Standing next to the news van parked under the trees was a beautiful woman. She was small, slender, Hispanic, with bronze skin and long black hair. Her designer sunglasses hid her eyes, but they complemented her facial features and her hair. She wasn't dressed for physical work, but rather wore a coffee and cream-colored sleeveless top that accentuated the color of her skin and showed off her strong, feminine arms. She moved with grace and energy around the truck as she spoke with a cameraman. Her jewelry, a gold necklace, earrings, and watch sparkled in the sunlight that filtered through the leaves.

Jack stood up and threw some bills on the table. "I guess we're done here." He walked past Ross towards the door, stopped, and looked back. "Junior... Ross, you coming?"

Jack crossed the street, heading straight for the woman as she and her news crew worked on readying the van for the press conference. A couple of cameras lay in the grass, the satellite dish was raised, and cables were pulled from the door. Ross trotted after Jack. "Where're you going?"

"We're going to a press conference, Junior."

"No," Ross grabbed Jack's arm, and nodded towards the woman ahead of them who walked around to the far side of the van. "Where are you going?"

Jack looked at Ross and exaggerated a nod in the same direction. "We're going to a press conference. Let's go."

Jack walked ahead; Ross followed a half step back. The noises of the crews and people preparing for the news conference grew louder and filled the air. When they reached the van, Jack circled it and stopped by the woman they had seen from the deli. She was talking on her cell phone. Ross stayed a few steps back and looked out over the rest of the small crowd of police personnel, maintenance people, and other news crews that had arrived and were preparing for the afternoon press conference.

The woman finished her phone call with a "Ciao" and put her cell phone in her pocket. She turned and saw Jack standing next to her and grabbed his hands in hers.

"Hi, Jack!" She pulled down on Jack's hands to force him lower, leaned forward, and kissed him on the cheek. "Nice sunglasses."

"Hey, Patty. When are you going to admit you're in Minnesota now and adopt our native ways? *Ciao* to say good-bye and a kiss for hello? Come on. What's wrong with see ya' and hi?"

"What's the saying, Jack? You can take the girl out of the country, but you can't take the country out of the girl. I drink your coffee and eat your food; let me hang onto a couple of things from my homeland." She leaned closer, still holding his hands. "Plus, how else am I going to get to kiss you?"

Jack didn't respond. For a second he didn't know what to say. Patty saved him. "Who's this with you?"

"Where are my manners? Junior, come here." Jack pulled his hands from Patty's and put a hand on Ross' shoulder. "Let me introduce you to somebody." Ross stepped over furtively and waited for the introductions. "Patty, this is Special Agent Ross Fruen. Owner of the sunglasses."

Ross' hand shot out in a peremptory move. "Nice to meet you."

Patty shook his hand with her right, but placed her left hand against the back of his right, gently holding his hand between hers.

"Hi, I'm Patty. It's nice to meet you too." She hung on for a few seconds before releasing Ross' hand. "It's too bad we need to be out in this dreadful heat today. I assume you're here for this?"

Jack responded. "This is Ross' case. He's new to our office so I'm assisting, showing him around, making introductions. I thought we'd check out the press conference. Show him how things are done around here." Ross stood next to Jack, staring at Patty through his sunglasses without saying a word.

"So are you part of this, or not?" Patty asked.

"No, we're not part of the press conference. We probably shouldn't even be here. One reason I came over to say hi was to ask a favor." Jack lowered his voice and stepped closer to Patty. The noise from the van and the crews preparing for the conference drowned out Jack's voice so Ross couldn't hear him. "What've we got, about 30 minutes until this starts? Could you have one of your camera guys swing his camera around and see who he can catch on tape before, during, and after the conference?"

"Sure, Jack."

"Ross or I will pick up the tape from the station later this afternoon."

"Or I could deliver it personally," Patty said.

Jack caught the hint but decided to try and stop it now. "You could bring it to the Bureau, but I'd rather we just picked it up."

"I didn't mean the Bureau."

"I know, but that's where I'll be." Jack grabbed Patty's hand, stepped back, and spoke a little louder. "Thanks, Patty, we'd appreciate it. We'll let you get back to work."

Jack stepped over to a clearing in the shade. Ross followed and glanced back at Patty. "She'd get a waiver from the GUD status."

"Well, Junior, maybe next time you can speak up a little more and let her get to know you. The second meeting you may even get a kiss on the cheek."

"What's her story?"

"Remind me on the way back to the office and I'll fill you in. Right now, we need to get to work." Jack stopped in the shade of a tree. "I want to split up and sweep the area, see if we spot anybody that doesn't belong, somebody who is too curious or maybe not curious enough. You'll recognize if somebody doesn't look like they belong. I'll take a stroll through the park and check out the boat docks; you walk back down by the shops across the street, look in the windows, and then swing through the parking lot at the north end of the park."

"I kind of stand out in these clothes. I look like a cop," Ross said.

"That's what we want. We want people to know we're here and we want them to know we're looking at them. Look for the one guy that stands out. The innocent will feel better and maybe the guilty will be nervous." Jack looked at his watch. "Let's meet back by the van here in about twenty-five minutes and catch the conference. See how the Wayzata police look."

The dry grass crunched under Jack's shoes as he walked through the park and meandered through the trees, checking out the crews that were prepping and testing their equipment. On a bench facing the lake, a couple of local older gentlemen were watching the commotion and debating what was going on, guessing who was going to talk and how long it would last.

Jack felt a little breeze off the lake as he approached the dock. He was thankful for the sunglasses, which cut the glare off the lake as the sun moved a little farther to the west. He stopped to admire a couple of the older wooden boats tied up to the dock. A lot of work had gone into their restoration and upkeep. They were beautiful. Not something he'd ever see on his government salary. At the end of the pier, Jack leaned on the railing and looked out over the lake. He looked back and forth, and with each pass his eyes moved out farther on the lake, scrutinizing the riders of passing jet skis, speedboats, and fishing boats. Nothing seemed out of the ordinary. He looked back towards the park and the activity on shore, then back out at the lake.

He tried to guess where their suspect may have gone if he left by boat. Across the lake he could see Excelsior, a small community of shops and restaurants. Staring at the far shore, he looked for the familiar landmarks and thought back to some of his early dates with Julie. They'd drive out to Excelsior beach on a hot summer evening and go for a swim, sit on the beach, and talk, kiss, swim some more. Holding hands, they would walk back through the small downtown and get an ice cream cone or a drink before driving back to the city. The memories were strong and good. He could visualize Julie in her bikini with her tan skin and shiny white smile. But, that was a long time ago. What had happened? He missed her laugh and the touch of her hand.

The chirp of Jack's cell phone brought him back to the present. Pulling it from his belt, he answered, "Miller. I'm out on the dock, Junior. I'll be right there. Sorry I'm late. No, I didn't see anything." Jack ended the call and headed back on the dock towards the park. "Nothing but memories," he said to himself.

5

There was a large white tent set up at one end of the park in the grass. The side of the tent facing the press was open. In it were two long tables, microphones standing in the center of each with cords running across the grass to a control station.

"We're ready to start." The spokesperson leaned forward into the closest microphone and repeated himself. At the tables were three men in a uniform of one type or another and a woman in business dress. Banners hung from the fronts of the tables announcing the offices they represented.

The press milled about on the grass, jockeying for final positions with the start of the news conference. The on-scene reporters lined the front across the grass from the tables, standing in the sun. Their camera personnel hung back and to the sides trying to get the angle and clear shot.

Jack and Ross stood a little further back next to a tree to be close enough to hear, but still be in the shade.

"Pay attention now, Junior. Here's your chance to learn how these things are done. One day you'll be up there for your field office," Jack said.

"OK, ladies and gentlemen, we're ready to start," the man repeated a third time. He looked out at the crowd, cleared his throat, and started.

"Good afternoon, I'm Rick Peterson with the Minnesota Bureau of Criminal Apprehension. With me today I have Chief Wolf from the Wayzata Police Department, Hennepin County Sheriff Palmer, and Special Agent Anderson with the FBI. Please hold your questions until after our update is complete." The four all sat stoically in their chairs while they waited their turn to speak. "Agent Anderson will start things off for us this afternoon."

Agent Anderson leaned forward, swiveled the microphone in her direction, and rested her elbows on the table.

"We're here on a somber occasion after a murder of a bank employee took place this morning. We wanted to quickly get information out to the public. There is a serial bank robber operating in the Twin Cities metro area and it has now escalated from robbery to violence. We will be releasing photos and video and ask that all citizens call in with any information that they feel may be beneficial. The Minneapolis FBI is working with other local law enforcement represented here to find this criminal as soon as possible." Agent Anderson held her stare at the group and then slowly returned to her original sitting position.

The BCA spokesperson took over again and reviewed how they were assisting and explained the roles of the Wayzata Police and the Sheriff's water patrol unit in the investigation.

Jack leaned over to Ross and whispered, "What do you think?"

Ross responded, "She's definitely in control."

"She's not that cold in person, but she's got a role to play and a job to do," Jack said. "They're wrapping up here. Time for them to get hammered with questions from the press. Let's go."

THE SUN WAS at their backs as Ross and Jack headed east on the highway back towards Minneapolis. The car was quiet except for the hum of the tires on the pavement and the fan set on high, blowing the cold air through the vents.

Jack broke the silence. "I guess you have your work ahead of you. The press was rabid for information. You heard them all start shouting questions as we were leaving. They know the public wants somebody to pay for these robberies and the murder of this mother and her baby. Watch the news tonight and you'll see a story you may or may not recognize. People are going to go nuts. When stuff like this happens in a place like Wayzata, nobody feels safe."

"I guess I better get busy. Weren't you going to tell me about Patty from the park?"

"Oh, yeah. You can start with her. I asked her to have her camera guy shoot some footage of everybody around the area this afternoon. She'll have the tape of that and the conference footage that won't make the news available for you at the station this afternoon."

"Great, but what can you tell me about her?"

"She caught your fancy, Junior? Well, you could see she looks great. She's a runner. She's been around the Cities for a few years, I guess. We've run into each other here and there on cases and stories and helped each other out from time to time. I'm not sure of her age, probably too old for you. She's always flirting, using that exotic beauty, her accent, and non-Minnesotan actions like that *ciao* and the kiss on the cheek to show she's different."

"Is she seeing anybody?"

"How would I know?" Jack asked. "I don't think she has time for a relationship. I think she wants to do a couple of big stories and move up to the next big market, either coast or maybe Chicago. A case like this can make it or break it for a reporter. You go see her this afternoon, get the tape, make some connections, maybe get yourself a kiss on the cheek. But remember, she has different motives for investigating and solving this case than you do. Be careful."

Ross laughed. "I can handle her." He drove on, silently looking ahead for a few minutes.

Jack looked at Ross. "What are you thinking about?"

"How many offices have you been in, Jack?"

"This is my third since Quantico. I wanted to start small, away from the Midwest, something different. Why?"

"It's what you said about Patty. Looking for that big story, or for us, that big case. What do a lot of brick agents want? Get lucky enough to get the big case and solve it, do a good job with it and move up to the next big office. I like it here so far."

"You haven't done winter yet," Jack interjected.

"I said, so far. Anyway, I'll get to work with some great people, like you, and learn a lot, but this could be one of those cases...for both of us."

"Junior, one thing you'll learn. Just take them as they come and do your job."

Ross pulled the car into the parking lot back at their office off Washington Avenue. "Thanks for driving," Jack said. "I think I'm going to head home and catch the five and six o'clock news from there. See you back here tomorrow about six thirty to head back out to the bank?"

"You're going home?"

"It's your case, Junior. I have my own. I told Patty you'd swing by and get the tape from the press conference." Jack winked at Ross. "Get the tape, take a break, work out, get ready for your race."

"I think I need to concentrate on this case."

"Take some down time. Let the subconscious gnaw on the details while you do something else. I'm taking a few hours off tomorrow afternoon to spend with my kids if it's OK with you. It's my birthday."

6

L ooking out the window of his condo, the man ate his late supper, some real Italian ravioli with a Gorgonzola and walnut salad from a restaurant down the street. The blend of cheeses in the ravioli melted in his mouth. The soft light of a dozen candles placed around the room was the only light as he listened to classical music and watched the muted television while he waited for the local ten o'clock news.

He often ate by candlelight to eliminate the glare on the windows so he could look out over the city. In the dark, the lights of downtown Minneapolis filled the void with their color. In the distance, the sun had fallen below the horizon and painted the western sky with a reddish glow. Closer, the Wells Fargo tower lit up the dark downtown sky, the lights showing the beauty of fifty stories of sandstone.

His eyes moved from object to object as they had so many other evenings as he looked over the downtown skyline and up and down the Mississippi River. He saw the Metrodome where the Vikings played football, the old mill buildings converted into condos, the Post Office along the west bank of the river, the blue-green lights atop the buttresses, and the lights on the cables of the Hennepin Avenue Bridge, the shortest suspension bridge on the mighty Mississippi. As always, he saved the best for last, his eyes drawn to the final object like a moth to light. On the other side of the bridge was the Ninth District Federal Reserve of Minneapolis. A modern brick building built in 1997, he knew it better than anything else he could see.

Out of the corner of his eye, he saw the transition to the news and turned up the volume of the television. The anchor was throwing out the teaser line before the commercial to keep the viewers from flipping to other channels. "A bank robbery and murder in Wayzata, details when we return."

The lead story covered the morning bank robbery and murder with a short take from the afternoon press conference. Wayzata, an upscale suburb of Minneapolis on Lake Minnetonka, was reeling from the murder. The story ended with a report on the string of robberies attributed to the same person. The anchor looked into the camera as he delivered his plea, "If you have any information pertaining to any of these bank robberies or to the identity of The Governor, please call the FBI at the number listed on the screen below."

At the commercial break, after the news and before the weather, the man swallowed the last mouthful of his favorite Merlot, cleared the dishes from the breakfast bar, and put them in the dishwasher before calling his dog.

"Vince, come on, let's go for a walk!" The golden lab trotted in from the other room where he'd been sleeping and headed for the door, the word "walk" his signal for action. Bending down to scratch Vince's neck, he whispered in the dog's ear. "There you are. Are you ready to go, my friend? Did you hear the news? They're calling me The Governor."

VINCE WAS a recent acquisition from the Hennepin County Humane Society. A two-year-old golden lab who was mellow, loyal to whoever fed and paid any attention to him, and the perfect cover for somebody who wanted to walk through neighborhoods or along River Road without drawing any attention from local residents. If you had a dog, walked it on a leash, and picked up after it, you were assumed to be a nice guy. The Governor had grown to appreciate the unwarranted affection and the company of somebody to listen to his plans, dreams, and accomplishments without interrupting; and he appreciated that he could live without fear of his companion telling anybody else.

Out on the street, Vince sniffed at the air and they headed out on their walk. The wind from the river was warm with the unique smell of the Mississippi, and flowed between the buildings, pushing discarded plastic bags along the ground. "Vince, you know where we're going, right? I just had to get a closer look tonight." As they crossed the Hennepin Avenue Bridge and walked beneath the superstructure, the Governor's pace quickened, along with his heart rate. Vince sniffed his way across the bridge, meandering where his nose took him, marking his territory along the way. As they got closer, the Governor stared at the Federal Reserve building, dreaming of the riches it controlled, both inside and moving between banks. It was an impressive, beautiful building. Its greatness more than beautiful architecture, it also represented money and power.

Arriving on the west bank of the river, they turned to the north, the Governor unable to take his eyes from the building. They didn't linger long. Even with the dog, the Governor didn't stop long enough to draw attention to himself. They had to keep moving. Only the homeless men that hung out on the benches along the bike path were invisible, unregistered by the rest of the population as long as they didn't bother anybody.

"Come on Vince, let's go home." They turned around and headed the other direction to complete their loop.

They headed south to the Stone Arch Bridge to walk back across the river. The bridge was a relic from the days that trains dominated transport of goods into Minneapolis, now converted to a pedestrian bridge. The Governor was deep in thought with his plans on how to penetrate the fortress. Starting across the bridge, Vince pulled on his leash and whined, breaking the Governor's trance.

"Hey, quit pulling."

Vince strained at the end of the leash, pulling the Governor to the side of the bridge, and peered through the railing at something down below. Three figures were clamoring along the bank towards the mill ruins. The Governor and Vince watched the trio dressed in dirty coveralls and tall rubber boots as they disappeared into one of the openings in the riverbank. "Where did they go?"

The Governor completed the loop with his dog and returned to the condo. He gave a couple of Milk Bones to Vince.

"OK, buddy. Take a break. I'll be back in a little while." Vince took the treats over to his dog bed, did the little spin dogs do before they lie down, and finally flopped down to eat his treat. The Governor locked the door and headed down to his car in the parking garage.

Firing up the Mercedes SUV, the Governor headed out and followed almost the same route he had just walked. He parked along the curb on West River Road, just south of the old mill buildings, got out of his car, and pulled a backpack out of the rear of the car. Flinging it over his shoulders, he headed down the bank towards the Mississippi, following the route he'd seen the trio from the bridge take. At the riverbank, he clamored along the edge and entered an opening that looked like a tunnel entrance. Inside, he flipped on his flashlight, shed the pack, pulled out a pair of dirty coveralls, and struggled to pull them on over his clothes. With assured movements that came from frequent practice, he zipped up the coveralls, grabbed a helmet out of his pack, put it on his head, and turned on his headlamp. Leaving his pack and coat along the wall, he looked into the tunnel and proceeded, following the lighted path from his headlamp and the flashlight in his hand.

Even though he was an experienced caver, he always had to focus to get himself to enter a cave, especially alone. He knew where he was going; he'd explored the maze of caves and sewers beneath the city many times. The draw was the beauty and quiet below the streets and buildings of Minneapolis. It was a pleasant place to explore. In the summer, it was cool and in the winter, it was warm with a temperature a constant fifty-three degrees Fahrenheit. Alone in a world of flowstone, mineral deposits, stalactites, and other beautiful, natural geological formations, he was a world away from any problems he had on the surface.

As long as he stuck to the naturally occurring tunnels and stayed away from the sewers, he could have been an explorer in one of any caves around the world. It was the sewers that let you know you were beneath the city. The smell always hit you first. The toilet paper, condoms, cigarette butts, and other junk flowing by in the sewer were additional reminders; that, and the rats.

He walked to the end of the cave, the circles of light from his headlamp and flashlight leading the way, and peered down into the hole he needed to squeeze through. After a couple of deep breaths, he bent over and entered head first, arms over his head, wiggling and pulling his body through the tight opening. He bent his body around the bend, squirmed, and turned, repeating the process until he wiggled his way through. Now, he was ready to belly-crawl through the tunnel. His headlamp lit the path ahead, but he couldn't see more than ten or twelve feet because of the bends in the tunnel. He dragged himself along with his elbows and pushed with his feet and his knees. The tunnel wasn't tall enough to allow him to crawl. He hated this part – the feeling that the ground was pushing in on him with him having nothing other than experience to gauge the distance he had traveled or how much farther he had to go.

With about thirty feet to go, he heard the muffled noise from up ahead. He shuffled and squirmed further, thankful for the noise and for remembering to put on the knee and elbow pads. With ten feet to go, he could see the light and he was able to hear the voices. His helmet bumped and scraped on the top of the tunnel, reminding him he was still in its grip. With five feet to go, he could hear the laughter, see the light, and smell the sweet, distinctive aroma of marijuana drifting up into the tunnel. Finally, he had reached the exit into the larger chamber of another cave. He stuck his head out and looked down. Twelve feet below were the three men he and Vince had seen earlier climbing along the riverbank. They sat on the floor of the cave passing a joint between them.

"Hey," he shouted. "What are you guys doing?"

One jumped and swung his flashlight up and shined it into his eyes. "Christ, you scared the shit out of me."

The others pointed their lights up. "Hi boss," they yelled in unison.

7

The Governor rolled onto his back and reached up to grab the handles affixed above the hole in the wall. He smoothly pulled himself up and pushed his hips out of the hole until he stood on the lip of the horizontal shaft. He found the ladder rungs below him with his feet and started down. At the bottom, he shook out his arms and legs, brushed off his knees and elbows, removed his gloves, and walked over to the trio.

"Give me that," he said, grabbing the stub of a joint from the mouth of the one who'd jumped earlier when he'd yelled down at them. He pinched what remained of the joint between his finger and thumb, put it to his lips, sucked in a lungful of the sweet smoke, and held it in. He dropped the soggy tip of the joint on the ground and rubbed it into the floor with the toe of his boot. He closed his eyes and fought the urge to exhale, feeling the calmness return. Finally, he exhaled, the smoke swirling in the beams from the headlamps of the crew. "God, I hate that crawl."

"You said it, boss, we call it the Mother Earth birth canal.

That bitch pushes us out of that hole and we enter this world head first." The three laughed.

The Governor looked at them. "OK, guys, what have I said about leaving the caves?" His head swung back and forth, the beam from his headlamp slashing across their faces as they sat looking up at him. "I think I've made it perfectly clear that you need to be careful. I saw you guys walking along the riverbank." He looked each one of them in the eye. "I don't want this operation put at risk. We've got too much riding on this."

They all hung their heads, their headlamps pointing at their toes, afraid to challenge their leader. The older of the two brothers finally looked up and spoke.

"We just needed a break, boss. You know how this underground shit can get to you after a while. We just decided we were due a little fresh air and a look at the stars."

"Plus, we think we've made some real progress. It was a little celebration," the younger brother added.

The Governor looked the three over. They did seem genuinely excited. "Well, lead the way. Let's see what you three have accomplished."

The Governor followed the three through the tunnels, the shafts of light from their headlamps and flashlights cutting through the darkness ahead of them. Leading the way was Dave, the tunnel rat. The Governor had run into him a couple of years ago on a journey into the tunnels and sewers on Nicollet Island, across the Mississippi from the Federal Reserve. Dave was experienced underground, beginning his expeditions into the sewers and tunnels of St. Paul when he was in high school. He expanded his reach into Minneapolis for new adventures and knew his way around the tunnels and sewers on both sides of the river. He showed the Governor the tunnels and routes he knew and they discovered new ones together. The Governor recruited him into the group with promises of a new adventure with great rewards at the end.

Steve and Rick were next. They were experienced diggers, brothers who were part of a local construction crew that specialized in digging through the layers of sandstone and limestone for various projects under the city. They were used to spending time underground in tight spaces and handling equipment used for digging. He'd recruited them from a bar in downtown Minneapolis as they sat and watched a woman take off her clothes. He bought the drinks and they talked about being underground, their dreams of the big project allowing them to end this life. Maybe buy a boat on an island and have a dive shop. He knew if he got Rick, Steve would follow. He did.

He was glad he knew how to pick people, read their feelings and desires. He was glad these three had agreed to join him. If they hadn't, they wouldn't have made it back alive from their first journey into the caves.

Forty-five minutes into the hike, the Governor and his crew reached the site they had been working. To reach it they had passed through a couple more caves and tunnels, traversed a river of sewage, and entered a gate they kept locked and covered with official looking signs describing the fines for trespassing into a posted city construction project. They weren't the only ones who were exploring the bowels of the city. The underground explorers and adventure seekers, like Dave, were around, but they were like rats; they tried to avoid detection and contact with others.

The four gathered in the opening where Dave stopped, their headlamps illuminating the walls and equipment and the hoses that ran along the ground into a dark opening in the floor. They were all breathing heavily and had beads of sweat running down their cheeks. After passing around a jug of water, the Governor walked over to the area of the most recent digging.

"Ok, let's see what you've done."

Steve was excited and started, "Boss, we think we've hit the old bridge cable-stay pits, just like you said we would." They were standing forty feet below the traffic that passed overhead, entering and exiting the west end of the Hennepin Avenue Bridge. The current suspension bridge that carried traffic across the Mississippi was modeled after similar suspension bridges that had been built here in the mid to late 1800's. The pits they had been looking for and discovered had anchored the cables of one of the past bridges.

He paused for some sort of response, and getting none, he continued. "So that gives us a pretty good idea of where we are, and we know where we're going, right? We just need to figure out how we're going to get there."

The Governor looked over the site with his hands on his hips, a slight smile spreading across his lips.

"Gentlemen, this is great. You were right; you did have reason to celebrate." He clapped his hands together. "From here, we find the shaft on my maps which will get us down to the next chamber and from there it's about another thirty or forty feet to the target. We're definitely making progress and we're right on schedule. Who has the papers?"

Dave pulled them out of his pocket and handed them to the Governor. He removed the papers from the zip-loc bag, unfolded them, and spread them out on a dry spot on the floor. They all knelt and trained their lights on the drawings, waiting for him to speak. The top sheet was a plan view that showed the street level of the area above them. The Governor folded back that sheet and shone his headlamp on the next. The second page showed the overhead view of the underground. Tunnel locations he and Dave had mapped, old cable-stay pits, forgotten underground foundations, and the black lines where he had drawn in the outline of the Federal Reserve vault.

The Governor pointed to their location on the map. "We should be about here, just like you said, Steve. Northwest of this location, about one hundred and twenty feet, and about twenty feet lower, is where we're going. Find a layer of sandstone and we should be able to dig our way there with spoons." He folded back the page to expose the next. "This is the goal."

Steve looked at his brother and then at the Governor. "Can you tell us about it again?"

The Governor looked at him, then closed his eyes and leaned back against the wall. He was a little light-headed. He didn't know if it was the pot, the hike in, or the excitement of the moment. He opened his eyes and looked directly at Steve.

"The Ninth District Federal Reserve vault houses twenty million dollars. It is a nearly impenetrable wall of solid concrete and steel with walls almost two feet thick, with one million pounds of rebar in four mats of number five bars, four inches on-center, staggered one inch per mat. But, there's an access door from when it was constructed. That's how we're going in."

Jack opened his eyes, but he didn't move. He stared straight up, taking in the shapes and shadows of the textured ceiling. The only sound he could hear was the beating of his own heart pounding in his ears, so loud he couldn't go back to sleep if he tried. The light was beginning to filter through the Venetian blinds, illuminating the dust moats floating overhead. He flattened his right hand onto the cotton sheet and slid it to his right, hoping, praying that it would bump into a warm body. All he felt was the coolness of the sheet on the bed next to him. He was alone.

He thought about sleeping in, a birthday present to himself, but figured it must be about time to get up. Turning his head to look at the alarm clock on the dresser across the room, all he saw was a red blur. Squinting made it a little better. Five something. Reaching for his glasses on the nightstand, his hand ran into last night's half-full glass of water, tipping it onto the floor.

He put on his glasses and looked at the clock again. 5:27.

It was strange how he always woke up right before the alarm went off.

He laid his head back down on the pillow, letting it settle into the feathers, and stared at the ceiling. What day was this? His eyes moved around the room. Pictures the kids had drawn at school hung on the wall, and the stripes of light leaking in through the blinds, creating stripes of light and dark across them. Next to them was his FBI Academy diploma. On the dresser, next to the clock were the photos: his parents' from the 25th anniversary party, the family shot from last summer's vacation to the Black Hills, Mount Rushmore in the background, the kids' birthday portraits. Things changed a lot in three months.

The buzzing started. Jack glanced at the clock. 5:30. Time to get up. He threw off the covers and swung his legs out of bed and walked across the room on knees that crackled with each step, to reach the alarm clock on the dresser. His fingers probed the clock until they found the button to end the noise.

He turned to face the full-length mirror on the closet door and straightened his back, grimacing as the pain shot through the lower vertebrae, part of his morning ritual.

"Happy Birthday, Jack," he mumbled. "Not too bad for 40." His gut wasn't too big, he still had some hair, and when he smiled, he wasn't bad looking. The dimples added something that his crooked nose took away. "Think I could get a date?" He turned sideways to the mirror and sucked in his stomach. Well, not if he was seen in this get up. He stood there in his ratty, old, college football jersey, the outline of number 84 still barely visible, and boxer shorts flaring at the waist with the elastic showing.

He looked back over at the pictures on the dresser. It would have been nice to have the kids wake him up with their giggles and birthday kisses. And he would have liked to wake up next to Julie too, but he didn't know if that was going to happen again.

At the end of the school year, before summer started, Julie had let him know where things had stood. She needed a break and for him to think things over. He hadn't been surprised that she was unhappy, but he was shocked when she told him she was leaving and taking the kids with her. She was moving out to the western suburbs into her parents' house. Ten years of being married to an FBI agent had taken its toll. The hours, his being gone for extended periods, the frequent moves to new field offices. She was home now, close to family and old friends, and she didn't want to leave. She wanted a commitment from Jack. A commitment that he would finish his career in Minneapolis and that they'd stay here to raise their family close to hers, to live a more normal life.

Jack struggled out of the clothes he wore to bed, put on his running shorts and a t-shirt, sat on the edge of the bed, and put on his socks and running shoes. Another part of his morning ritual. He stood up to stretch, twisted slowly from side to side, and bent over to touch his toes. His fingertips reached just below his knees. He rolled his head a couple of times clock-wise and reversed direction a couple of turns and shook out his arms. He was ready to go.

When he opened the door, the heat and humidity imme-diately enveloped him. Better to go out now than later when it really had time to warm up. He slowly jogged towards River Road and the paths along the bluffs of the Mississippi River.

Jack crossed the paths and scrambled down through the woods to run on the trails that ran next to the river. The bike paths above were nice, but below the bluff was another world. A world removed from the city. Woods, the river, and few noises other than squirrels foraging for food in the grass and leaves on the ground.

Jack liked to run to think, and running down through the woods along the river brought him even deeper into the recesses of his brain. Jack thought about the day ahead. He dreaded working on his birthday. He wanted to spend it with the kids. They were excited to see him, to give him his gifts, and to sing Happy Birthday. It was all they had talked about on the phone the past two days. If he didn't have to work, they'd go to Como Zoo to see the polar bears swim or the Minnesota Zoo to see the dolphins. If he could make it through the day, they'd have fun tonight. Maybe this weekend they'd get to the zoo or go bowling. He'd let the kids pick.

Fifteen minutes into his run, Jack reemerged from the woods and followed the path up to the Ford Parkway Bridge. He was in the zone now, running without thought or effort, autopilot. The sun was peaking up on the east horizon, causing him to squint as he crossed the bridge. Sweat ran down his face and arms as one foot plodded in front of the other. Thirty more minutes and he would be home, ready to shower and face another day.

9

The Governor jerked. Startled, he reached out from beneath the blankets and felt around on the nightstand to find the source of the repeated blaring. Finding the alarm clock, he rolled onto his back and brought it to his face while he pushed various buttons, trying to make the sound stop. The numbers glowed silently in front of his eyes, 6:03, while the noise continued. His heart beat hard in his chest.

"It's your pants...cell phone," Sandy mumbled. "Make it stop." She grabbed the pillow and pulled it down over her head to muffle the noise.

The Governor got out of bed and grabbed his pants. Sandy had thrown them across the room last night before a long night of unbridled "body exploration," as she called it. He felt as if he had been explored and conquered. The ringing had stopped before he got the phone out of his pants pocket, but he held it in his hand and sat in a soft chair by the window, waiting for the telltale beep indicating the caller had left a message.

The phone beeped; the display showed a message was waiting for him. He glanced back at the lump on the bed and debated retrieving the waiting voice message or climbing back under the sheets for some additional needed sleep, his thumb playing with the numbers on the face of the phone while he tried to make a decision.

The window air-conditioner unit kicked into life to catch up with the rising temperature of the apartment. Sandy snorted and pulled the pillow tighter over her ears.

Walking into the living room, the Governor looked out the window as he pushed the button to retrieve the message. Waiting for the call to go through, he studied his naked reflection in the window. He was happy with how he looked. At fifty, he was fit, looked good in and out of his clothes, and was able to attract and bed women much younger than himself. His short, black hair was speckled with gray, giving him an air of class. He followed a regimen of yoga and tried to watch what he ate. Sandy had even got him to start running around Lake Calhoun with her.

The voice in the phone told him to enter his password. Once he completed this, he heard a familiar voice. Listening, he looked out the window at the world coming to life.

"Damn," he breathed. He pushed the button to end the call, gathered the rest of his clothes, and got dressed.

He sat on the edge of the bed and gently pried the pillow from Sandy's hands to reveal her face. "Princess, I have to go." He reached out, brushed the stray hairs off her cheek, and tucked them behind her ear.

Sandy's eyes opened slightly. "What?" she asked. "What time is it?"

"A little after six. I have to go. I wish I could stay, but I have to go meet some people. Something's come up." He ran his hand down her arm. "How about we meet for lunch? One o'clock, the New French Bakery?"

She rolled over again. "Sure, one o'clock."

Gently rubbing the back of her neck, the Governor tried to recall their conversation from the previous night.

"What was the name of the agent that questioned you at the bank?"

"Special Agent Ross Fruen. He was kind of cute," she teased.

"Cute. Right." The Governor squeezed her neck. "I'll see you at one."

After stopping at Caribou Coffee for a badly needed cup of coffee, the Governor continued driving up Hennepin Avenue towards downtown Minneapolis to follow up on the phone call he had received. Hot coffee wasn't what he really wanted on a morning that was already hot and sticky with the rising sun, but he needed to be alert.

With the air-conditioner blowing on him as he drove by the Walker Art Center towards the Basilica, he dialed his cell phone and spoke into the hands-free headset he wore. "Vadim, it's me. Yeah, I know it's early. Sorry."

The Governor signaled and moved over a lane to the right as he listened to what had to be Russian cursing.

"Listen, Vadim. The Feds are getting a little nosy and I need you to get something done before we meet tonight. What? No, nothing like that," the Governor said, shaking his head. "Just let your fingers do their keyboard dance and see what we can learn and how you can mess up a life a little so a certain agent has other things to worry about.

"He's Special Agent Ross Fruen, late twenties. OK, how long will it take? That's it? Great. I'll see you tonight. And bring the information we discussed." The Governor ended the call and placed the cell phone in the seat next to him. "Welcome to my game, Agent Fruen," he said to the windshield as he continued towards downtown Minneapolis to take care of his other issue.

10

The Governor pulled his SUV into the parking lot off West River Road and backed into a parking spot so the tailgate would face the bike path and the woods that ran along the west side of the Mississippi. He sat in his car for a couple of minutes with the newspaper in his hands. The headline of the Metro section, above the fold, was "Who is this man?" over a picture of him from the bank. The story contained details of the bank robbery. The weather info on the back page of the paper confirmed that the heat was here to stay, with rain in the forecast every day for the next week.

The Governor casually looked around to get a feel for the morning people and car traffic. A biker pedaled by. Across the parking lot, an elderly man and his grey-faced lab were walking away from him. Just a couple of people out trying to beat the heat that was sure to get worse in the afternoon. Checking his watch, the Governor grew anxious.

It was almost 7:00. He had to get to the site, deal with the problem the crew had called him about, get home to shower, and get back Uptown for lunch. When the old man and his dog rounded a bend in the path and were out of sight, the Governor got out of the SUV and grabbed his duffel bag out of the back-end. He took one more glimpse up and down the bike path before crossing it, and headed into the woods and down the bank to the river.

This was the long way to the site where his crew was digging. Above ground, he was about a half a mile north of the Hennepin Avenue Bridge and the Federal Reserve. That wasn't bad, but underground it was a maze of passages and turns with no direct route to where his crew was working. It was a longer hike than the mill ruins entrance by the Stone Arch Bridge, but he didn't dare enter the underground caves from there during the day since the bridge was a popular spot for walkers and bikers.

He stood in the sand at the edge of the Mississippi and looked across it to the Boom Island landing. Everything was quiet. The river flowed silently by, its surface shimmering in the morning sun. No paddleboats were loading at this time of day to take sightseers down river through the lock and dam and back again.

The strap of his gear bag dug into his shoulder, reminding him why he was there. He wiped the sweat from his brow and rearranged the strap farther up his shoulder before he turned and continued walking downstream along the bank until he got to the spot he was looking for. The concrete apron for the storm sewer jutted out of the woods, breaking up the wooded shoreline like a scar, an unnatural opening into the earth. It reminded him of an entrance dug by a large underground creature.

He entered the sewer pipe, more like a cave at this point, and moved far enough in to get out of the light, where he was able to change into his caving gear without being seen from outside. The dark sewer, providing a respite from the heat that had been building since he'd woken up, also offered a transition back into the underground.

The Governor hurried through the sewers and tunnels to the site. Almost ninety minutes after he started his trek, he found his small crew watching over a man sitting against the wall.

Standing in the middle of them, the Governor tried to catch his breath. The sweat that had formed on his neck and back under his coveralls was now a cool trickle as it ran down to gather at the small of his back, where it was stopped by the belt around his waist. He nodded at Dave to get him away from the rest of the group so he could get up to speed on what had happened.

Dave walked over and the Governor put his arm around his shoulders. "Who's our friend?"

"He came up on us while we were working. Caught us by surprise. We're not sure what he knows or heard." Dave glanced over at the young man sitting along the wall. "I told him we're a city crew and that he's trespassing. Told him I was contacting the supervisor. That's you."

The brothers, Steve and Rick, watched nervously.

"OK. You did the right thing. Let me talk to him. Go calm those two down." The Governor walked over to the young man, knelt down, and smiled.

"Good morning, I'm Mr. Peterson. What are you doing down here? It's pretty dangerous, especially alone."

The young man kept hugging his legs. "I was just exploring. Can I leave now?"

"What's your name?"

"Mike. Mike McDonald." The twenty-something man looked into the Governor's eyes and then at the others. "Listen, I know what I'm doing. I can find my way back out. I'm not hurting anything. Can I just go?"

"Tell you what. I can't just let you go out on your own. This is a great place to explore with all of these caves and passageways, but what if you got hurt on the way out? You'd sue the city; we'd lose our jobs." The Governor nodded at the others. "You have to understand where we're coming from. Are you alone?"

"Yeah, just thought I'd explore a little up this way, stay cool in the caves. Trying to find some new routes to show my friends."

"We need to get you out of here. We'll all go out together. These guys need a break anyway." The Governor rose and put out his hand.

He pulled Mike up and turned to his crew. "Hey, guys. I think it's time for a break. We'll escort our new friend, Mike, out and I'll buy us something to eat before we get back at it." He winked at his crew. "You guys lead us out. Mike and I will follow. Let's go out by the Chute. I want to check something out on our way."

The group made their way through the tunnels. The Governor could tell their intruder knew what he was doing. He had the right gear, knew how to move, where to look, how to crawl through the tight spots. Somebody like this could be useful if he was interested in joining them, but he was also dangerous now that he'd seen them.

A low rumble turned into a constant roar as they turned down a passageway.

"The Chute landing is up ahead!" Steve called back.

In the next chamber, they all stood next to a river of water that flowed quickly past them through a half-pipe of concrete before disappearing with a roar through an opening in the far wall.

The Governor took off his hard hat and wiped the sweat from his forehead. He leaned over and spoke in Mike's ear.

"Mike, you've been exploring these caves before. Have you ever been to the Chute?"

Mike just shook his head.

"No? Well, a couple of crazy guys rode this river in a rubber boat. Went through the Chute and lived to tell about it. Said it was the dumbest thing they ever did."

The Governor's crew had worked their way to block the passage ahead and the passage from which they had come. Mike McDonald looked one way then the other and then stared at the Governor.

The Governor stepped back from Mike and yelled.

"Mike, we're going to give you a chance to make history!" The Governor looked from the young man to the river. "How would you like to be the first to make the trip without a rubber boat?"

Rick, the crazy younger brother, giggled.

"What?" The rest of Mike's thought hung in the rumble of the passage. He looked towards Rick standing in front of the path they had come from, and Steve in front of the path they were to follow. "Who are you guys?"

The Governor shook his head and pulled a gun from his pocket. "Does it matter?"

Rick giggled again. He took a step forward. "Come on, man, jump in!" he yelled.

The Governor had his light and gun trained on Mike. Mike squinted from the light in his eyes and stood his ground. He turned and looked towards Steve. He shuffled his feet and kept his back facing the wall across the water behind him. Mike took a step to his left and there was a blast. Mike froze, Rick screamed a laugh. Rock dust and sand flew off the wall behind Mike from the bullet that crashed into it.

The Governor pointed the gun at Mike's chest. "I'm

going to count to ten. You can take a ride down the Chute with or without a bullet in you. One, two..."

Mike took a step back, looked at the Governor and his gun, then at the dark water that ran by. He faced the Governor again and raised his hands up. "OK, enough. I'll leave. Just let me go." He took a step towards the exit.

"Three, four," the Governor continued, and pulled the trigger. The flash filled the darkness and the noise echoed through the tunnels.

"Wait!" Mike screamed. He was about twenty feet from the entrance of the Chute, where the water in the stream poured over the edge into a pipe taking the water deeper into the ground. He squatted down and tentatively put his right foot into the stream, trying to get a grip on the bottom while he leaned his arms on the edge for balance. The water was just above his knee. He shifted his weight to move his left foot into the water and his right foot slipped. He splashed into the water which then swept him downstream. The Governor and the crew hurried to the edge and searched for Mike with the lights on their helmets. They spotted him as he bobbed to the surface on his back, arms wrapped around the helmet on his head, the current carrying him along through the wall and out of sight.

"God, he did it!" shouted Rick. He looked at the others. "Fuckin' crazy!"

"I think that kid was crazier than you, little brother," Steve said. "He said somebody had gone over this before. You don't think it was him, do you?"

The Governor continued staring at the wall where the river disappeared. "He was crazy, but he gave himself a shot. He went feet first."

11

J ack pulled the car into his spot in the parking lot outside the building that housed the FBI in downtown Minneapolis and turned off the engine. Looking in the rear-view mirror, he ran his hands through his short, dark hair and checked his tie. Jules had taught him how to dress; 100% cotton shirts, starched and pressed, silk ties with a Windsor and a dimple, dark wool suits, polished black shoes, simple socks, and a belt that matched the color of his shoes. It served him well as an accountant out of school and carried over in his career at the FBI.

"Happy Birthday to me," he said, and got out of the car.

Jack left the stairwell, and turned to head to his office, but stopped when Ross yelled, "Jack, I've got the videos from the three bank robberies set up in the conference room. Are you ready to look at them?"

Jack turned to face Ross. This kid was anxious. "Junior, we're going to Wayzata. I'm going to get my coffee and we're out of here."

"I've got coffee in here and I might have something. Come take a look."

Jack shook his head. Just like his kids, no focus. As he turned into the conference room, the singing began.

"Happy birthday to you..." Somebody pulled him into the center of the room, where he stood smiling, enduring being the center of attention. He jabbed a finger at Ross, raised imaginary batons in the air, conducted the group, and joined in at the end, bellowing, "Happy Birthday to me." Jack looked into the faces of his friends and colleagues. "This is what I was waiting for. Not the singing, but the official breakfast of crime fighters, fresh doughnuts and real coffee. Thanks, everybody."

As people left, they wished him happy birthday, gave him a hard time about turning forty, shook his hand, or gave him a hug. Everybody here was family. Barb, his assistant, was last. She gave him a squeeze and a kiss on the cheek.

"Thanks for pulling this together, Barb. Did you let everyone know it was my birthday today?"

"Not everyone, a couple of people are on vacation. Happy birthday, Jack."

Ross stood at the table. "They made me do it. Happy birthday."

Jack held a chocolate covered donut in his left hand and a cup of coffee in his right. "Thanks. I think I needed that today. Did you really have the videos ready?"

"They're ready to go," Ross said.

JACK AND ROSS watched the videos from the other bank robberies. "Well, that was a bust, nothing new. What's next, Junior?"

Ross looked at his watch. "There's a temp from the

Wayzata bank I need to interview. She lives over by Lake Calhoun. I'll call her to make sure she's there. We'll drive my race course on the way over, conduct the interview and I'll buy you a birthday lunch."

"Sounds like a plan. I'll get to see your interviewing skills." Jack said.

12

Jack held his palm up over the air vent to check and see if it was cooling yet. "We're sitting inside for lunch. It's too hot to sit outside. Especially in these suits."

Ross drummed his fingers on the steering wheel as they drove around Lake of the Isles. Jack looked out the window and watched the world go by. His mind was a mess. His thoughts jumped from his kids and his birthday plans with them to what he and Ross had seen at the bank. He was struggling with coming up with an explanation for why the Governor had killed that woman. He thought their trip to the scene was going to help, but nothing had jumped out at him.

"Jack, a dollar for your thoughts."

Ross' voice snapped him out of his trance.

"What?" Jack asked.

"What are you thinking about?"

"Too many things, that's the problem." Jack rolled his head to loosen his neck. "Tell me about this woman we're stopping to see."

Ross smiled. "She's about twenty-eight, long legs, blonde hair, and blue eyes."

"Very observant, Junior. What else do you happen to remember?"

Ross tried to get serious. "She's a temp. Works in the back room handling faxes, some data entry, etc. She worked pretty closely with the victim and seemed to take this whole thing pretty hard."

"So, why are we stopping to interview her?" Jack asked. "Because she's cute?"

"Well, that doesn't hurt," Ross said. "But like I said, she was pretty broken up by this and I wasn't able to get much info from her when I interviewed her at the bank. She was too distraught."

"Any other theories on why The Governor killed the woman at the bank?" Jack asked.

Ross shook his head.

"One thing you don't want to do is let your theories totally drive your questioning and investigation. Keep the theories flowing, but try to let the evidence and facts point you in the right direction." Jack looked out the window. "I'll see what other words of wisdom I can come up with to pay for my lunch."

Jack looked out the window again while his mind drifted to thoughts of the kids and Julie, wondering what they were doing.

As they drove by the Lake Calhoun boat marina, Jack looked out at the kids learning how to handle the sailboats and the winds. A couple of kids were standing on the side of a boat tipped in the water, struggling to right it. It was apparent they were going to have to recruit a few more bodies to have enough weight to right the boat.

"Hey, Jack. I think that's her." Ross signaled to a woman

in sunglasses, a sleeveless shirt, khaki shorts, and sandals walking on the sidewalk ahead of them and across the street.

"You're right, she's pretty. You know what you're going to say?" Jack looked at Ross. "Just don't blubber and drool. You're a Federal Agent for God's sake."

Ross laughed and pulled the car over. "Got it." He put the car in park. "You coming?"

Jack shook his head. "Too hot. Leave me here in the air-conditioned embrace of La Reina. You go talk to her. We'll debrief over that lunch you're going to buy me."

Ross grabbed the door handle to get out of the car.

"Don't take too long, Junior. I'm hungry."

Ross got out of the car. "Ms. Hoffman..." the rest of his words cut off as the car door slammed shut.

Jack watched as Ross trotted over to the young woman. She looked up in surprise, then recognition. Jack saw she was a flirt from the start. She laughed, dug her toe in the dirt, and tilted her head as Ross asked her questions. Jack hoped Junior could concentrate.

After a couple of minutes, Ms. Hoffman glanced at her watch and touched Ross' arm. Ross nodded, walked her to her car, and opened the door for her before turning to head back to where Jack was waiting.

"It's nice in here," Ross said as he got back in the car.

"You get what you wanted?" Jack asked.

"Like I said, she was a temp. Didn't know many people at the bank except the deceased. Feels bad for her family. She's been there a couple of months."

"You got that out of her?" Jack chuckled. "I thought you were coming back to tell me you had a lunch date with her and you were dumping me. If it wasn't so hot out you'd still need the AC to cool off after that conversation."

"It wasn't like that. She had to get going to meet a friend for lunch. She can't believe what happened at the bank and isn't sure she can go back to work there. She's going to go talk it through with her friend."

"It's a bummer, but she'll be OK. So, where are you taking me for lunch? Remember we both need someplace cool."

DURING LUNCH, they tried to take a break from the case. Ross asked Jack more questions about his history at the FBI. Jack had been around long enough and in enough different field offices to have more than a few stories to tell. They watched the scenery walk by and Ross joked with Jack that his kids were going to grow up to look like the tattooed and pierced bodies that walked by the window.

The waitress took Ross' credit card to pay for lunch. Waiting for her to return with the receipt, Ross asked, "Jack, have you ever dated somebody from a case?"

"Don't even think it, Junior."

"Not during the case, Jack, but how about after? I meet her at a bar, she asks me to dance? There's nothing wrong with that, is there?" Ross stuck out his hand to take the bill from the waitress as she returned. "I mean, she was coming on pretty strong, Jack. And she was gorgeous."

"Sir?"

Jack and Ross both looked up at the waitress. She wasn't handing the bill over to Ross.

"Do you have another credit card, sir? There seems to be an issue with this one."

"What do you mean, an issue? Must be something wrong with the system."

"We tried it a couple of times."

Ross dug another card out of his wallet. "Can you try this one?"

"Sure, I'll be right back. Won't take a minute."

Ross held the card and looked at it. "Wonder what's happened?" he asked. "I just got this card." Ross looked back at Jack. "So, theoretically speaking, could I ask her out?"

"Theoretically speaking, if the case was all wrapped up and she approached you...I'd call her a groupie, but I think you could go out with her."

"Sir?" The waitress was back at the table.

"That one worked, didn't it?" Ross hoped.

"This one has exceeded its limit."

"That's impossible." Ross took the card from the waitress. He turned the card over and looked at both sides. "Exceeded its limit?"

Jack took some cash out and handed it to the waitress. "Keep the change. Sorry for the problem. Thanks for the birthday lunch, Junior."

"I don't understand what's going on, I haven't used this card," Ross said.

"Let's go. I have to go pick up my kids and you can call your bank."

13

"Hey, where are you? I'm right here."

The Governor snapped from his daydream to the hand waving in front of his face. He grabbed the hand and held it gently in his, stroking it with his thumb. "I'm sorry, babe." He smiled. "There's no excuse. How could I be thinking about something else with a beautiful woman sitting across from me?" He looked at Sandy Hoffman, his gaze moving from the designer sunglasses covering her eyes, down a long, tan arm, to the hand with the manicured nails, held in his hand.

"I don't know, but you were a long way from here. What were you thinking about?"

"It's nothing. Just the morning. But that's taken care of and behind me now." The Governor reached out to hold her other hand, his fingers playing with the silver ring on her finger. "I'm all yours now. Please forgive me." He looked at her eyes, hiding behind the dark sunglasses and smiled. "What were you saying?"

She waited for a bus to rumble by. They sat on the sidewalk outside of the New French Bakery on busy Lyndale

Avenue. "I was saying all sorts of things." She pulled her hands back from his grasp and crossed her arms. "I was saying it was hot. I was saying that after lunch I'd like to go for a drive out to Lake Minnetonka and take your boat out, maybe go for a swim. I was saying last night was great."

"OK, now I'm listening. Go on." The Governor took another drink of his iced coffee and leaned forward, resting his elbows on the table.

Sandy leaned forward to meet him and quietly said, "I was going to ask why you killed her."

The Governor looked over her shoulder and then glanced over his own. Then he put a finger to her lips to keep her from saying anything else. "We'll talk about that later when we're alone. What else do you want to talk about?"

She grabbed her iced tea and settled back into her chair. "I thought we could go away for a weekend. Relax. Spend some time alone. Talk."

"That sounds great. I'd love to spend an uninterrupted weekend with you. Have any ideas?"

Sandy crossed her legs, one bronze leg swinging as she talked. "I was thinking the North Shore, north of Duluth. A resort on the lake. Some hiking, walks along the shore, camp fires at night."

The Governor nodded, his eyes hiding behind his sunglasses. "I'd like to hike the falls down to the lake. See the lighthouse."

"That would be fun," Sandy said. Another bus went by and she continued. "There are some great antique shops up there too..."

His thoughts started to drift with her words. He couldn't shake the vision of the kid floating away towards the chute. The nagging feeling he had that the kid had survived the fall. He went feet first. Could he have survived a fall? From what Dave had told him about the Chute, he wouldn't survive the fall, would he?

The muffled words of his beautiful companion continued. "I had a visitor today." She paused. "Special Agent Fruen stopped by to see me."

"What?" The vision of the kid floating away popped.

"Have you been listening?"

"We were talking about the North Shore and then you said something about Agent Fruen?"

"Special Agent Fruen stopped by as I was leaving my apartment to meet you for lunch. Can you believe they wear those ties and suits all of the time? In this weather?"

"What did he want?" She had his full attention now.

"Just some follow-up questions about what happened at the bank."

The Governor stood up. "Come on, let's take that drive out to Lake Minnetonka and you can tell me all about it. We'll take the boat out for a spin and jump in the lake to cool down."

14

Jack pulled the car over next to the curb in front of the third house from the corner, the brick rambler with white trim, birches planted in the front corner of the lot, and colorful flowers accenting the picture window flower box. He put the car in park, closed his eyes, took a deep breath, and prepared to see his kids. They never failed to show him what was important and what wasn't. He needed the distraction and the big dose of reality.

Squeezing himself out of the car, he walked up the sidewalk to the door with the mixed feelings of dread and excitement. At the door, he hit the awkward moment; ring the bell or walk in? He felt strange just walking in; he was here at his in-laws where he'd walked in many times before, but now it was different. He didn't belong. As he stood there trying to decide what to do, he was saved as the door flew open to shrieks of "Daddy!"

He bent over as the two pairs of arms encircled his neck. He stood up with a grunt as the kids hung on so they wouldn't drop to the floor. "Hi guys, how are you, I missed you!"

"We missed you too, Daddy."

"I missed you more than he did."

"No, she didn't."

As the argument ensued over who had missed him more, Jack looked at Julie who stood in the hallway, watching.

"Hi, Jules."

"Hi, Jack. Looks like you have your arms full. You're right on time for a change. What are the plans?"

Jack absorbed the dig without reacting. "I thought I'd take these monkeys here to the Como Zoo. I think they've escaped. We got a call at the office to be on the lookout for two monkeys running loose in this neighborhood."

"Did you really, Daddy?"

"Sure did. If we're going to the zoo, you better get your monkey shoes on and get in the zoo mobile."

The kids ran back into the house to get their things. Jack jammed his hands back into his pockets. "So, how are they doing?" he asked as his eyes moved from hers to over her shoulder to watch the kids.

Jules leaned against the doorframe, her arms crossed. "They're doing OK, but they miss you. A little confused why we're here and you're back at the house." She glanced back over her shoulder. Looking back at Jack with concern, she softly said, "You look tired, Jack. Are you doing OK?"

"Yeah, I'm doing OK." He thought, but couldn't say, *I miss you guys*. "Getting into a new case, helping out a new agent. It's the Governor bank robber case. You hear about it on the news?"

Julie nodded. They fell into the comfortable banter Jack remembered, talking about a new case, the people involved, where he thought the case was going.

The kids were hunched down at Julie's feet making monkey noises. "Take us to the zoo," they squeaked.

Jules took a step forward and kissed Jack on the cheek. "Happy birthday, Jack."

"Thanks."

Jack took a hand from each of the kids into his to walk to the car. As they walked down the sidewalk, Jack called back over his shoulder, "Don't worry about us. We'll be back late, we're going to eat too much monkey food and wake you up when we get back." Then he bent over at the waist and started walking and grunting like an ape. The kids took the cue, swung their arms, and screamed like chimpanzees.

Jack was looking forward to the afternoon. As he drove, his eight-year-old, Lynn, rambled on about the new friends they'd been playing with in grandma and grandpa's neighborhood. Willy, six, sat quietly in the back adding details to the conversation when Lynn would let him. Neither had asked the tough question yet about what was going on between mommy and daddy, when they were moving home again, why they'd left?

A couple of miles from the zoo, rain started to pepper the windshield and forced a change in plans. The kids picked the St. Paul Children's Museum and Jack didn't care as long as he could spend some time with them and have some fun.

At the museum, the kids explored the exhibits. Jack followed the kids into the room with the anthill exhibit and stood off to the side with other parents as the kids put on the ant costumes and climbed through the tunnels of the kid-sized anthill. There were chambers with ants, their enemies, eggs, and tunnels to educate the kids. Lynn and Willy popped up on one side and waved before ducking back in to climb around. Jack felt content and almost normal as he watched and listened to his kids play. It was hard to believe that when the day was over he wasn't taking them home.

Lynn ran up and grabbed his hand. "Come on, Dad, Willy wants to show you something." She dragged him over to the anthill entrance, dropped to the ground, and scampered in. Jack lowered himself to his hands and knees with a groan. "Come on, Dad," pleaded a voice from inside. "Hurry up."

"I'm coming," Jack said. He started crawling in on his elbows and knees, anxious to play with the kids and see what they had to show him. He reached the dead end of the tunnel where Lynn and Willy were impatiently waiting.

"Dad, isn't this cool?" Willy asked. This is where the ants keep their food.

Jack patiently listened, lying on his side, while he was educated on the eating and food storage habit of ants.

"Dad, you have to see the eggs," Willy said.

"Yeah, Dad, turn around and we'll take you over there," Lynn said.

"Easier said than done, kids. This tunnel's more for ants your size." Jack tried to turn around, but the tunnel was too narrow. His knees and elbows were sore from the carpet. The kids were impatient and were trying to squeeze by and hurry him out. He tried another move to get out and hit his head. His pulse quickened and he started to breathe harder. His throat shrunk and he gasped and started to sweat. He pushed the kids roughly back into the end of the tunnel. "Wait a minute," he said a little too loudly.

Jack closed his eyes and tried to slow his breathing. He'd had claustrophobic attacks before, but it had been a while. He lay still and tried not to think of where he was.

"Dad, are you OK?" Lynn asked.

"Yeah," Jack responded. "Just a minute. Don't move. I

have to back out of here." He lay there without moving for a few more seconds before he slowly backed out of the tunnel. Once out, he pushed himself up onto his knees and took a deep breath. The kids slowly crawled out and looked at him, not sure how to act.

"Come here, guys, give me a birthday hug." Jack was on his knees with two ants hanging on his neck, wishing it could always be like this.

"I think it's time for us to go get some people food and celebrate my birthday with some cake before I take you back to Mom."

15

The Metro club was always dark. The Governor stopped just inside the entrance and heard the low buzz of voices and the clink of glasses as his eyes adjusted to the darkness, allowing him to see where the noises came from. The Metro was the Minneapolis/St. Paul gathering place for the men in the Russian community. It was here that they spoke quietly in Russian, traded information, made deals, and strengthened relationships. The power brokers controlled who got jobs, what work was done here or in Russia. Small groups of men sat at the bar, others at tables surrounded by mahogany walls and soft lights. The Governor had been to the Metro before and knew he didn't fit in. He had dark hair like most of the men here, but he was tall and lean. Most of the men looked like the one that was approaching him, a little shorter with short, dark hair, a round face, maybe a mustache and dark clothes, with a cigarette in his hand.

"May I help you? You are here to meet someone?"

The Governor looked at the man and then out into the room. This man was more than a greeter. He was the first barrier into the room for the uninvited. He had a gentle smile and a demeanor that put people at ease, but he also commanded attention through the intensity of his gaze. The Governor saw through the smoke that many of the men were looking back at him. "I'm here to see Vadim."

"There is more than one Vadim here, I am sure. Can you be more specific?" The man took a drag from his cigarette and blew the smoke up into the darkness.

"Vadim Skarbov, he should be expecting me."

"I'll go see if I can find him for you. Why don't you have a seat at the bar?" It wasn't a suggestion. The short Russian accompanied the Governor to a seat at the bar before going to find Vadim.

A small glass appeared on the bar in front of the Governor. Holding the glass in his hand, he looked into the mirror behind the bar to see what was going on behind him while he waited for Vadim to appear. He took a sip and smiled. One thing the Russians knew was their vodka and they shared the good stuff with whoever frequented the Metro.

A couple of years before, Vadim had introduced the Governor to the Metro and to good vodka. Vadim had been in town for a national computer hacker's convention as a speaker on a panel talking about the security of financial information and his past intrusions. He was known for attacking financial companies around the world, accessing information and funds, which he exploited for his own benefit and the benefit of his relatives in Russia. He had served his time after being caught. There wasn't a lot of publicity outside of the hacker community; banks and companies didn't acknowledge their losses. To do so would ruin the confidence their customers had in keeping their savings with them. The Governor was able to talk with Vadim at a reception and they developed a partnership of necessity, neither able to succeed without the other, on the plan the Governor had proposed.

After another glass of vodka, the Governor saw the greeter in the mirror standing behind him. "You can follow me." Walking through the restaurant, he noticed the conversations at the tables ended as he approached and began again in his wake.

At the table in the corner, a man with long, black hair tied back in a ponytail dropped his cigarette in an empty glass and stood when they approached. "Hello, my friend."

The Governor shook his hand. "Vadim, it's good to see you."

Vadim shooed the greeter away with a nod of his head. "Sit. We have some things to talk about. You brought me something?"

"We're almost there, my friend." The Governor pulled a package from his pocket and placed it on the table. He pushed the bubble-wrapped item across the table. "I should have the last, most important piece of the puzzle soon."

Vadim grabbed a knife and slit the tape that held the package closed. He tilted the package and let the contents slide into his open hand. It was a computer hard drive, like the others the Governor had given him. "Do you know what is on here?"

"Vadim, we each have our roles here. I research and steal, you figure out what is on these and how we're going to use them. No, I don't know what is on there."

"None of these is any good without the last piece," Vadim said.

"Like I said, we'll have it soon, in the next day or two." The Governor looked across the table at Vadim. He called him his friend, but he wasn't a friend. He was a partner. One he had to trust to get what he wanted.

"You wanted something, too," Vadim said. He pulled an envelope from the seat next to him and placed it on the table. "Your list of agents in Minneapolis."

"Thanks. I'll get back to you soon." He slid back his chair to stand. Vadim reached across and placed his hand on the envelope.

"When you get to your car, look in the envelope and listen to your voicemail. I don't like what I have found. We are too close to put this at risk. There are two people you can trust. You and me." Vadim sat back and pulled a pack of cigarettes from his jacket pocket. He placed the unfiltered Camel between his lips and lit it. "We will talk soon."

The Governor started his car in the parking lot to get the air-conditioning going and opened the windows a few inches to let the hot air escape. His fingers slid along the envelope as he contemplated what Vadim said. What was the risk? He tore open the envelope and pulled out the sheets of paper. The first two sheets were an alphabetical list of agents, their addresses, and phone numbers. He found Ross Fruen on the list and looked to see where he lived. Then he looked at some of the other names on the list. They were primarily male, a variety of names, titles, and pay grades. Nothing special, but he had the names he needed to be aware of.

He examined the other two pages and tried to decipher the information they contained. They were phone logs indicating incoming and outgoing calls, duration, source, and destination numbers. One sheet was for Sandy. The other for Ross Fruen. There were some numbers highlighted on each page. He studied these entries and determined that they had called each other. Nothing wrong with that, was there? Agent Fruen was conducting an investigation; she was returning his calls.

The Governor slid the pages back into the envelope and pulled his cell phone from his pocket. Vadim had said to check his voicemail. He looked at the face of the phone and saw that a message was waiting. He didn't remember any beep indicating a message had come in. He pushed the message button, put the phone to his ear, and waited for the message to begin.

What was he listening to? The message was from Sandy, but it wasn't for him. He listened once to the whole message, and then listened again from the beginning.

"What the hell?" He pushed the button to listen to the header to see when the call came in and shut his phone to end the call. He yanked the sheets from the envelope again and ran his finger down the list of calls from Sandy's phone. This morning, with Agent Ross Fruen, thirty-six seconds. What was she thinking?

16

Jack decided to start his day with a run downtown. After changing into his gear at the YMCA, he ran down Nicollet Mall, the main street through downtown Minneapolis, about twelve blocks to the Mississippi River. The morning was already hot and sticky, the sun peaking between the office buildings as it rose. He weaved through the pre-caffeinated crowd heading into work, dodging the groups of young men in suits, accountants or attorneys, he guessed, and the odd street people as they moved between prime sitting locations on the mall and the bus stops. Smokers stood outside the buildings getting their morning fix of nicotine. He tried to focus on his running path through the crowd so he wouldn't run into a light-post, a tree or a bus, but his attention drifted as he approached the groups of young females wearing less than they did during a Minnesota winter. Summer was his favorite season since he moved to the Twin Cities.

As he passed the IDS Crystal Court, he flipped a thumbs-up to the man sitting on the stool on the sidewalk singing God Bless America, a patriotic tune for the upcoming Fourth of July and one that might trigger an increase in tips.

Deep in thought, Jack kept running, his breathing regular, and his pace constant. He ran across the Hennepin Avenue Bridge, past the Pillsbury flour mill buildings, past the Stone Arch Bridge.

Exhaustion and dehydration brought his thoughts back to focus on his own immediate condition. He was still moving at the same pace, but it was getting harder and he was thirsty. He started thinking about pushing himself to finish the run and hooking up with Junior to plan their day.

Passing the Guthrie Theater above the lock and dam, he was trying to remember where a drinking fountain was when he came upon a group of people and patrol cars at the top of the bank overlooking the old mill ruins. He stopped to look over the scene, standing with the rest of the gawkers.

"Hey, Miller."

Jack looked to his left for a familiar face, but the glint of the rising sun reflecting off a squad car windshield blinded him.

"I hardly recognized you in your running gear."

Squinting, Jack stepped to his left and put out a hand to block the glare and to find a face to put with the voice. Searching, he found the face that was looking his way.

"Hey, Patty, there you are. You blinding me on purpose?"

"It's just my sunny disposition. Come on over."

Jack walked around the street sign wrapped with the yellow crime scene tape and over to the car. "You have any water with you? I'm dying."

"Sure, in the van. And the AC's on too; want to sit inside?"

"No, I don't want to get your seats all sweaty, but the water would be great."

Patty came back with a bottle of spring water and handed it to Jack. "Here you go, courtesy of yours truly. It's car temperature."

He took the water bottle, unscrewed the top, and chugged the cold water. It ran from his chin and down his chest. Pulling the water bottle from his lips, he raised it and poured some over his head. "Thanks, I really needed that."

"No problem, just remember who you got it from."

Jack held the cold bottle of water against his neck and nodded towards the police tape. "So what's going on over here that's important enough to drag you out on a hot day like today away from breakfast in the air-conditioned bistro?"

"Screw you, Miller. Give me back my water."

Jack laughed and held the bottle out and away from her. "Very eloquent. I always said you had a way with words. Really, what's going on?"

"Pay any attention to the news?" Patty walked towards the edge of the bank to the yellow tape keeping the public away from the scene and looked down to the river's edge. Jack followed.

"I've been busy."

"Well, a body was found down along the river bank. Just past the old mill ruins down there." Patty pointed down towards the park along the riverbank. "It had to have been there a while. We haven't heard how long yet."

"Somebody fall into the river?"

"Yeah, something like that. Well, they strung some crime scene tape to keep the strollers and joggers out, hoping to be done before the people came out to start their day. Didn't make it. The ambulance was here to get the body and the detectives are still looking around. Somebody called it into the station and I got a text to get out here."

Jack looked down at the activity below and took another swig from the water bottle.

"There was a guy here giving the uniforms a hard time. He's the developer of these condos here in these old warehouse buildings. It's a big part of the rejuvenation of this area. He threatened to call the mayor."

Patty was on a roll, so Jack just took another drink and looked at the buildings behind them. The condos in this development were going to have a draw as the river front development continued. The view was great. The Guthrie Theater right here and the new Twins outdoor ballpark a short walk away.

Patty continued on. "Well, mister dog walker, developer has his undies in a bundle. Wonders when the tape is coming down. He's got some big open house planned for the night of the Fourth to showcase the condos. Wants to show off the views, treat the potential buyers to the balcony view of the fireworks across the river and sell some units." The frustration was showing in her voice. "There's a dead guy down here, maybe foul play, and he doesn't care. He has to sell some units. I'd love to tell the story about that."

"Well I'm glad you're here; you saved my life. Doesn't sound like a federal case so I think I'll finish my run and get back to work." Jack handed her the empty bottle. "Thanks."

"You're welcome." Patty grabbed the bottle, but didn't pull it away. She stared into his eyes in a way that made him blink. "I heard you might be looking for a running partner. I like to run in the morning."

Jack thought he caught her meaning. "I kind of like running alone right now."

"Well, if you're looking for company or another bottle of water, let me know."

Jack didn't know how to respond. Nobody had seriously

hit on him in a long time and seeing other women hadn't even entered his mind. He let go of the bottle, mumbled, "Thanks, good luck with this mess," and turned to head off down River Road to complete his run. His legs were a little stiff from the stop that had let the lactic acid build up in his muscles, and had left his brain spinning from Patty's offer.

17

The Governor sat in his car listening to the classical music station, not wanting the words of others to interrupt his thoughts. He needed the classical music to soothe him.

Anything harder and he was afraid he'd punch the window or tear the steering wheel from the column.

He was torn. Walking Vince this morning, he'd discovered that it looked like Mike McDonald hadn't made it. The police had cordoned off an area down by the river and there was a body in the water. From what he could see, the clothes matched what Mike had been wearing and the Chute would've dumped him in the Mississippi. That had turned out OK.

But, Sandy had shocked him at lunch yesterday. First, she asked the question about the murder of the woman at the bank. Then, she told him about Agent Fruen's visit. He couldn't believe she had been talking with the FBI agent again. It worried him. She was attracted to the man in the suit and she wasn't as smart as she thought she was. She might say the wrong thing. Playing detective against a trained agent, she would probably give up more than she learned about the bank investigation without even knowing it.

Now here she was at the club working out with the agent. She had served her purpose. With her temp jobs in banks, she had been able to get information, learn who's who, office configurations, and routines. Her beauty and brains went well together to gain the trust of others as she worked the inside helping him. She was a good worker. And, as a temp, she would be hard to track. She needed to quit working, to disappear.

The blue car he had been waiting for pulled out of the club parking lot ahead of him. The Governor followed in the stolen Tahoe. Its tinted windows served two purposes today. It helped keep the interior cooler as he sat in the sun, and those on the outside couldn't see who was inside. From the vantage point of the large SUV, he could keep an eye on the car ahead of him, looking over the smaller cars on the road.

He stayed back, but close enough to keep track of where the car was going. He switched the radio station from classical to something harder to match the quickening of his pulse and the anger surging from deep inside his body. His head nodded with the beat and his hands kept time on the steering wheel as he followed the car off Highway 100 towards the Uptown area by Lake Calhoun. He got closer now that they were off the highway. He didn't want to lose the car at a traffic light.

The Governor worked to control his fury; he couldn't make a mistake now. He took a deep breath and dialed his mobile phone as he tailed the blue car through the intersection and they pulled onto Lake Street by the parkway on the north side of Lake Calhoun. There were bikers and joggers out on the trails and at the intersections, but the Governor was barely aware of them as he focused on the car ahead of him.

He listened intently in his earpiece, waiting for the ring as the cellular system linked his phone to the one he dialed. As the cars hit the section of road that divided into six lanes of traffic, three in each direction, around the north side of the lake, the Governor heard a ring, maneuvered into the lane to the right of the blue car, and pulled up alongside. He glanced over and kept pace with it. He could see a hand digging in a bag on the seat looking for the ringing phone. He turned down the radio and waited for an answer.

"Yeah?" the Governor heard in his earpiece and glanced to his left.

"Haven't you heard it isn't safe to talk on a cell phone when you're driving?"

"Who is this?"

Without answering, the Governor accelerated and swerved left driving the large Tahoe into the side of the blue car. Both vehicles continued left until the wheels of the car bounced off the curb dividing the east and west bound traffic. It all seemed slow motion, surreal, as the Governor felt the jolts, and heard the sounds in his vehicle and the sounds in the car next to him through the earpiece of the phone. There was cursing, but he couldn't be sure of the source of the words. Was it the agent or himself?

He pushed left and accelerated again, first driving the left wheels of the blue car onto the curb and with a final twist of the wheel, up and over it. Horns honked and tires squealed and finally, there was a tremendous crash as the blue car collided head on with a large furniture store delivery truck. The Governor continued eastward on Lake Street with only a glance into his rearview mirror to assess the chaos behind him. He moved quickly to the right lane and turned right onto a neighborhood street, accelerated, and turned right again at the end of the block where he quickly pulled into an alley and parked next to a dumpster behind an apartment building.

He glanced down the street as he pulled the latex gloves from his hands and put them in the fanny pack/water bottle carrier. The Governor broke into a jog towards the lake. It was a hot day for a run, but he was just another jogger as he headed for the trail system along the chain of lakes he was going to follow on his long run home. He heard the sirens and headed towards the lake and the scene of the accident to see what had happened.

18

Jack ran by the bronze statue of Mary Tyler Moore throwing her hat into the air on the Nicollet Mall in front of the Macy's store. He tried to block it, but couldn't stop it. Damn it. The theme song from the old television show burst into his brain. *You're going to make it after all!* It happened every time. With just a few blocks left to reach the YMCA and a shower, the song played in his head, threatening to be there all day. The second verse started, then a voice called out, "Jack!"

Jack slowed and looked back over his shoulder, first at the statue, at the hat still just leaving Mary's hand as she flings it into the air, and then he scanned the faces behind him on the sidewalk. The lunch crowd on Nicollet Mall had thinned as the downtown office workers returned to the land of the cubicles in the surrounding office buildings.

"Miller, over here."

He looked to his left and saw Patty sitting in the passenger seat of the news van next to the curb. She motioned him to come over to the car, the look on her face telling him she wasn't here just to offer him water again.

He jogged a few steps over to the car, nodded at the driver, looked at Patty, and asked, "What's up? For a minute I thought Mary was calling my name."

"We got a call, Jack." Patty locked her eyes on his. "One of yours, an Agent Ross Fruen's been in a car accident."

"Where is he? Is he OK?"

"He's over at HCMC. That's all I know. We heard some calls over the radio, thought you'd like to know so we came to find you."

"I need to get there. Hennepin County Medical Center handles all the trauma cases. Can't be good." Jack looked anxiously up and down the mall.

"That's why we're here. Jump in."

"You sure? It's just a few blocks. I can run there."

"Come on, Jack. Let's go."

Jack settled in the back seat of the van among the video equipment and leaned forward in his seat. "So we don't know anything?" Jack asked.

"Sorry, Jack, you know what I know. But we'll be there soon enough."

The driver took off.

"So who's Agent Fruen?" Patty asked.

"You met him when we were in Wayzata."

"The new agent? Shy guy with the sunglasses?"

"That's him." He looked at Patty. "I wonder what happened."

They pulled up in front of the emergency room at the hospital and rocked to a stop. Patty climbed out and opened the back door for Jack. "Thanks," Jack said. "I have to get inside."

"I'm coming with you." Patty gave a wave to the driver and told him she'd call him.

"There goes your ride. I didn't even thank him."

"Don't worry, Jack. He knows. He's glad to do it and he's used to waiting around." Patty started for the door and grabbed Jack by the elbow to get him moving. "Let's go on in. I'll hang around if you need me for anything. A call, another ride, anything."

Jack followed Patty inside. Once they were in, Patty headed for a chair while Jack went up to talk to a couple of agents in suits who were leaning against the wall.

"How is he?"

"Hey, Jack." The closer of the two agents kept leaning against the wall, hands in his pockets while he spoke. "He's not dead, that's about all we know. We're waiting for the doctor. He's supposed to be out soon."

The second agent stood with a Diet Coke in his hand. "It's a miracle Junior's still here. You know what saved him?" He took a big swig of soda and waited for Jack to answer. When all he got was a shake of the head, he let out a quiet belch and continued, "That piece of shit car of yours. The Rino or whatever you called it. Should've called it El Tankay, 'cuz that tank took a beating but saved Junior's ass."

The doctor had approached the group.

"Gentlemen, you're with the FBI?" The first agent quickly flashed his badge in answer.

Jack answered, "Yep, that's us. How is he?"

The doctor looked at the second agent. "You're right that the car probably saved him. That, and he's young and in good physical shape. He's beat up. He'll be bruised and sore, but I think he'll be fine. We want to keep him overnight, treat the pain and observe him, let him rest, but he should be able to go home tomorrow or the next day."

The agents all looked at each other and then at the doctor. "That's great, doc," was all Jack could say.

"He was asking for Jack," the doctor said.

Jack nodded. "That's me."

"Follow me. I'll take you in to see him."

Jack looked at the other two agents. One took a swig of soda while the other pulled out his mobile phone. "We'll call the office and give them an update. Tell them Junior's still kicking. We'll wait here or at the cafeteria to get an update from you."

Jack stepped over to the drinking fountain and took a long drink of water. When he was done, he looked over at Patty and gave her a "thumbs-up" then he looked at the doctor. "All right, let's go."

Jack walked beside the doctor, their shoes squeaking on the floor. The rhythm and hum of the ER worked its way into Jack's thoughts now that he knew Ross was OK.

As they walked by the desk, the doctor stopped to talk to the nurse. "Can you get an extra-large top sent down to room 2?" He continued down the hallway with Jack following. "A hot day to run. I hope you're hydrating."

"I was just heading to the showers when they picked me up to bring me here."

The doctor stopped outside room 2. "We'll get you a dry top. Don't stay in there too long. He's OK, but he needs his rest to help him recover and we have him on some strong stuff for the pain. He may be a little dopey."

Jack followed the doctor into the room. Ross smiled when he saw Jack, but it quickly turned to a grimace from the pain. Jack almost grimaced along with him because Ross looked terrible. His arm was in a sling, his face bruised from the air-bag, and there were cuts on the side of his head. He sucked in air as he fought the pain, and the sound triggered the sympathetic reaction in Jack.

"Remember, not too long," the doctor said before leaving.

Jack was ready to keep it light, make sure Junior was OK. He started to say something, but Ross beat him to it.

"Jack, it was him, the Governor."

"What do you mean, it was him?"

Ross spoke softly. "My phone rang, I answered it and boom, somebody's playing bumper cars with me." He shifted in bed. "It was him on the phone Jack. He said something to me about how I shouldn't talk on the cell phone when I'm driving and then he hit me."

"Slow down, Junior."

There was a knock on the door. A nurse came in and handed Jack a green surgical top before approaching Ross' bed and checking the IV's and other equipment surrounding him. Jack took off his t-shirt and put on the dry top. "Can I keep this?" he asked the nurse.

"Sure. I'll come back in a couple of minutes to make sure you leave our patient alone." She smiled at Jack, but underneath he saw she was serious. He didn't have a lot of time.

"OK, Junior. You're sure about this? This isn't a dream induced by the meds? The doctor said you'd be a little dopey."

"It was him."

"We must be making him nervous for him to try this. I have to go find your car. Get the crime team to figure out what hit you. Find your phone."

"Are my clothes here?"

"Junior, you're not going anywhere."

"The phone, it might be in my coat pocket."

Jack looked around the room, but didn't see anything. "I'll find them, Ross. They have to be around here somewhere."

The nurse pushed open the door. "The party's over boys. The patient needs some rest."

Jack looked at Ross. "I'll be back later, Junior. I'll see what I can find out about the phone, car, and witnesses. Maybe you'll remember something." He headed for the open door and the glares of the nurse.

"Jack," Ross hoarsely whispered.

Jack looked back. "Yeah?"

"Sorry about the car."

"Don't worry about her, Junior. She saved your life."

19

The room had a quiet buzz from the equipment and the soft clicking of fingers on keyboards. The only light in the room came from the computer monitors spread across work surfaces, which wrapped around the outer wall of the room and formed an island in the middle of it. Jack stood a couple of steps inside the door, waiting for somebody to notice him. Nobody even looked up so he walked over to one of the faces glowing in front of a huge monitor and looked over the shoulder of the operator. ESPN's website was up in one of the windows. "How are the Twins doing?" Jack asked.

The computer operator's head jerked slightly to the left towards Jack's voice. "If you're a betting man, bet against them."

Jack looked around the room and settled his eyes back on the sports fan. "Who can tell me how we're doing with the Governor case and the accident with Special Agent Fruen?" He threw in the "Special Agent" to get this guy's attention and the attention of anybody else listening. He wanted to make it known how he felt about the agents pounding the pavement versus these guys pounding their keyboards.

The man in the chair spun it around to face Jack. "And who are you?"

"Special Agent Jack Miller. Can you tell me who you are?"

"Sure thing."

Jack stared at the man, waiting for an answer. He wasn't going to ask again. He looked at the computer screen again and some papers on the desk. The man had been working on some spreadsheets; game stats were on the papers. He looked at the man again. The corners of his mouth had turned up into the smallest of smiles.

"OK, Sure Thing, can you tell me where things are at with our investigation or are you just looking for those sure thing bets."

"Well, Jack, we've been busy down here. What do you want first?"

"Let's take them all in order." Jack sat on the edge of the table, keeping his elevated status over the man in the chair. "Bank videos, mask, Agent Fruen's credit cards, and his accident and cell phone call."

"Bank videos, that's Goose's assignment. The guy over there with the red hair." Jack looked in the direction that Sure Thing had nodded. The blob of curly red hair glowed with the reflection from the computer monitor.

"The Governor is a man, five foot ten inches tall. He's right handed. The coat he was wearing was nice, but too big for him. Trying to make him look bigger than he is. One hundred sixty-five pounds."

"That's it? I could get most of that." Jack looked across the room at Goose.

"And he prefers boxers."

Jack looked at the Sure Thing with a grin and raised his eyebrows.

"OK, that's his guess, but if I was a betting man I'd bet boxers." Sure Thing spun around in his chair, fiddled with the mouse, and brought up two pictures on his computer monitor of the Governor in his mask. "I'm sure you know this already too. This mask is good. It fits well and the likeness isn't perfect but it's very close. If you got a glimpse of him on the street or in the car next to you on the road you might think it was the governor." Sure Thing got up from his chair and walked a few steps. He returned with a glossy printout of what was on the screen, gave it to Jack, and sat back down. "That's for you." He scribbled something on a piece of paper. "Take this too."

Jack looked at the scrap of paper with a name on it.

"That guy's the best in the business. He's at the Guthrie. With his contacts and a little digging, he can probably find out who made the mask. You can get there tonight?"

Jack nodded as he looked at the picture in his hand. Sure Thing had been talking a mile a minute and wasn't slowing down. Jack was afraid to interrupt him and throw him off track. Sure Thing reached under his worktable, brought out a bottle of Mountain Dew, and twisted the cap to open it, releasing the carbonated gas.

"You want one?"

Jack shook his head.

"I'll leave him a message that you're coming. Make sure he'll talk to you." Sure Thing took a big swig of the green soda, put the bottle on the table, and belched out of the corner of his mouth. "OK, what was next?" He answered his own question without waiting for Jack to answer. "Credit cards. I gave that to Squeaky."

Jack looked around the room, trying to guess who

Squeaky was. Everybody was still staring at computer monitors and typing.

Sure Thing called out, "Hey, Squeaky!" A hand popped up from behind the monitor across the aisle, flipping them off.

"What do you want, asshole?" The origin of the nickname Squeaky became apparent as the voice carried around the room, a combination of the voice somebody gets after breathing helium and the sound of fingernails scratching a blackboard.

Jack looked at Sure Thing and tilted his head at the sound, like a dog hearing a high-pitched whistle. "Asshole?"

"She loves me." He waved his hand through the air. "Come here, my love!"

Squeaky pulled herself away from her station and walked over. She was about four foot, eight inches tall, barefoot, and had an unlit cigarette tucked behind her ear. She sat down in the chair next to Sure Thing, spun herself in a circle on its swivel, and asked, nodding at Jack on the next revolution, "Who's your friend?"

"This is Jack. He's here to find out about Agent Fruen's cards and finances."

Squeaky jammed her feet to the ground to stop the gyrations of the chair. She slowly positioned herself to face Jack, leaned forward, and with a new, serious look on her face asked, "Who did he piss off?"

"I don't know. That's what I'm hoping you guys can help me with," Jack said.

"Whoever it is, I definitely wouldn't want that person for my enemy. Fruen's money is gone; his credit rating is annihilated. Whoever did it was good. They covered everything; his credit cards, credit rating, checking account, savings account, the couple of investments he had. It was all done in a very short time frame yesterday morning. Smells Russian to me, but that's all I've got is a smell. Nothing obvious, no signature, no point of origin for the request that leads me to who did this. But, it smells Russian. It was clean, quick, somebody who really knew what they were doing. We've seen something similar before. Coders have a signature, a style, an accent, like with any language. This is Russian. They were after Fruen and didn't bother to leave a false trail."

Jack looked at Sure Thing. "Still doesn't tell me a lot, does it?"

"I think it confirms that it's all tied together. The Governor is smart and connected to some people that know how to get things done in the world of finance and technology. He is able to, or knows people who are able to, get into the systems of the banks and related financial institutions discreetly, but he's still going in to banks physically for something."

Sure Thing nodded at Squeaky. "And if she says it smells Russian, it's probably Russian mob. Woman's intuition. Something you and I don't have."

"That's something, I guess. Let me think about it," Jack said. "Thanks, Squeaky. You done or still turning over rocks?"

Squeaky got up. "I'm still turning over rocks. There's always something out there hiding, I just haven't found it yet." She left and returned to her workstation.

"If there's something out there, she'll find it," Sure Thing said to Jack. "Just be glad she's on our side." He spun his chair around and faced his monitor; his right hand moved the mouse around, waking up the computer from its screen-saving mode. "Come here. We've got one last thing to discuss."

Jack pushed himself up from the edge of the table to look over the sports fan's shoulder. A map of Minneapolis was depicted showing the region around the Uptown area lakes; Lake of the Isles, Calhoun, and Harriet.

Sure Thing touched the screen with his finger. "This is approximately the location of the accident. Let me walk you through this. Agent Fruen's phone was tied into a tower located here. We've contacted the cell phone company the incoming call was made from. The tower it was communicating through was the same one. Which means the call was made from the same area. That corroborates Agent Fruen's story."

"Did you have to do that?" Jack asked.

"Just dotting the I's and crossing the T's. That's just the beginning. The phone is still on and it's still in the same area."

Jack leaned forward. "Where is it?"

"Right here," he pointed out the location on the map.

"I was just in that neighborhood."

"It's a few blocks from the accident. I doubt the Governor is still there. Looks like he just cut off of Lake Street and dumped the phone. The van's out getting the exact location right now and a tactical team is there just in case The Governor is still around."

"Tell them not to touch it." Jack took a step for the door, turned back, and said, "Come on. Let's go."

20

"Where is it?" Jack stood in front of the tactical van parked on the street.

The agent in charge, Stephan Ramirez, was dressed in black and ready for action. He had his tactical weapons around his waist and an earpiece with a microphone for directing the on-site team. Sweat glistened on his cheeks. The warm morning was becoming a warmer afternoon. The sun turned the humid air into a sauna. He nodded to his left. "We have men in the bushes with eyes on the truck. It's parked in the apartment parking lot down the street."

"OK, let's go get it."

Stephan touched the earpiece to activate the microphone and said one word, "Bingo."

Down the street, Jack watched as a team of people, in dark pants with t-shirts under bulletproof vests that said FBI on the back, converged on the truck. They approached the vehicle but didn't touch it. On either side, agents peered through the windows, inspecting the interior. The left side of the vehicle was dented and scratched. This was the correct vehicle and their equipment told them the phone that had called Ross was inside it.

Jack looked at Sure Thing, who was leaning against the van. "Let's go. Looks like they've secured it."

Jack cupped his hands to cut the glare and looked in the windows of the truck himself. "Take your time. We don't know why he left this here. Make sure there aren't any surprises. He went after Special Agent Fruen today with this truck."

"Sure Thing, I'm going to take a little walk. You've got this. Let me know when they're through."

Jack walked around the apartment building. He looked up at the back of the building. Across the street, some youngsters were standing on the sidewalk, watching the team working around the van. Standing on the sidewalk in front of the apartment building, Jack looked at it with a feeling of recognition. He slowly turned around and surveyed the street. About halfway through his turn it hit him. This was the street where Ross had talked with Sandy. He took out his phone and dialed a number.

Jack stared at the apartment building while he waited for the phone call to connect. The building was an old, three-story brick building. Many of the apartments had window air-conditioner units and most of them were running to ward off the hot, sticky air. The call went unanswered and forwarded to voicemail. He ended the call and walked up the steps. He looked through the front window to examine the names on the mailboxes. Most of them just had last names.

Jack instinctively patted his pockets. What was her last name? The card that Junior had just said Sandy. He tried to dig back through his memory, but couldn't remember her last name, just what she looked like. He looked at the mailboxes again. She hadn't answered her cell phone. Could she be home? Did she even live in this building? Was it a coincidence the car the Governor had used was parked behind this apartment building?

Jack called the number posted over the mailboxes that was for the residents to call to report problems with the building. After three rings, a voice answered in a whisper, "This better be important."

"My name is Special Agent Miller with the FBI. I'm standing outside your building on the front steps. I'm trying to track somebody down and I think she may live in this building. Could you come to the front door and let me in and answer a few questions for me?" Jack started nice, but firm, hoping it would get him the results he was looking for.

"I'll be right down," the man answered.

"Great, I'll see you in a minute."

Jack stood on the front steps in the shade and slapped at the mosquitoes that buzzed his ears. A man with a shaved head wearing a gray, sleeveless t-shirt and faded, maroon gym shorts with the gold University of Minnesota M on the thigh came to the door. He was somewhere in his thirties. The man pushed open the door and stepped outside. "You're with the FBI? Can we talk outside so I can have a smoke?"

Jack showed the man his FBI credentials and agreed, thinking that the cigarette smoke would help keep the bugs away. "Did I wake you?"

"Late night. I bartend over here in Uptown."

"Sorry I had to wake you, but I'm looking for a woman that lives in this neighborhood and I think she might live in this building." He described Sandy, the car she drove, and said she might work at a bank. The man blew the cigarette smoke up into the air and ran his hand over his shaved head.

"You've got the right building. Sandy Hoffman is her name. Lives in 4A. She's got a great body. Been living here for about a year. What do you need her for?"

"Thanks. I just need to talk to her. Before we go inside to see if she's home, I need to show you a car in your parking lot out back and see if you know who it belongs to."

The man took another drag from his cigarette and followed Jack around the building. "Holy shit, what's going on back here?" the man asked.

Jack looked at the people surrounding the SUV. The driver-side door was open and a tow truck was preparing to load the vehicle onto the bed to take it away.

"Do you recognize that vehicle or know if that parking spot is assigned to anyone?"

"I've never seen that car before." The man looked at Jack and took another long drag from his cigarette. "The lot is first-come, first-serve for those who pay to rent off-street parking. The spots aren't assigned to anybody."

Agent Ramirez and Sure Thing walked towards them. Jack nodded to the man and said, "Excuse me. I'll be right back."

Ramirez said, "We tracked the owner down. A couple from Anoka reported it missing yesterday morning. We're taking it to the lab. The phone was under the seat."

"Thanks. I'll be ready to go in a minute." Jack turned to the building supervisor. "Can we go back and see if Ms. Hoffman is in? You don't have to let us in her apartment, but I would like to ring her apartment and see if she's in."

The man dropped his cigarette on the ground and

stepped on it. "I can tell you she's not in. She gets up early and works out."

"Then she goes to the bank?"

"I don't know about working at a bank. But I know she's a dancer at Sheiks, downtown."

21

"Junior, it's me, Jack." He could hear Ross fumbling with the phone.

"What time is it?"

"It's lunchtime." Jack heard Ross clear his throat and get a drink of water. "Are you awake now?" Jack asked.

"Yeah, what's up?"

"Somebody's messing with you, Junior, and we need to find out who and why. I was in the lab his morning with the geeks; they don't sleep. I have some good news and some bad news. First, your credit is shot. Somebody messed with your credit cards, your credit rating, and your bank accounts. Your finances are a mess and it'll be a major headache to get it all fixed."

"They got everything?"

"Yep, they pretty much wiped you out."

"Well, what's the good news? There wasn't that much money. They assumed my debt too?"

"No, what I told you was the good news."

"Great."

"And we found where the Gov ditched the truck and the phone."

Ross yawned. "Sorry, I'm not awake. Did you tell me the bad news yet?"

"Junior, this guy didn't just come across you on the road. He followed you from somewhere. Where were you coming from? Who knew where you were going to be or where you were going?"

"I worked out at the gym in the morning with Sandy."

"And?"

"And nothing. I had some follow up questions for her and this morning was a good time for them. She's been a little stressed out so I thought if she felt comfortable talking to me at the gym I should take advantage of it."

Jack shook his head. "And you wanted to see her again and seeing her in her gym clothes was a bonus."

Ross didn't argue. "That's about right."

There was silence on the line and then Ross yawned again. "Junior, stay with me a little while longer and then you can get some sleep," Jack said. "OK. Somebody either followed you or knew where you were going to be. You went straight to the gym this morning?"

"Yeah. Got up. Went to the gym to meet Sandy and work out."

"You didn't see anybody follow you. What do you remember?"

Ross took a deep breath. "I talked with Sandy while we worked out. Didn't learn much. I left the gym. Decided to take the scenic route back by Lake Calhoun, the phone rings and boom, I'm here." He yawned again.

"Well, I told you we found the truck. It was parked behind Sandy's apartment building. I don't think it's a coincidence."

"You think she's involved?"

"Yes, look at the facts. She worked at the bank, you worked out with her and got attacked, and we found the truck behind her apartment. What do your investigative skills tell you from that?"

"Oh man, Jack. Just a second."

Jack listened to the silence.

"Since we don't know who the Governor is, I guess I need to start with Sandy. See what she can tell us." Ross took a deep breath and puffed it out. "I have her number in my phone."

"I called her and it went straight to voicemail. Her phone's off. We can't geotrack her." Jack paused. "She's working tonight. I was thinking, if you're up to it, we should go visit her."

"Working? There's a bank open?" Ross asked.

"Um, no. She's got a second job."

"What is it?"

"Junior, she's a stripper, or exotic dancer. She works at Sheiks."

"What?" Ross asked. "No way."

"We're at her building. We found the truck that hit you parked in back with the Governor's phone under the seat. The super for her building said that's what she does and she's working tonight."

There was silence on the phone.

"Junior, you still there?" Jack asked.

"Yeah. When are we going?"

"I'm going back to the lab with the truck and phone to see what we can learn. Then I have a dinner date with my wife. I can't miss it. I'll pick you up after that. Get some rest."

～

"ANYTHING?" Jack asked.

Two men and a woman dressed in white coveralls were examining the vehicle inside and out.

"Nothing so far. Looks like he wore gloves. No finger-prints on the door handle or steering wheel or keys. We've swabbed the windshield and steering wheel for DNA in case he sneezed on them."

Sure Thing walked over to join them. "Nothing on the phone, Jack. It's a throw away. Made a couple of calls."

"He left it there to taunt us," Jack said. "He could've just as easily taken it with him. The only reason he left it was so we'd find the vehicle. He's feeling pretty superior right now."

Jack and Sure Thing stood in the garage, looking at the side of the truck with its scratches and dents. "Any ideas?" Jack asked.

"Nothing comes to mind, but we'll keep working."

"If Sandy's phone comes on, locate it and call me. I'll be having dinner with my wife."

22

The doors of the lock and dam opened and six larger boats and two kayaks slowly exited single-file, traveling south down the Mississippi, bypassing the impassable concrete apron and falls that made this part of the river famous. The people on the stone arch bridge watching the process waved to the people in the boats below before continuing on their walks across the bridge. Everyone was enjoying the break from the rain.

"Well, what do you think? Can't you see yourself living here, close to work, low maintenance, and impressive architecture, one of the best places to live in the Twin Cities?" the Governor asked. The balcony of the condominium offered a great view of the river. At this time of day, there were shadow outlines of the buildings across the ground, extending across the river as the sun traveled across the sky to the west.

"It's nice. I thought it'd be noisier."

"We're too high. Once in a while you hear the locks bell ring or a tug horn signaling, but all the other sounds pretty much stay down below." The Governor pulled a leather case from the inside breast pocket of his jacket and removed two cigars. He handed the cigar and cutter to the man leaning on the balcony railing. "Here, try one of these. I think you'll like it."

The man pulled the cigar along his upper lip, below his nose, and smelled it. "Nice." He snipped the end of the cigar and put the freshly cut end in his mouth like a lollipop, wetting the rolled leaves prepping for a light. "Tastes good too."

The Governor struck a wooden match on the side of the matchbox in his hand and held the flame under the end as the man rolled the cigar between his fingers for an even burn. The man inhaled and exhaled a few times until the end glowed, the smoke rolling around above their heads before the breeze carried it out towards the river.

Leaning against the railing, the Governor lit his own cigar. "Listen, James. You can't afford not to buy this place. The view is great. Besides the location, the elegance, the area, the history, it's a great investment. Development will be going on all around you. You'll be one of the first ones in. Stay here two years. You don't like it, sell it. You'll make a killing."

James laughed. "Hey, I think this is great." He swung the cigar in his hand from the condominium balcony windows out towards St. Anthony across the river. "I'd love to live here. But, what did the sign downstairs say, from two hundred fifty thousand to a million? I'm sure this place isn't at the lower end."

"It's not at the upper end either. You can afford it." The Governor sat in one of the chairs on the balcony. "What's this talk about money? You work at the Fed. You just walk in and print yourself up some money, right?"

"Right. I just walk in and say, I'll take a million today,

Charlie." James joined the Governor and sat in the other chair on the balcony. "It's amazing. Millions of dollars flying around on wires from this bank to that, but what do I get? My paycheck from Mr. Fed Chairman. I do all right. But, with the divorce, she took me to the cleaners and still gets more than her share every month. I don't know how I could afford it."

The Governor listened to James ramble as he enjoyed his cigar. He knew more about James than James did. He knew about the bank accounts James kept hidden from his wife, about the affair James' wife was having with the neighbor in their suburban Burnsville home while James was at work and their daughter was in school. He knew how much James and his wife owed on the house they used to share and he knew why James' wife asked for a divorce. In fact, he had sent the photos. The photos of James with his administrative assistant after work, and with her in the hotel room over lunch.

"Take another look at this view. It won't be your last. Do you have any plans for the Fourth of July? We're having an open house for special guests that night. Good food, beverages, a view of the fireworks over the river. Plenty of beautiful women."

"I don't know."

"Think about it. It'll be a great night." The Governor stood. "Let's go get some dinner and we can talk about financing options, I know some people. We'll get this done for you and then we'll celebrate at Sheiks and see if your favorite red-head is dancing tonight."

23

The reflection of the candle flames dancing in Julie's eyes mesmerized Jack. Julie sat across from him, eating her garden salad and bread with garlic and olive oil. He missed this; eating with her, talking with her, her smile, her laugh. She looked up and caught him staring. She looked to see if she had spilled something down her front. He tipped his wine glass to her and swirled the merlot before taking a drink. Julie started to say something but the waiter interrupted her when he stopped by to scrape the breadcrumbs from the tablecloth.

"Jack, when you asked me out for dinner I didn't expect something so nice. A sports bar or that Mexican restaurant you like would have been fine."

"I know, but I thought you might like someplace a little quieter for a night away from the kids. Plus, I wanted to be able to talk to you." Jack put his wine glass down and leaned forward. He wanted to reach across and take Julie's hand, but he wouldn't push it yet. First, a nice dinner, a conversation about their situation, what he might be able to do to get things back to normal, then he could push it a little. "I miss you, Jules, and the kids. Any thoughts about coming back yet?"

Julie raised her eyebrows. "Yet?" She settled back in her chair and crossed her arms. "Jack, it's not like the kids and I went on a little vacation and we're coming back next week. We left for a reason."

"Yeah, I know. Well, I think I know." How was he going to get this out of this rut? Trying to find something to do with his hands, he fiddled with the silverware and then grabbed the wine glass again. He tilted the glass from side to side and watched the wine slowly flow down the sides of the glass. "It's the job. I've tried to spend more time with you and the kids and give the cases the time they need." He looked up at her for some sort of acknowledgement. Getting none, he continued. "If it's not that, you need to tell me. I'm trying, but I don't know what's not working."

Julie uncrossed her arms and leaned forward. "I was so happy when you got assigned to Minneapolis, Jack. I know what your job is, what it means to you, why it's important. It's one of the things I love about you."

Jack stopped swirling the wine at the L-word.

"Yes, Jack Miller. I love many things about you. But when you came home with the offer from the SAC to move to New York and said you had to think about it...." Julie looked away and gathered a thought. "I had to do something. I thought you got it, that I wanted us to stay here with the kids. No more moves. But, when you said you had to think about it? It just showed me we weren't on the same page about where we're at with our lives, what we want. I had to do something. I had to give you something else to think about."

Jack knew Julie well enough not to say anything. It was best if he just paid attention and let her talk. They sat at the table looking at each other. Jack took another drink of his wine. Julie shifted in her seat. When the awkward silence became painful Jack decided he better say something. "Jules..."

The waiter interrupted him as he swooped in and placed their dinners in front of them. Jack rolled his eyes and glared at the waiter, and Julie giggled. The waiter stepped back and put his hands together. "Will either of you be needing anything else right now? Some more wine, water?"

"No, thanks," Jack said. Julie held her napkin to her mouth to cover her smile and shook her head.

After the waiter left, Julie put her napkin in her lap. "Did you pay him to come then?" she asked.

"Good timing, huh?"

"Changed the mood, that's for sure." Julie held up her wine glass and reached across the table. "Happy birthday, Jack."

Jack touched his glass to hers and looked into her eyes. "Thanks, Jules. Thanks for coming to an early dinner with me tonight; thanks for being such a great mom to our kids, and thanks for loving some things about me."

They ate their dinners. Jack tried some of Julie's salmon and she tried a bite of his steak. They fell into a comfortable conversation talking about the Governor case, and Jack's new partner, Ross.

"You call him Junior?"

"I've had worse nicknames."

Julie laughed. "I'm saving those for when I really need to get you. I'll just tell the kids what nicknames you had."

Jack almost choked on a bite of his steak. "Please don't. Can you imagine?"

Jack finished eating and placed his napkin on the table. "The Fourth of July's almost here. What do you say to the family thing at Nicollet Island for the day? Tonight shows we can still get along. It's a tradition I would love to keep going."

"Let me think about it." Julie looked at her watch. "I better go."

"Yeah, me too," he said. He stood up and walked Julie to the valet stand out by the front door. They stood at the curb waiting for Julie's car to arrive. "Give the kids a kiss for me."

"I will. I almost forgot I have to report back to them. What do you think about getting a dog?"

"A dog? I guess it depends what Grandma and Grandpa think. But I'm OK with it as long as they help take care of it."

Julie's car pulled to a stop in front of them. Julie turned to Jack and put her arms around his neck. "Happy Birthday."

Jack held on to Julie, his arms around her waist. He didn't want to let go. Her hair brushed his cheek and he could smell a familiar mixture of shampoo and perfume. It was her smell and he missed it.

Julie ended the hug and pulled away. "I have to go, Jack. I'll let you know about the Fourth." She took her keys from the valet, got in her car, and drove away.

"Sir?"

Jack pulled his eyes from the taillights of Julie's car. His Cougar was waiting for him. He tipped the valets, squeezed into his car, and looked at his watch. Time to go pick up Junior and see if they could find Sandy.

24

The pounding music and the flashing lights of the club created an atmosphere that the men liked. It was electric. The room oozed energy, lust, hormones, smoke, and money. The Governor and James sat at a table drinking scotch while they watched the women work the groups of customers in the room. The women were practiced. They could read the look in a man's eye, his dress, his mannerisms, the style of his haircut, the condition of his hands and skin, and tell if he had money or not, if he was from out of town looking for fun and whether he was willing to trade some money for their attention.

James and the Governor were left alone. They belonged to somebody else.

James looked around the room. "Where is she?" He licked his lips and knocked back his drink. His words were beginning to slur and he was getting more boisterous. "I need some of that lovin' tonight. And maybe a little celebration if I decide to buy that loft."

The Governor signaled the waitress for another round of drinks. "Don't worry," he said. "She's on tonight. She'll be here. And, I'm sure she's looking forward to seeing you. You two have really seemed to hit it off." He looked at his watch and then around the room. Where was she? He looked at his watch again; to be late, tonight, of all nights. His hand instinctively slid to his belt and felt for his cell phone. Should he call her?

The waitress set their drinks on the coasters in front of them on the table. James leaned over to talk in the Governor's ear. "Where is she?"

The Governor tried to avoid the spittle he felt pepper his ear and started to answer James' question when he felt an arm around his shoulder. He looked back over his other shoulder and saw Sandy's beautiful smile.

"Good evening, gentlemen." Sandy spoke between James and the Governor so they could both hear her. She kissed James on the cheek and then kissed the Governor. "I'm so glad to see you both tonight." Sandy walked around to face the men, dragging her fingertips along James' neck, eliciting a shiver from him. When she got to the other side of the table, she leaned forward to talk to James, bracing herself with her arms on the table top, pushing her barely covered breasts together to further enhance her cleavage. "Is there anything in particular you had in mind for this evening?"

James stared at Sandy's chest across the table, and then he looked up to her eyes. "We were just waiting for you."

The Governor grabbed James by the arm. "Come on, James. Tell her the news. We plan to celebrate tonight."

"Celebrate? Celebrate what?" Sandy asked.

James looked questioningly at the Governor.

"James, come on, tell her about the loft."

"I'm thinking about buying a loft over by the river."

"Thinking about it?" the Governor asked. "There's

nothing to think about. It's yours. We'll sign the papers tomorrow, but we're celebrating tonight."

Before James could protest, Sandy grabbed his hand and pulled him up from his chair. "Well, if we're celebrating we need to move to some place more comfortable." She started to lead James back to another room.

"Wait a minute. I need to visit the restroom before I get comfortable. I want to be able to give you my undivided attention. I'll be back in a minute."

The Governor and Sandy sat on the couch waiting for James. "Can you leave?" the Governor asked. "I want to take him to the boat?"

"If you pay for the time, we can leave."

"OK, when he gets back, it's your idea to go out there. It's a beautiful summer night." The Governor reached over and gave her hand a squeeze. "We get this info tonight and we're home free."

The Governor saw Sandy's eyes move and turned his head to follow her gaze. James was wobbling back towards them with a couple of drinks in his hands.

James handed the Governor a drink and flopped down onto the couch, spilling some scotch onto his shirt. "Shit, that's a waste of good scotch," he said. He put his arm around Sandy's shoulders. "A toast to kick off my celebration. To my friend, for finding me an investment, a home, a new start on life, and this beautiful woman." James clinked his glass with the Governor's. "Thanks."

"Salud." The Governor sipped his drink.

Sandy put her arms around James' neck and spoke into his ear. "James, if tonight's so special, why don't you ask if we can go out on his boat and celebrate. It's a beautiful summer night."

James looked at the Governor, his eyes unfocused. "Hey,

buddy. I've never been out on your boat. Why don't we go out there and seal the deal tonight?"

"For some of my clients I take them out on my boat to celebrate. Why should tonight be any different?" The Governor looked at his watch. "Can you leave early and come out to the lake with us?" he asked Sandy.

"I'll meet you at the door," she said.

James turned to the Governor and put his arm around his shoulder. "Thanks, buddy. This is going to be a great night."

25

"Turn out the light!"

Tim flipped the switch to turn off the light that hung over the side of the small fishing boat, just above the water. The darkness of Lake Minnetonka immediately enveloped them. Clouds blocked out any moonlight. The only visible lights were the yellow electric lights from houses on the lake or flickering flames from fire pits along the shore. Plus, a few boats prowling the lake.

Tim and Matt were brothers, sixteen and fourteen years old from Excelsior, a small town on the south side of the lake. This summer they had decided they liked to catch fish and found the best way to do it consistently was to go at night and hang a light over the side of the boat. They set up a lantern with a shade around it, directing the light down into the water, just the way their grandfather had taught them. They had doused the light a few times tonight when boats had passed them. They had been sitting on the edge of a weed bed, illegally shining light into the water to attract the fish. They also didn't have any running lights, which were required out on the water after sundown.

Tim looked to the front of the boat where he knew Matt was sitting and waited for his eyes to adjust so that he could see him.

"What's up?" Tim whispered.

"There's a cruiser coming. Port side. Over there." Matt pointed across the boat.

Tim couldn't ever remember port from starboard and followed Matt's outstretched arm to see what he was looking at.

The boys sat and waited as they did the other times this night, waiting for the boat to pass so they could get back to fishing. "It's stopping. What do you want to do?" Tim asked.

The large, white, Sea Ray Sundancer coasted to a stop about one hundred and fifty feet from them. The boys crouched in the camouflaged duck boat and peered through the reeds at the cruiser glowing in the dark with the lights on the bridge and rear compartment blazing. The voice of Frank Sinatra carried over the water from speakers somewhere on the boat.

"Sit tight. I don't think they saw us. Let's just wait and see what happens. We can leave if we need to." Matt said. The waves from the cruiser rolled across the lake and rocked the boys in their boat. They reeled in their fishing lines and waited.

In a few minutes, they saw two men with drinks in their hands gather at the rear of the boat. The soft murmur of voices and the occasional laugh carried across the water. A woman joined them.

"Whoa, check her out."

"I wish I had my binoculars."

"You don't need binoculars to see those. She has her own personal flotation devices if the boat goes down."

The boys could see Sandy standing on the lit deck in her

yellow bikini top. They watched as she talked to the men. She turned and started to walk away.

"Wait, come back." Matt said a little too loudly.

"Shh, you idiot. You want them to see us?"

"Where'd she go?"

"Probably to take a piss or get another drink."

"Looks like they'll be there a while. Should we go?" Matt asked. The music drifting over the water changed to something more upbeat and Sandy reappeared with something in each hand. She crossed the deck and handed each man a fresh drink. Then she started to move with the music.

"We're staying." Matt said.

"No argument here, bro."

Sandy spun around the deck, her long hair flowing behind her. She danced and moved provocatively in front of the men seated on the bench seats in the rear of the boat. Finally, she straddled a man, gyrating and grinding in his lap. She stopped and reached back behind her neck, untying the bikini top and letting it fall.

"You see that?"

"Definitely not real."

"No, but very nice."

"No tan lines."

"Who's the lucky guy?"

"I wouldn't mind trading places with him."

"In your wet dreams."

"In my fantasy tonight."

"Shh."

The brothers continued to watch as the man and woman ground together and kissed. Finally, the woman stood up, took the man by the hand and led him out of sight. The second man remained seated and finished his drink. He looked at his watch, and put something in his mouth. A flare lit the night as the man held a match up to the end of the cigar and puffed to light it.

The smell of the cigar carried across the water. "Poor guy's left alone with a drink and a stogie."

"I think the show's over and they aren't going anywhere soon. Let's go."

Tim quietly pulled up the anchor and Matt started the nearly silent electric trolling motor and the brothers quietly pulled away from their fishing spot to head home for the night.

26

The Governor took another long pull from his cigar, causing the ember on the end to glow red against the black sky, and watched as Sandy led James below deck. He looked at his watch. They'd been slowly cruising the lake for most of the evening, drinking and looking at the large homes on the shores. He had time to enjoy his cigar and the other work he had planned for the night. He stood up and looked out over the lake. It was a quiet night and the temperature out on the lake at night was bearable with the light breeze.

This might be the last night he would spend on Lake Minnetonka and he wanted to enjoy it. The next hour or so would determine his fate. If all went according to plan, he could be on another boat looking over a larger body of water with a warm, salty breeze and perhaps a Cuban cigar in his hand. A boat in the summer would make the heat of the islands bearable and the winters would be like heaven. He had dreams of captaining his own boat, not one he had leased for the summer. Sailing his own boat from island to island, meeting new people, inviting women to travel with him from time to time.

The Governor looked at his watch again to check the date. Where the three should have been, the small window had a two in it. July 2nd. The team in the tunnel had been making progress and was in the position according to the timeline he had planned. Vadim had most of the information he needed to complete his part of the plan. There was one final piece of information they needed and James was the key. The Governor flicked his cigar into the night and watched the red glow tumble through the dark until it hit the water and went out with a hiss. He had business to do and it was time to get to it.

At the bottom of the stairs, the Governor leaned against the wall with a drink in his hand.

Across the cabin, James and Sandy lay on the bed; James was on top telling Sandy how great it was, how beautiful she was, how lucky he was.

Sandy rolled James onto his back and straddled him. "It's my turn now." Sandy bent over and kissed him on the lips. "I know what we should try," she said. She reached over James' shoulder and pulled up a rope with a loop on the end. She slipped the loop over his right wrist and pulled it tight. "I think you're going to like this."

The Governor swirled his drink and the ice cubes clanked against the sides of the glass. James looked at the Governor with a quizzical look on his face. Sandy put a finger on James' lips. "Shh, let's let him watch, OK?"

The Governor winked at James and held his drink up in a toast. James smiled and leaned back and rested his head on the pillow on the bed. Sandy took his left arm and tied it in place over his head. Then she moved down to the foot of his bed and repeated the process, tying each of James' ankles to a corner of the bed. He was naked, spread-eagle on the bed now. Sandy lightly dragged a fingernail up the inside of James' leg from his ankle to his crotch. James squirmed, his limbs pulling on the ropes, and groaned.

Sandy left the side of the bed, walked over to the Governor, and kissed him on the lips. "He's all yours," she said.

The Governor held his free hand against Sandy's cheek and stared into her eyes. "Thanks, I made you a drink, your favorite." He handed her the drink. "Why don't you go up on deck and relax."

Sandy took the drink, kissed him fully on the mouth, and went upstairs, closing the door behind her.

THE GOVERNOR WALKED over to the side of the bed and pulled a knife from his pocket. He unfolded the six-inch silver blade from the handle until it snapped into place.

James pulled on his arms and kicked his legs. He was securely tied to the corners of the bed. "What are you guys doing? Teasing me? Cut me loose."

"I don't think so, James. The party is just beginning," the Governor said.

"Hey, come on." James face started to grow red as he pulled harder with his arms and then with his legs against the bonds, tightening the loops, making them dig further into his skin. "This was fun, but I'm not into guys. Cut me the fuck loose!"

The Governor calmly responded. "James, I'm going to get right to the point." On James' protruding, curly black hair-covered belly, the Governor stood the knife, the point of it supporting the knife about three inches above the navel while the handle rested between his fingers. The weight of the knife was enough to make a dimple in the white skin, but not enough to break it. "I don't want to hurt you, but you have some information I need."

James sucked in his gut and tightened his stomach muscles reflexively to avoid the pain. His eyes locked onto the knife. "What are you doing? That hurts. Quit screwing around."

The Governor remained calm, but spoke with authority. "James, look at me." He stared at James, waiting.

James was breathing in short breaths, afraid to take his eyes off the knife handle. He pressed his back into the bed trying to avoid the sharp point he couldn't see, but could feel, on his stomach.

"James, look at me."

James turned his eyes up to look at the Governor, but he didn't turn his head.

"Relax. You'll be OK. I just want you to know that I'm serious. That I really want you to think about what you're going to tell me."

"What do you want to know?" James' eyes flicked to the knife and back to the Governor. "I didn't do anything with her that she didn't want. Why are you doing this?"

The Governor twisted the knife on James' belly. "This isn't about her. I want you to relax and think about what I am going to ask you. I want you to know that I'm serious. But, if you give the right answers, I'll let you go. If you don't..." the Governor slid the sharp blade against the skin, shaving a patch of skin bare, "I'll hurt you." The Governor lifted the knife off James' stomach and held it in his hand where James could see it, black, curly hairs hanging from the silver blade. He waited for James' breathing to calm down a little and watched as James' brain sorted through the panic and the facts, knowing he would begin to figure some of it out.

The Governor planned to start simple, like a lie detector test. Let James give out information that was private, but he was willing to give up; information like his birthday, his employee ID, maybe his ATM PIN. He was going to test him, show him the process, and demonstrate how this game was going to work. After a couple of penalties for information that was too slow in coming or incorrect, James would be more likely to give up the rest.

James was weak. The Governor held a pillow over his face to smother some of his screams. He had made an initial show of strength, vowing he would never give up the information the Governor wanted, but after a couple of slight nicks and cuts on the stomach and a penetration into the shoulder joint with the blade of the knife, James was willing to tell the Governor anything he wanted to know.

The Governor listened to the recording he'd made during the interrogation to make sure he had all of the information on tape. "Did we forget any important piece of information James?" James was sucking in breaths against the pain in his shoulder. He shook his head weakly from side to side. The Governor put the backside of the blade against James' neck. "If I find out this information does not get me what I want, you will die. Let me ask you again. Did we forget any important piece of information?"

"No," James said quietly. "You can get what you want with that."

"OK, I believe you." The Governor walked across the room, opened a drawer, and took out a roll of duct tape. "I want to go up on deck, but I'm sure you understand that I need you to keep quiet. I'm going to put a strip of tape over your mouth to make sure you don't make too much noise." He pulled a strip from the end and let the roll dangle at the end of the strip stuck to his finger. He slashed through the tape easily with the knife and let the roll fall to the floor. The remaining twelve-inch strip of silver tape hung from his finger. The Governor put the handle of the knife in his mouth and held it between his teeth. He grabbed the free end of the tape to keep it from sticking to itself. With his right hand, he pressed the end of the tape to the counter top and pulled the strip taut with his left. The twelve-inch strip became two strips as he sliced through the tape.

The Governor walked over to the side of the bed. "Put your lips together James." James complied and the Governor placed the strip over James lips. "Can you breathe through your nose?"

James' cheeks sucked in as he reflexively tried to breathe through his mouth. His breath whistled as it passed in and out through his nostrils.

"Just relax. You don't want to hyperventilate." The Governor walked across the room, took his mobile phone out of his pocket, and dialed a number. As he waited for an answer, he glanced at James, whose breathing was slow and regular through his nose. What would happen next would depend on how this call went.

"Alo'," someone answered the phone in Russian.

"My friend, it's me. I'm sorry to call you so late, but I have some information I need you to verify." The Governor looked over at James who stared at him and nodded his head as he listened to him tell the person on the phone the codes and passwords he had told the Governor earlier. The Governor walked back to the side of the bed and stood over James as he listened to the phone. "OK, call me back once you've verified everything that you can."

The Governor ended the call and put the phone back in his pocket. He looked down at James.

"You're sure you can breathe OK?"

James nodded yes. The Governor smiled. "I'm going up on deck while I wait for my friend to call me back. You lay here and just relax. If you told me the truth, everything will be fine."

"Hey, beautiful, where are you?" the Governor asked to the night air as he walked to the back of the boat. He looked around. On the bench were her sweatshirt and towel and next to that the empty glass from the drink he gave her. Her phone was on the deck of the boat. He picked it up. A missed call from Ross Fruen. "Damn it." What was she thinking turning on her phone?

He'd expected to find her passed out on the bench or floor of the boat after she finished the drink with the roofie in it. "Damn it." He peered over the side of the boat. She must have gone for a swim, but with the date rape drug in her she'd probably drown. Not that that was a bad thing. Made his life easier. He walked around the perimeter of the boat, looking out over the water. He wanted to know for sure where she was. Shining a flashlight out over the water was out of the question. That would draw attention to the boat. He went into the cockpit and turned off the party lights, leaving just the running lights on.

He looked out over the water to see if he could spy the lights of any other boats. He hadn't heard any boats and he couldn't see anything. "Sandy," he hissed out over the water. "Where are you?"

∽

Ross led the way as he and Jack walked up the steps. "You been here before, Junior?"

"Maybe once," Ross answered.

The man at the door eyed Ross, Jack, and then Ross again. He opened the door and held it open for the agents to enter. "Welcome back, sir," the doorman said to Ross. "I hope the other guy looks worse."

"Thanks," Ross mumbled. "Car accident." They stepped inside.

"Maybe more than once, Junior?"

"Really, Jack. Once, maybe twice, when I first got to town." Ross looked back towards the closing door. "I probably look like somebody."

The door shut, removing the last source of natural light into the room. The crowd was ramping up and Sheiks was starting to come alive for the evening.

"You called her?" Jack asked.

"Straight to voicemail. Phone's off." Ross answered.

"Let's see if she's here."

The darkness turned to light as their eyes grew accustomed to the interior lighting. Ross wasn't moving, so Jack led the way to the bar where he leaned forward on it, supporting his weight on his elbows while he waited to catch the attention of one of the bartenders working behind the counter. Ross stood next to Jack, but with his back to the bar so he could scan the crowd.

"What can I get you guys tonight?" the young bartender asked as he expertly spun a bottle through the air and caught it at the neck. "Special is Cuervo shots. And if you're in the mood to tip tonight, I'd recommend a body shot from one of these lovely young ladies."

Ross turned to face the bartender with Jack. The bartender did a double take when he saw Ross and almost missed the bottle that was spinning through the air. Jack smiled and said, "He was even scarier looking before the accident."

Before Jack could say another word, Ross blurted out, "Is Sandy working tonight?"

"Sandy? I don't know any Sandy," the bartender answered.

"Maybe she didn't go by Sandy here." Jack tried to get control of the situation again and laid his credentials on the bar along with a twenty-dollar bill.

The bartender leaned forward, looked at the credentials, and grabbed the twenty. "Who was it you were looking for?"

"Sandy. Sandy Hoffman," Jack said.

"She was here earlier, but she left with two of her regulars for a private party."

Jack put another twenty on the bar along with a business card and picked up his credentials. "Do you know who they are?"

"One's a real estate guy, developer. The other, don't know. They come in together pretty often to see Sandy."

"Thanks. If she comes back, or if you think of anything else, give me a call." Jack turned to Ross. "We missed her."

"We have to find her, Jack."

"I know. Let's go." They pushed out through the doors into the hot, night air. Jack pulled his phone from his pocket and dialed while he walked towards the car. "Sure Thing, it's Jack."

"I was just going to call you, her phone's on. Sandy's."

"Where is she?" Jack asked.

"What's going on, Jack?" Ross asked.

"Sure Thing, just a second."

Ross opened the passenger door and stuck out his good arm. "Give me the phone. I can talk one-handed. You're driving."

Jack got in the car and turned the phone speaker on. "You hold it so we can both hear it." Jack got in and started the car.

Sure Thing's voice came from the speaker on the mobile phone. "Would you two quit fighting and get going?"

"Just tell me where to drive," Jack said.

"Did you bring your swimsuit?" Sure Thing asked.

"Why?" Jack asked.

"Looks like she's on Lake Minnetonka. Head to Excelsior out on Highway Seven. It's about a thirty minute drive," Sure Thing said. "I'll stay on the line."

THE GOVERNOR THREW Sandy's purse overboard, with her phone inside it. Then he called Vadim. "It's good?"

"Yes, that info all checks out. We have everything we need."

The Governor smiled. "That's great news. I need to tie up a couple of loose ends. We're set until tomorrow night. I'll talk to you then."

James was still tied to the bed with the tape over his mouth. His breathing slightly whistled through his nose. The Governor sat on the edge of the bed. "Your info checked out. I won't hurt you anymore." The Governor reached his hand up to the tape on James' mouth, stopped, and then pinched his nose between his thumb and forefinger.

A yell rumbled in James' throat and he thrashed on the bed. The Governor held the nostrils shut with one hand and used his other hand to hold James' head in place. He climbed on top of his chest to lessen the thrashing. James' eyes were wide open and panicked.

James thrashed for a few minutes. The Governor intently watched his face. He could see the resolve melt away as James accepted his fate. He struggled hard a few more times and then passed out. The Governor continued to hold on to James' nose until he was sure he was dead. Then he turned out the exterior lights on the boat and dragged James' body to the rear deck. There he tied an anchor to his waist, lowered the anchor over the side of the boat, and then lifted and dropped James into the water.

He was still curious where Sandy was, but was happy to move on with his plan without her. He started the boat and headed for the marina on the other side of the lake.

"SURE THING, we're standing here looking at the lake. Where were they?" Jack asked.

"Somewhere between you and Big Island."

"Come on. It's dark out here. Where's that?"

"Look straight out, perpendicular from the shore."

Jack looked out over the dark water. A little to the left and then to the right. "You see anything, Junior?"

"A few boat lights. That's it," Ross said.

"You know where I am, Sure Thing?" Jack asked.

"Yeah, I have you pinpointed on the map from your phone signal. Her phone disappeared about five hundred yards out from where you're standing."

"If she was on a boat, it's not there anymore," Jack said as he paced along the water's shore.

"Jack, the boat still has to be on the water. This is a big lake with lots of bays." Ross reached for Jack's phone. "Sure Thing, how many Marinas on this lake?"

"There are about a dozen."

"That's it, Jack. We need to check them out and see if we can figure out which boat went out earlier or see which comes in," Ross said.

"Get us some help and let's go. We're so close," Jack said.

"This is a bust, Jack. We've visited three marinas and no boat."

Jack and Ross stood in the gravel parking lot under the humming lights and swatted at mosquitoes. "Let's get in the car away from the bugs and call the Sheriff, see if they have any better news."

Ross yawned while he spoke. "We need to get some sleep, Jack."

Jack started the car, checked the air-conditioning was on, and called the Sheriff.

"Sheriff, this is Miller, we just finished visiting our third marina and we got nothing."

"Nobody has anything yet," Sheriff Looney replied. "Assuming they were on a boat, they either came ashore on private property, docked before we got around and snuck out, or they're still out on the lake. I've got a couple of boats out on the water and we'll keep patrolling the landings."

"Thanks, Sheriff. Agent Fruen and I are going to get some sleep. Give me a call if you find anything," Jack said and ended the call.

"Junior, why don't you just come crash at my place and we can get right back on things in the morning."

"Won't your wife care?" Ross asked.

"She and the kids are staying with her parents for awhile." Jack spun the wheels on the gravel and pulled out of the lot. "I've got a couple of spare beds right now."

"Want to talk about it?" Ross asked.

"No, I just want to get some sleep and solve this case."

THE NOISE JERKED Jack from his dream. He grabbed the alarm clock on the bedside table and hit the snooze. The noise didn't stop. He peeked through his lids at the numbers on the clock. Five twenty-three. What the hell? He grabbed the phone. "Yeah?"

"Agent Miller?"

"Yeah." Jack cleared his throat and tried again. "Yeah. Who's this?"

"Agent Miller, this is Deputy Sheriff Looney."

"Looney." It felt like he just went to bed. Jack looked at the clock again to make sure what time it was.

"I think we got something you'll want to see."

Jack cleared his throat again. "You find the boat?"

"No. A fisherman found a body out on Lake Minnetonka. Young woman."

"I can be there in forty-five, maybe thirty minutes."

"Make your way to Deephaven, southeast end of the lake, and call me. I'll talk you in from there. I'll text you my number."

"Right, I'll be there soon. Thanks." Jack hung up the phone and went into his son's room. "Junior, get up."

"Geez, Jack. Do you know what time it is?"

"Just got a call. They found a body out on Lake Minnetonka. We're going to check it out. Back where we were last night. Leaving in ten minutes."

27

Vince was curled up on the passenger seat, nudging the Governor's elbow.

"Shh, Vince."

The Governor sat behind the wheel and looked out through the windshield. According to the list, Jack Miller lived in a house on the next block up from where he and Vince were parked. And the info said he was a regular morning runner. From their vantage point, he could see the house and one end of the alley that Jack might come out of when he drove to work. He didn't know what he looked like, but Sandy had described him so he thought he would be able to pick him out.

A shade went up in an upstairs window of the house he was watching, grabbing his attention. Vince noticed the change in his master and sat up in his seat. The Governor scratched Vince's neck. "Down, boy. Nothing to get excited about yet." Vince groaned and settled down into the seat.

The Governor watched the house as he scratched Vince around the ears. The front door opened and a man stepped out wearing khakis and a polo shirt and looked up and down the street. "Doesn't look like he's dressed for a run this morning, Vince." A second man stepped through the door. "Special Agent Fruen." The Governor reached under the steering column and touched his car keys. He wouldn't start his car until they had started theirs so as not to draw any attention.

The two agents walked down the sidewalk and got in the car parked at the curb. They pulled away quickly.

"Vince, they're in a hurry to get somewhere."

28

J ack pulled to a stop outside of the police tape stretched across the driveway to the boat launch, rolled down his window, and slid his sunglasses down to the tip of his nose so the officer controlling access could see his eyes. He held his credentials out the window, facing away from him.

"Special Agents Miller and Fruen. They're expecting us down there." Jack jabbed his chin towards the lake where the ambulance and a couple of police cars were parked. "Can you let me in?" The officer lifted the tape so Jack could drive under it, onto the driveway, and down to the group of vehicles parked at the water's edge.

Jack and Ross walked over to the group standing at the shore. A big bass fishing boat and a Sheriff's water patrol boat were nosed in resting on the sand. A man of about sixty sat at the wheel of the bass boat. He had a tanned face with white strips extending back to his ear on either side of his head where the sunglass temples had protected his skin. A deputy was questioning him.

"Hi, Sheriff." Jack shook his hand. "This is Special Agent Fruen."

Ross stuck out his left hand, his right arm in a sling.

"You the one in the car accident?" the Sheriff asked.

Ross nodded.

"We keep meeting over dead bodies, Sheriff," Jack said.

The sheriff was in uniform and beads of sweat were forming on his forehead. "It hasn't been the best of circumstances. I wouldn't normally have called you. We get a few drownings every summer. But with what happened at the bank I thought we should at least clue you in on anything happening out this way."

"What do you have?" Jack asked.

The sheriff started walking towards the ambulance parked down by the water's edge. Jack and Ross fell in step next to him. A black body bag lay on the stretcher in the heat of the morning sun.

"The man in the boat there, talking to my officer, went out to go fishing this morning. Was trolling this bay, casting for bass. Found this girl floating. She was dead. Called us on his cell phone and met us here." They stopped next to the stretcher.

"We don't know who she is. Just had a swimsuit on. Nobody has called to say she fell off a boat during a party last night. We'll put out a story today on the news and see if anybody comes forward. That's how it works, once in a while. Somebody wakes up the next morning with a hangover and a guilty conscience and gives us a call." The sheriff stared at Jack and glanced at the body bag. "I think we've got a drowned party girl, but like I said, I just wanted to make sure you're in the loop on anything that happens out here for a while."

Jack dragged his palm over his forehead, back through his hair to get rid of the sweat that had formed since they got out of the car. "What do you think, Junior?"

"Let's see who we've got here."

Jack looked at Ross. "You don't sweat, do you?"

Ross shook his head and stared at the body bag.

"He's from the East coast, likes this weather," Jack said to the Sheriff.

The Sheriff handed Jack and Ross purple latex gloves and put on a pair himself before grabbing the zipper of the bag in his right hand and the top edge of the bag in his left to allow the zipper to open smoothly. "I really don't like this," the Sheriff said.

Jack nodded and looked at the bag in anticipation. "Nobody does."

The Sheriff took a deep breath and slowly zipped open the black body bag about halfway before spreading the bag to reveal the body. Jack stood and looked at the face and hair.

"Damn it," Ross said. "It's her." He turned and walked to the lake.

"Who?" Jack asked.

Jack looked back at the girl and a sense of recognition came over him.

"He knows her?" The Sheriff's voice drifted quietly past him. "People don't exactly look the same dead as they did alive. The life force is gone. No muscle tone and the skin looks grey. Plus, she's been in the water."

Jack closed his eyes. "No other clothes, jewelry?"

"No."

"Tattoos, piercings?"

"Nothing obvious, but we didn't look too closely, yet."

The Sheriff's voice got a little tighter. "You know who she is? Think she's linked to the bank murder?"

Jack stood up and closed the body bag until just her face showed. "We know her. She worked at the bank."

"Ross, you OK?" Jack joined Ross and they both stood at the shore, looking out over the lake.

"I'm OK."

"This is where we were last night," Jack said.

"It's not a coincidence that she's here, is it?" Ross asked.

"I don't think so. I don't believe in this kind of coincidence. She works at the bank. You work out with her and get attacked, and now she's found here. I think the Governor has another victim."

A jet ski came roaring towards them, slowed as it got closer to the scene, and paralleled the shore about fifty yards out. The teen boy driving looked over the scene.

"Those look fun to ride," Ross said.

Jack watched the kid as he answered. "My father-in-law hates them. He's got a cabin up north. They're loud and create havoc in his sanctuary."

Jack took a step towards the lake and started waving the kid in. "He's out here this early, he probably lives on the lake; let's see if he knows anything."

The kid got a look of panic on this face, turned the Jet Ski out to the open water of the lake, and accelerated away.

Jack yelled to the men behind him, "Sheriff, we got a runner!"

"God damn it. Stevie, go get him!" the Sheriff yelled out to the officer in the water patrol boat. The deputy accelerated away from the group in pursuit of the Jet Ski.

Jack pushed the bass boat off the shore and high-stepped through the water out to it, yelling over his shoulder, "Junior, let's go!" Jack grabbed onto the side of the bass boat so it wouldn't drift away. The water was up to his crotch. He looked at the 225 hp motor mounted on the back of the boat. Ross splashed through the water behind him, wading out to the boat. "Hi," Jack said to the man behind the wheel. "We're with the FBI. What's your name?"

"Bert."

"Bert, you can catch that kid with this, right?"

Bert smiled and said, "Not a problem," and turned the key. The motor started with a throaty roar.

"How am I supposed to get in?" Ross asked, waving his right arm in the sling like a broken wing.

Jack crouched and intertwined his fingers under the water. "Step here, like you're getting on a horse."

Ross held the boat with his left hand, stepped into the stirrup Jack had created, and swung his other leg into the boat without kicking Jack in the head. He climbed into the seat to the left of the driver.

Jack grabbed the side of the boat, pushed himself up and in as it rocked down, scrambled up to the front deck, and sat on the floor. "Let's go!"

"Hang on," Bert said. The nose of the boat rose into the air as the motor thrust drove the back end forward and the nose up.

Jack was thrown onto his back and struggled against gravity and momentum to right himself until the boat planed out. He scrambled to his knees and grabbed onto a rope as they raced across the smooth surface of the lake, following the wake of the Sheriff's patrol boat in pursuit of the teen on the jet ski.

"Are you OK, Jack?" Ross asked.

"I'm fine. Can we catch him?" Jack yelled back.

Bert inched the throttle further ahead and the boat accelerated. "His top speed, if he's gutsy enough to push it, is fifty or sixty. We're faster. We'll catch him."

The teen was out in the middle of the lake with nowhere to hide, making a beeline for the other side of the lake. He was about three hundred yards ahead of the Sheriff. Bert steered to the left out of the Sheriff's wake and passed him.

"Let's swing out and cut him off. Show him he can't outrun us." Smiling, Jack turned and looked at Ross. "You OK, Junior?"

"I'm fine."

Bert ran parallel to the teen. "Hey, kid!" Jack yelled. "Stop! We just want to talk to you!"

The kid veered to the right.

"He's more maneuverable than we are," Bert said.

Ross chimed in. "Let's cut him off and make some waves. He has to slow down for the waves."

Bert circled the boat to the right. Jack rocked left and grabbed onto the side.

"Hang on, Jack," Ross yelled.

The bass boat was on the tail of the jet ski; it passed it on the right side and then turned left, making waves in front of the jet skier, forcing him back in the direction they had come from. The kid hit the waves, jumping the machine into the air. The jet ski motor groaned and screamed as it left the water and reentered.

Jack was on his knees on the front of the boat. "Come on, kid. We're with the FBI and just want to talk. You aren't going to lose us!"

The boy sat atop the idling machine as it bobbed in the

water and looked at Jack, then over his shoulder at the Sheriff's boat that was approaching.

"Turn it off and we'll come over and talk," Jack added.

The boy turned off the jet ski and the sound of the idling motor stopped. "Is she dead?" he asked.

"Let's go talk to him," said Jack.

29

Jack spoke slowly and quietly to control the emotion and to keep Junior focused on procedures and the job ahead of them.

"I think somebody killed her. You heard what the kid told us. She was on a big boat partying the last they saw her. We'll know more by the end of day after the ME makes a ruling. If this was related, we need to keep doing our jobs and find the Governor."

Jack opened and closed cupboard doors in the kitchen. "Where are your glasses, Junior? I need a drink of water."

Ross walked into the kitchen, grabbed a glass out of the cupboard and handed it to Jack. "We don't know shit, do we?"

"Not yet, Junior, but we will." Jack drank his glass of water, thinking about how to calm Ross down. "Junior, you get changed and then you and I are going to Mrs. Humphrey's funeral to see if anybody shows up there that shouldn't be there, besides us. Then we're going to see what else we can find out about Sandy. The Sheriff will keep looking for the boat."

In the kitchen, Jack pulled his mobile phone from his pocket and called the Sheriff. While the phone rang, he refilled his water glass, walked into the living room, and sat on the couch. Ross had an apartment typical of a new agent; small, sparsely decorated, used furniture, his road bike parked in the living room, and boxes lined up against the wall, still not unpacked.

"Chief, it's agent Jack Miller. Find that boat yet or learn anything else new from the boys?"

"We've been checking landings, assuming he docked it. We're moving out into the lake now to see if it's anchored. Got a better description of the boat from the boys. That's about it."

"You'll call me if you find something?" Jack asked.

"I got your number," the Sheriff answered.

Ross walked into the living room.

"That was quick," Jack said.

"We aren't going to solve this case sitting here in my apartment. Let's go."

"I see you haven't unpacked yet," Jack said pointing to the boxes against the wall. "Have a good camera or binoculars in any of these?"

"No. Those just have crap in them I don't need; winter clothes, books I don't have time to read. Stuff like that."

"OK, we'll swing by my place. I'll change clothes and grab some equipment we'll need." Jack stood up and put his water glass in the kitchen sink. "Let's go, Junior. You're right. We aren't solving this case sitting here."

Cars, vans, and pickups lined the edge of the
narrow road that snaked through the cemetery.
Each parked vehicle had two tires in the grass and
two on the pavement. Jack drove slowly along the line while
Ross pointed the video camera through the passenger
window to capture the license plates of each of the cars. An
analyst would review the tape later and identify the owner
of each of the cars for them. At the end of the row of cars,
Jack pulled onto the grass, angling the car so Ross would
have a good view of the area around the funeral party and a
good vantage point for capturing faces on film when they
returned to their cars after the burial ceremony.

Jack checked his hair and tie in the mirror. "I'm glad I
found my sunglasses, Junior. I wouldn't have worn yours to a
funeral."

"You look good, Jack. Nice, but official. You'll blend
right in."

"Thanks." Jack handed Ross the camera with the long
zoom lens. "You shouldn't have any problem getting everybody's picture with this. I'll leave the car running with the

AC on for you so you don't die. Be polite. Don't let anybody see you taking their picture."

"Don't worry about me. I'll be waiting for you right here," Ross said.

The heat was almost unbearable. By the time Jack walked across the grass from the car to the gravesite, he was sweating. His shoes crunched through the dry grass, a sound amplified by the quiet of the cemetery. A couple of people glanced at him as he took up position at the back of the group of thirty or so people all facing the pastor preparing to perform the ceremony. Jack bowed his head while he waited for everyone's attention to return to the pastor. Then he looked up and started his surveillance of the group in front of him.

Nobody appeared not to belong. Family, friends, and coworkers were here to provide support and pay their last respects. The pastor said something that got Jack's attention. *Take these persons into your kingdom?* Jack shifted to his right and looked over the shoulder of the man in front of him. Two caskets, side by side, identical in every detail except for their size, sat supported over the holes in the ground into which they would be lowered. The mother and the baby. Jack felt a knot in his stomach. He closed his eyes and turned his face up to the sky. He wanted to swear, but not here. He controlled his anger and returned his attention to the service to pay his respects.

At the conclusion of the service, some people shuffled off to their cars, while others milled around to support each other. Jack waited off to one side in the shade of an old oak tree watching the people around him. A few people had formed a line offering condolences to the husband. Jack waited for most of the people to head to their cars before he approached.

"Mr. Humphrey?" Jack extended his hand. "I'm Special Agent Jack Miller with the FBI. I'm very sorry for your loss. I'm a husband and a father, but I can't imagine what you're going through. I just wanted you to know that we're doing everything we can to catch the man that did this." Mr. Humphrey nodded and Jack turned and strode back to the car.

31

The brown, leather satchel rode smoothly on its side on the seat next to the Governor. He laid his hand protectively on it and gently rubbed the smooth surface. Soon his dreams would come true; his problems would be behind him. He knew this day would come. A quick glance at the satchel proved what the touch of his right hand told him. It was still there.

Months of planning, learning, plotting without knowing if what he dreamt of could come true. His business was a failure, he would soon have to file for bankruptcy, but now it didn't matter.

He drove down a long, winding driveway lined with crab apple trees and hostas. He had been here before, in the spring, when the trees were flowering and filled the air with their intoxicating smell and the pink petals created a path to the house. Vadim provided a newly emigrated Russian family with housing in exchange for their keeping up the property. They worked hard in exchange and also served as guardians. One of them appeared from around the corner of the house as the Governor pulled into a parking spot in front of the garage. When the gardener recognized the Governor, he relaxed and walked over to the car and opened the door for him.

"He's at the pool, sir. Can I help you with your bag?"

The Governor held tightly to the handle of the satchel. "I'll take it, thanks. I probably won't be long."

The sun shimmered on the surface of the swimming pool. A light breeze pushed a blue air mattress around in the corner of the pool where it gently bumped against the side. Vadim looked up from his book and waved the Governor to join him in a lounge chair next to him. A table between the two chairs held a pitcher of something cold. Its sides dripped with condensation from the humid air. "Hello, my friend. Join me. Can I offer you some lemonade?"

The Governor sat down in the chair and gently set the satchel on its side at his feet. "I would love a glass, thanks." The Governor drank half of it and put the glass on the table. With the pleasantries completed between them, he couldn't wait to get on to why he was here.

"Vadim, I have been successful in obtaining the final piece."

Vadim closed his book and sat up. "You got it?"

"Yes, but I have a small problem I want to take care of."

"What is it?" Vadim asked.

"One of the FBI agents who's been trying to solve the bank robberies. He's getting closer than I would like him to be. I have a plan to take care of him and I think the distraction may be beneficial to our other endeavor."

"How can I help?"

"I need a gun, and a rifle with a scope." The Governor sat up and turned to look at Vadim. "I need it tonight, and I need to practice some. It'll be about a quarter mile shot."

"Let me get somebody to take care of it for you."

"Thanks, but it's something I need to do." The Governor forced himself to relax and speak evenly. "It's safe. I won't put the job at risk, but it's something I need to do."

Vadim swatted a yellow jacket away from the lip of his glass of lemonade. "You are sure I cannot have somebody take care of this for you?" The question hung in the air. "It would be no problem."

The Governor shook his head.

One of the gardeners appeared from behind them through some bushes. Vadim and the gardener exchanged some words in Russian before Vadim turned to the Governor.

"Follow him. He will get you everything you need. I will take the satchel. Is everything I need here?"

"Everything but the password."

32

The line of oak trees created a horizontal shadow in the distance from the setting sun. Above the shadow, the hill in the background formed a backdrop of greens and oranges as the sun reflected off the grass and wild flowers. In the shadow below, the greens were darker or gray. A series of white discs hung from branches, appearing to hover in mid-air. They hung by monofilament line attached to large branches, twisting lazily in the air like a giant mobile, out of place in the natural setting. The plate on the left turned slowly showing a circle, and then a line as its edge faced the trees and then again, a circle. Then it shattered, leaving a cloud of plaster dust in its place and a loud explosion sounded and echoed off the hill.

The Governor exhaled the remaining air in his lungs and took another breath, as he lay prone on the ground, his eye still at the eyepiece of the scope attached to the rifle cradled across his left arm.

"Very nice. Good timing, just left of center," the voice said from behind the Governor. Vadim had arranged for the Governor to visit a shooting range run by one of his friends west of the Twin Cities metro area. The men he met here had a variety of rifles for him to choose from and were providing him with some instruction. "Try again. The next plate. Remember to watch the target, anticipate, breathe, relax. It is not too much to remember, no?"

"I've got it," the Governor responded as he watched the plate spin in the circle of the scope, trying to keep the cross hairs centered on it as it came into full view with each revolution.

"When you are near ready, take a full breath, release part of it, and gently pull the trigger."

The Governor tried to relax as he lay on the ground, the rifle resting on a dead tree that had fallen, and was bare of bark. He wanted to practice in as close to real conditions as he could create. The plate turned slowly, approximately a quarter of a mile away. Taking a deep breath, the Governor tried to ignore the sweat that ran down his temples and back. He exhaled slowly, held his breath. The circle in the scope turned to a line and started to form a circle on the next revolution. He gently pulled the trigger, increasing the pressure on it, feeling it resist until the force of his pull overcame it and the rifle barked, ramming its stock back into his shoulder, causing the Governor to blink. He refocused on the plate and saw it spinning rapidly, a small chip gone from its edge.

"Try again. That is good enough for your purposes. Three more plates and we'll move on to another exercise."

The Governor repeated the process, hitting the target on each of his subsequent tries. The rifle began to feel more comfortable in his grip and his confidence grew. The barrel of the rifle felt warm against the skin of his hand. He sat up and reloaded to prepare for the exercise his teachers had planned for him next. The ammunition was not large. He was using smaller rounds to keep the sound down, a quieter "pop" instead of a louder "boom." The bullets would be effective despite their size.

IT HAD BEEN A LONG DAY. Ross needed somebody to talk with so Jack had hung out with him at his apartment for a while when he'd dropped him off. The injury, its effect on his ability to sleep, what had happened to Sandy, it was all taking a toll on Ross, whether he was ready to admit it or not. It was mostly Sandy. Ross had really been interested in her and he was going to get hit hard over the next couple of days by the pain in his heart.

At home now, Jack looked at his watch and swore. It was too late to call the kids and wish them a good night. He tried to remember when he'd talked to them last. The days were a blur for him too. He grabbed a beer from the fridge and a bag of pretzels off the counter and sat on the couch in front of the television, using the remote to flip through the stations to catch up with what was happening in the rest of the world. The Twins beat Detroit six to three, rain was in the forecast...again, no tornados had been spotted today, fireworks displays were planned around the metro area whether it rained or not, and there wasn't any mention of a bank robbery or a homicide. The Governor and the bank robbery/murder were already old news unless something new happened that the public needed to know. Jack thought he better talk about public relations with Junior tomorrow.

The funeral today had been tough. He missed his kids as they spent the night with Julie at her parents' house, but he couldn't imagine what he would do if they were killed. Mr. Humphrey was going to have a tough summer ahead of him. It would be a while before the memory of the small casket didn't stir up strong emotions in Jack's soul, having two kids of his own.

Jack tipped back the beer and drained it. A small belch escaped his lips. The news ended and went to the introduction to the Late Show with David Letterman. Jack couldn't decide if he wanted another beer or bed until he heard who was going to be a guest tonight. Salma Hayek was on to promote her new movie so Jack got up at the commercial to get himself another beer from the fridge.

After popping off the bottle cap from a Bass Ale, Jack picked up the phone and debated whether or not to call Julie and talk about the Fourth of July. He put the phone to his ear and heard the multiple beeps indicating he had a message. He punched in the code in the handset of the cordless phone as he walked back to settle down in front of the television again. Jack smiled at the message on the phone and followed that up with an excited exclamation of a whispered "all right". Julie had decided that the four of them should get together for the Fourth of July celebration on Nicollet Island, keeping the family tradition alive. He replayed the message three times before saving it to make sure he heard it right and also just to listen to his wife's voice. The second message was from Patty. She said she had some information for him on the Governor case and wanted to talk with him tonight.

Jack dialed Patty's number. It was ten-forty. It might be late, but she wanted to talk with him tonight. He leaned back in his chair, listening to the phone ringing and waited for her to answer.

She answered on the second ring. "Jack."

"Hey, uh, yeah. How did you know it was me? I'm the only one calling you this late?" he asked.

"Caller ID, Jack."

Jack closed his eyes and rested his head back against the throw pillow. The beer was overcoming the effects of the day and he was suddenly very tired. "Right. You have some information for me?"

"I do, but I don't want to share it over the phone."

"It's been a long day, Patty. You'll have to tell me over the phone or share it with me tomorrow. I need to go to sleep."

"Tomorrow's fine. If you're running in the morning, I can be outside your house before the sun comes up. We'll get out while it's not too hot and I can share the information with you."

She wasn't going to give up. Jack thought about the first call on his voicemail from Julie, and inhaled and exhaled through his nose. He told himself Patty's call meant nothing. She had some information she wanted to share and if it took a run with her to get her to share it, he would do it.

"Jack, you still there?" Patty asked.

Jack opened his eyes. "Yeah. If you're up for six miles, be outside my house at five thirty and I'll show you some nice paths along the river."

33

Jack slowly opened his eyes. Empty beer bottles stood in a row on the coffee table in front of him. The pillow was wet against his face where he had drooled. He flipped the pillow over and closed his eyes, but his bladder coaxed him back from entering his dream. On his way to the bathroom, he squinted at the microwave in the kitchen and saw the blue numbers showing 5:12.

On his way back from the bathroom, he grabbed his running clothes. He sat in his living room, laced up his shoes, and thought about the call from Julie the night before. She wanted to get back together, at least for a day. It was a start. The four of them together for the day at Nicollet Island celebrating the Fourth of July, Jack was excited about it. He glanced at the phone in its cradle and thought about the message, tempted to listen to it again. Maybe it was more than a start.

In the kitchen, Jack drank a large glass of water. The thermometer on the counter said it was already seventy degrees outside. Jack pinched the small roll on his stomach and decided to wear a tank top since he'd be running with Patty, if she showed up.

Jack pulled the front door shut behind him and positioned himself on the steps facing the house. His toes were perched on the edge of the concrete steps as he lowered himself to stretch out his calf muscles. He felt the calves of his legs slowly burn as the muscles lengthened like rubber bands.

"So you decided to show up," Jack said to Patty's reflection in the window as she walked up the front walk behind him.

"I didn't think you'd be up this early. Seems like you've had some late nights lately with this investigation." Patty stopped on the sidewalk and bent over into her own stretch, knees locked, her forehead pressed against them as she grabbed her ankles.

"Show off," Jack said.

"Yoga, you should try it." Patty put her hands out in front of her on the sidewalk and posed in an inverted vee.

Jack took the opportunity to check out Patty's back, butt, and legs. Her black hair was tied back in a ponytail. The white top showed off her brown skin and the muscles of her back, shoulders, and arms. Her legs were well proportioned from her taut hamstrings down to her defined calves.

Then he bent over to reach towards his toes, his fingers reaching his shins. "Whatever. You ready to run? I usually go down by the river, through the trees. Kind of gets you out of the city."

Patty rolled her head from her left shoulder, to her chest, and to her right shoulder. Then she windmilled her arms in large circles. "Lead the way, Miller."

By the time Jack reached West River Road, the sweat started to trickle from the pores of his head and his chest.

Patty ran to his side or slightly behind him. "How's this pace?"

"Six miles?" Patty asked. "This will work."

Jack looked over at Patty. She was running easily alongside him, breathing without a struggle. "Am I the only one that sweats?"

"I don't sweat, I glisten."

"Well, you're not glistening yet."

Patty laughed.

The birds were flitting about singing their morning songs as the sky to the east warmed to an orange glow. Jack wiped the sweat from his forehead with his hand and jogged automatically onto a path that led down into the woods, deeper into the Mississippi River gorge. A sign at the head of the path said "Winchell Trail."

"This way," Jack said and motioned down the hill through the trees.

Jack had explored the trail with his son, Willy, before. Its history was that it was an old Indian trail used to move up and down the bank of the river. Willy imagined the past as he walked down the trail with his dad and they found routes down to the river. The well-worn path through the brush and trees at spots had been paved or had chain link fences erected to keep people from falling down the steep slope.

The path offered some relief from the heat with the cooler night air trapped among the trees, but there was no breeze to evaporate the sweat from Jack's skin and help to cool him. As he worked his way along the trail, he looked about twenty feet ahead for rocks, roots, and holes to avoid. He hadn't sprained an ankle yet on a morning run on this trail and he wasn't going to start today.

Jack also found that if he focused on the trail and where to step, that kept part of his brain busy and the other part of his brain found something else to keep it occupied, usually his cases from work. Patty hadn't told him yet what she wanted to share with him and he was trying to decide if he should wait or push for the info.

"You were right, Miller."

Jack yelled back over his shoulder. "What's that?"

"This path down here is great!"

"Don't tell anybody. I don't want to share it."

34

The sun was coming up, but the Mississippi River Gorge was still in shadows. The rays of color from the rising sun just touched the tops of the oaks and elms lining the top of the gorge on either side of the river. The river's surface was ninety feet below the tops of the trees, carrying water from northern Minnesota to the Gulf of Mexico.

The Governor was sweating as he worked his way down through the trees from the street to the riverbank below. He was in a hurry to be set for when Jack ran by. Vadim's surveillance said Agent Miller ran most mornings, leaving his house at five thirty. Vadim's cohorts had also scouted out this spot for the Governor to shoot from.

He wrapped the rifle in a jumble of fishing rods he carried in one hand, a plastic pail filled with ammunition and his camouflaged gillie suit in the other. At the edge of the river, he checked the time. Jack should be running across the river from him in about five minutes.

The Governor stood in the sand along the riverbank and dumped the contents of the pail by a tree. He put the plastic pail upside down on the shore for a stool, and propped up a fishing pole next to it with the line in the water.

A large log was half-buried in the sand. Weeds and brush grew up around it. He pulled the gillie suit over his shoulders and lay behind the log. He was almost completely out of sight. He looked up and down the opposite bank of the river. Seeing nobody, he looked to the south, up at the Ford Parkway Bridge, the only place somebody may be able to see him as he was exposed from above.

Under the netting, leaning on the log, he felt secure, hidden. He wiggled and shifted to move the sand until it conformed to his body. The rifle barrel rested on a branch from the fallen tree. He held the stock against his shoulder and moved his eye to the scope. The trees across the river were suddenly in focus. The Governor looked through the scope and scanned slowly up and down the river to make sure he could move the rifle freely. He also assessed the path through the trees to identify the best spot to execute his plan. He didn't want his prey to have a place to hide. He wanted him in the open, trapped. The Governor looked up and down the opposite bank, took a deep breath and exhaled to relax. Any minute.

THE CRACKED blacktop path curved up the slope and merged with the bike path before turning back down into the woods farther ahead. Jack slowed and Patty caught up with him.

"Here's your chance, Patty. We've gone a mile. You can turn around here or it's another mile before we come out of the woods again up by the Ford Parkway Bridge."

"Let's keep going."

"You going to tell me what info you found out?"

"Later." Patty ran out ahead of Jack. "Follow me."

Jack followed Patty into the woods. She was running faster than he had up to this point and he was breathing heavier than he had before. "So what was it... you found out?"

"Shut up, Miller, or I'll run faster so you can't talk at all."

Jack stayed quiet and ran on the path behind Patty. Running with somebody else wasn't so bad, if it was a beautiful woman and she was running in front of you. He tried to guess what she might have found out, running different scenarios through his head. Back down the slope in the trees, it was quiet again; the only sound was their feet pounding along the path. Jack felt himself pushing to keep up, running at a faster pace than normal.

"How can somebody as short as you run so fast?"

"I don't have as much gravity pulling on me. Just move the legs fast, Miller."

The walking path ran along the river about halfway up the slope between the river and the road above. A dirt path veered down the slope to the river.

"Follow the path down the hill," Jack panted. "We'll get down closer to the river."

Patty slowed and worked her way down the steep dirt path to a path that ran along the Mississippi River. They ran in the same direction as the river flowed.

"This is great being this close to the river. I feel it's pulling us along with it."

"Down here can be a different world," Jack said, having a chance to catch his breath as they slowed, coming down the slope. "I've seen deer, fox, and a coyote."

Patty kept running ahead, her feet crunching across the dead leaves on the dirt path. "I haven't seen the Ford

Parkway Bridge from down here before," she yelled back over her shoulder.

"I told you, everything is different down here."

THE GOVERNOR CAUGHT some movement through the scope. He blinked hard and settled in behind it. The runner in the crosshairs was a woman. She was attractive, and ran smoothly along the trail. She turned her head and it looked like she was saying something. It was almost as if she was talking to him.

He stopped tracking the woman and saw his target, as Special Agent Jack Miller ran into his view. The Governor was surprised to see him running with somebody else this morning. He needed to think quickly. He had planned options, but two runners hadn't been one of them.

His plan wasn't just to shoot Jack without warning. He wanted to toy with him. Draw out the fun so Jack knew the Governor was in control. He focused on controlling his breathing and caressed the trigger with his finger.

Jack entered the shooting zone, the area where the running path squeezed between the steep wall and the river with no place to hide. The Governor centered the cross hairs on his target and then pivoted the gun on top of the log it was resting on, tracking to the left to keep pace with the runner, and moving the crosshairs slightly ahead just as he had with the tires during practice. He slipped off the safety, took a deep breath, exhaled part of it, and squeezed the trigger.

35

J ack continued to watch his step, but he was also watching Patty. Her strong legs carried her ahead of him down the trail. The straps of her jogging top framed her shoulders. He could see the muscles shift under the skin as her arms pumped forward and back.

"Rock!" Patty shouted back over her shoulder.

Jack saw it as she passed over it and stepped quickly around it.

"We have to run back up there?" Patty asked, nodding at the bridge ahead of them sixty feet above.

"I didn't say it was a flat six-mile run."

Patty held up her right hand and flipped him the bird. Jack was laughing to himself when Patty screamed and went down on the trail ahead of him, rolling across the dirt. A bang sounded and echoed in the river gorge. Jack ran up to Patty, suspecting she'd sprained her ankle, but then the sound registered. Jack pushed Patty's head down onto the ground and shielded her body. "Stay down."

"I'm bleeding!" Patty yelled. She was holding her leg. Blood covered her hands and ran down her thigh.

Jack pulled off his tank top and wiped off her leg. A small dot showed in the hamstring on the back of her leg. "I think you've been shot. Put this on it."

"Shot?" Patty asked, confused and in pain. She tried to sit up.

Jack held her down. "Stay down." He scanned the far bank of the river from the water to the trees to the road above the river gorge. "I don't know what happened, but you need to stay down until we figure out what's going on. It's not bleeding too bad, so we stay down for a little bit."

"Somebody shot me?"

"Shh, you'll be OK," Jack tried to calm Patty. "Probably some freak accident. Just hold my shirt over the wound."

Jack tried to assess their situation. This wasn't some freak accident. People didn't shoot guns down in the river gorge early in the morning and accidentally hit somebody who happened to be running by. She had definitely been shot. He could tell by the entrance wound in her leg. Small caliber, meant to hurt. It had to be the Governor.

He didn't like where they were. He went back through all of his training and experience as an agent. He had to assess the situation and make some decisions. There were a few trees around, but they were on a part of the path down by the river with the steep wall behind them. They were kind of in the shadows, but in a short time, the rising sun would expose them in a brighter light, making them easier targets. The path was worn enough that it was a small trough. With Patty lying flat in it, it offered some protection.

Why did he shoot Patty? He'd been waiting for him to go out on his morning run. The Governor had been watching him. Patty being here was a surprise. She wasn't the target. The Governor was playing some sick game with Jack.

"Jack. I'm going to kill whoever shot me," Patty said between clenched teeth.

"Listen. I think he wants me, but we can't just sit here all morning. We're off the usual path down here, but somebody else might come along."

"They can go for help for us," Patty said.

"Or he'll shoot them too."

Patty continued lying on the path, sucking breaths between her teeth against the pain. "Not good. So what do we do?"

"I'm going to run a little farther down the path. When he starts shooting, you go back the other way and try to get behind a tree. Stay in the path. Stay down."

"He's going to shoot at you? Why hasn't he shot you sitting here?"

"He either can't see me or he's toying with me. I don't think he was shooting at you. I think he was shooting at me. But with us running it threw him off."

"I'll kill him," Patty said.

"You ready?" Jack asked. He wanted to move while Patty was worked up and mad, using her anger to get past her pain.

"Yeah."

"Stay low." Jack jumped up and ran farther along the path, away from her. The wall of the gorge ahead of him puffed dirt as a bullet hit it and Jack heard the report of the rifle echo down the river. Jack kept running. A second bullet hit a branch on a tree to his right. The Governor had hit Patty when she was running. Jack didn't want to give him the chance. He hoped Patty had used this chance to run the other way for cover. Jack veered left in his run and after three strong paces, dove from the riverbank into the river.

The shallow dive brought Jack out into the river away

from the riverbank. The cold water instantly gripped him and carried him along with it as it made its way south towards the Gulf of Mexico. When Jack surfaced, he looked back and saw Patty scrambling and limping the other way. She quickly became smaller as he was carried the other direction in the current. She'd be safe.

Jack did a dive and got below the surface, out of sight, where the water could carry him safely farther downstream away from the Governor. He held his breath and counted, trying to imagine how far he had moved down river. He wanted to get back to shore and get out near the base of the Ford Parkway Bridge. From there, he could make it up to the road for help.

When his head broke above water for the second time, Jack wiped the water from his eyes and looked back across the river, trying to see if he could tell where the Governor might be. He heard another shot but couldn't tell where it hit. He turned and swam hard towards the bank. He made some progress, but was moving downstream much faster than he had anticipated. For each stroke towards the bank, he moved further downstream. It didn't look like he would be able to reach the riverbank at a point where he would be able to crawl out.

The river pulled him towards the locks on the west side of the river. There were two locks side-by-side for moving barges and boats past the dam used to provide electricity to the Ford truck plant. He floated by the concrete walls along the riverbank below the bridge. There was no way to get out of the river from here.

A loud bang sounded as a bullet ricocheted off one of the steel lock doors. The shot wasn't close to him, but served notice that the Governor was still there and Jack was still within range. Jack dragged his hand and foot along the wall, trying to slow his progress, trying to allow himself time to examine the wall for a ladder, a hand hold, something to help him get out of the river. He floated below a red button on the wall. The button was used by boat drivers to signal the lock operators to open the locks for the boats. Jack kicked his legs to propel his body out of the water and stretched his right arm up the wall, but he was still four to six feet short of reaching the button.

Jack put his thumb and second finger just inside his lips and blew, whistling a high-pitched shriek, just as his uncle had taught him thirty years before. He had to get the attention of somebody working at the locks or somebody passing over on the bridge. He didn't have many options left. Swimming east, past the locks would put him in a position where the river would carry him over the dam, almost certainly killing him as the churning water would hold him in its grip at the base of the dam until he drowned. Here in the calmer water in front of the lock, he was open to a shot by the Governor. Jack swam to the lock door and positioned himself in the corner between the steel door and concrete wall between the two locks. His exposure to the Governor was minimized. He treaded water, shivered, and whistled.

THE GOVERNOR TOOK one last shot at Jack, aiming more for the steel doors, certain he wouldn't hit him from this distance. But he wanted Jack to stay pinned in the corner by the steel lock doors. After the shot, the Governor turned the scope back up stream to see what the woman was doing. She was still behind the tree, using it for protection from the shooting.

The sound of a horn echoed up the river gorge walls. The lock operators must have learned somebody was in the water and sounded the alarm. The Governor decided it was time to leave and pulled the camouflaged netting off. Then he stood, wiped the sand from his clothes, and threw the rifle, netting, and fishing equipment into the river.

He took a last look towards Agent Miller and then his running partner before turning and walking through the trees, and then entered the opening of a storm sewer that emptied into the Mississippi River.

36

The St. Paul police cordoned off East River Road and were investigating the trees along the riverbank with dogs, trying to find the shooter and the site from where the shots had come. The Sheriff's department had launched a boat from the University of Minnesota two miles upstream and was patrolling the river from there to the Ford Parkway Bridge, looking for signs of the shooter. The shooter had to go up the bank to the road or north along the river. The only way south was the way Jack had done it, in the water, and from the east side of the river, a swimmer would be swept over the dam.

The FBI dispatched a tactical team to Jack's location and took up positions on the west side of the river to provide protection to the paramedics who were tending to Patty. Jack and the tactical team's lead waited at the ambulance parked on the bike trail at the top of the river gorge, next to the road. Somebody had given Jack a t-shirt and he sat on the bumper of the ambulance, trying to recover from his time in the river and the effects of the adrenaline leaving his system.

The lead was listening to a report from the radio, the earpiece keeping Jack from listening in.

"What is it?" Jack asked.

"A couple of things. Your running partner is going to be OK. She's on her way to HCMC. She's pissed and says you owe her." The lead smiled. "She's feisty."

"That word fits. What else?"

"They found the shooting site. The shooter positioned himself in the sand on the other side of the river. Looks like he was laying behind an old tree on the riverbank. That's it, no shooter, no gun, nothing else." The lead stood in front of Jack, arms crossed over his Kevlar vest. "There's a vehicle in the parking lot above there. May have been the shooter's. We're checking it out." Drivers on their way to work slowed their cars as they drove by on River Road to see what was going on. "What do you have for me, Jack?"

"It's got to be the Governor, the bank robber. He was waiting for me. I usually run alone along this route in the morning. I don't know why he shot Patty. Hit her by accident or just messing with me." The words poured out of Jack. "They haven't found anything?"

"Not yet."

"Where's Ross?" Jack asked.

"He's coordinating services from the office. You want to talk with him?"

Jack leaned back against the door of the ambulance and closed his eyes. He started shivering.

"Hey, Miller. You OK?" The lead shook Jack by the shoulder. "Jack."

Jack opened his eyes. "Yeah, I'm OK. Just really tired."

"You're wet, a little dehydrated, and coming down from the adrenaline rush." The lead kept a hand on Jack's shoulder to make sure he didn't faint or fall to the ground.

"Let's get you home to your family; you need to sleep a little." The lead motioned to the paramedic to come to the back of the ambulance.

Jack's head snapped up at the mention of his family. If the Governor knew who he was, he may know he had a family. "Get me Ross on the radio."

The lead handed Jack his radio and earpiece. Jack asked him to get him a ride to his house and then spoke into the radio. "Junior, it's me."

"What's going on out there? You OK?"

"I'm fine. Listen. Get the St. Louis Park police to go by my in-laws' house and watch it, but not to go in. I want to make sure Julie and the kids are fine and stay that way. Tell the police I'm coming to check out the house."

THE MERCURY COUGAR skidded to a quick stop in the driveway. Jack was out before it had rocked back into place and settled. On the way over, he had called his in-laws and nobody had answered. Then he tried Julie's cell phone and it went straight to her voice mail. He cut the twenty-minute drive to fifteen by speeding the whole way, but it still seemed to take forever. Jack had called ahead to the patrols that were around the house and had them looking for any individuals that didn't seem to belong. All was quiet and Jack told himself that everything was fine. The Governor was after him, not his family, and probably wouldn't know they weren't living with him.

Jack got out of the car wearing his FBI windbreaker over his running gear. The jacket, blue nylon with the three letters on the back in gold, was the only clean thing Jack was wearing. Two police officers followed him up to the door, pulling their guns from their holsters and holding them

down at their sides, taking Jack's lead. They looked at him as
he stood there and exchanged a look. Jack was still muddy
from the top of his head to his shoes. He smelled of sweat,
river mud, and adrenaline and he had a look in his eye. He
hadn't said a word to them yet. He tried the door and found
it locked.

One of the officers cleared his throat to get Jack's attention. "What do you want us to do?"

Jack looked through the window of the front door and
then turned. "We're going to go in and clear the house."

"Do we have a warrant?"

"Something better." Jack tipped up a flowerpot on the
corner of the front step and grabbed something from under
it. "We have a key." He glanced through the front window
again. "Here's the deal. My in-laws live here, a couple in
their late sixties. My wife and children are visiting. I believe
they may be in danger." Jack looked from one officer to the
other. "I think the house is empty, but we're going to make
sure. You ready?"

Both officers swallowed and nodded.

"OK, let's go. And try not to shoot each other." Jack slid
the key into the lock and slowly opened the door.

THE HOUSE WAS quiet and the air was cool from the air-
conditioning. Jack went first, searching through the living
room and kitchen. He sensed nothing. It didn't feel like
there was anybody there. Everything was in its place. He
noticed a couple of the kids' things in the house, reminding
him that they were living here now. Lynn's book, a fantasy,
lay open on the kitchen table and Willy's toy cars were
parked under the coffee table. The officers went down the
hall to the left and checked out the bedrooms and bath-

room. Jack opened the door leading to the attached garage and looked around. It was a two-car garage with the items of suburban life stored neatly inside. The lawnmower and snow blower were against the far wall. An extension ladder and a six-foot ladder hung on the wall next to snow and garden shovels. A Chevy Malibu was parked in the spot closest to the door where Jack stood. The spot next to it was empty. Julie's dad's pickup truck that parked in that spot was gone.

"Anything?" one of the officers asked from behind Jack.

"One of their cars is gone." Jack turned and pointed at the officer that was doing the talking. "You stay here. We're going to check out the basement."

The basement was dark and just as quiet. Sunlight came in through the small windows. Clean clothes were neatly folded in clothes baskets in the laundry room. The officer rejoined Jack after checking out the shop area under the stairs. He sniffed audibly once, cleared his throat, and backed a step away from Jack.

"Do I smell?" Jack asked.

"Maybe a little."

Jack pulled out the windbreaker from his chest, stuck his nose down inside it, and sniffed. "Maybe more than a little. Sorry, it's been a long morning." He shook his head. "There's nobody here. Let's go."

Out on the lawn, Jack thanked the officers and asked them to keep an eye on the house in the future. He put the key back where he found it and sat down on the front step. Where the heck was everybody? His in-laws may be at their cabin. They never planned their time away. They just went. But, they weren't answering their phone. Julie and the kids should be around. He pulled the left sleeve of the wind-breaker up so he could see his watch. He wiped off the mud-covered face with his thumb so he could read it. Just two hours since he woke up this morning. Where were they? He was just about to call Ross and update him when the phone in his pocket rang. He fumbled around in his pocket for it, flipped it open so he could see who was calling, and hit talk. "Jules, where are you?"

"Jack, I got your message. What's going on?"

"Where are you? Are the kids with you?" Jack was pacing back and forth in front of the house.

"We're in St. Paul. We went out for breakfast on our way to the Como Zoo." There was silence between them as Jack didn't answer, relieved that they were OK. "Hello? Jack, you still there?"

"Yeah."

"What's going on, Jack?"

"Nothing."

"Jack?"

"Well, something." Jack sat down on the step again. "You may see it on the news tonight. Somebody took a shot at me while I was out for my run this morning." Jack heard Julie suck in a breath. "Don't worry. I'm OK. I think it was the Governor. I don't think he knows where you guys are staying, but I came over to your mom and dad's to check it out. To make sure he didn't come over here. Where are your mom and dad?"

"They decided to go up to the cabin."

"That's what I figured. Are you going up there?"

"We were planning to stay here for the Fourth, remember? We're going to Nicollet Island together," Julie said.

Together, she said together, Jack thought. They should be safe in a crowd and if he was with them he could keep an eye on them. "Sorry, with all this stuff going on I forgot what day it was. I can't wait for the four of us to hang out together, but I don't want you staying at your mom and dad's and," Jack hated saying it, "I don't think you should come home. Where else could you stay tonight?"

"Jack, I can't put somebody else out tonight. It's the Fourth of July weekend. People have plans. You don't think we'd be OK at Mom and Dad's?"

"I'd sleep better tonight knowing you weren't here. How about you guys go down to the Marriot at the old depot downtown, the one with the waterpark. I'll get you a room and bring you your clothes and swimsuits. The kids can swim and you can sleep in."

"You know what we need?"

"I'm sitting at your parents'. I'll throw some stuff together and drop it off for you at the hotel. You'll have fun, I'll sleep better, and I'll pick you guys up in the morning and we'll walk over to Nicollet Island to spend the day."

Now it was Julie's turn to be quiet. Jack listened to the silence on the other end; the only sound was the voices of his kids in the background arguing over something.

"Jules?"

"OK. We have some other stuff to do today. We'll get that done and go to the hotel."

"Pinky promise me you're not coming over here."

"I promise," Julie said.

"I'm really serious, Jules. You have to stay away, lay low, take it easy."

"I promise, Jack."

"OK. I'll get the stuff, leave it at the hotel, and I'll pick you guys up tomorrow morning at nine? We'll get some breakfast together."

"The kids are looking forward to tomorrow."

"Me too. Turn off your phone and check for messages at

the hotel. This guy knows his stuff and he'll track you if he knows your phone number."

"Really?"

"Yes, I'm serious. Turn your phone off. I'll get you a different one."

"OK, Jack. Talk to you later. Be careful."

"Always am."

Jack held the phone to his ear to make sure Jules wasn't still there, not wanting to let go. Finally he flipped the phone shut, got up, and got the key out again from its hiding spot and went in to gather his family's things for the next few days.

37

"Junior, any news?"

"There's a team working the river sites. Nothing's turned up yet. You OK?"

"Yeah. I'm cleaned up and ready to get to work. You ready for some field work?" Jack asked.

"What's the plan?"

Jack pulled his car into the convenience store lot and stopped at the gas pump. "I have to get some gas and cash and then I'll pick you up. Be ready to go in fifteen minutes. Bring the files with you so we can take a look at them."

Jack stopped the Mercury Cougar outside the door of the FBI offices to pick up Ross. "Come on, Junior," Jack said to the windshield. There was a lot to do and he wanted to get going. He took another drink of the convenience store coffee and grimaced at the bitter taste of the lukewarm beverage. He opened the car door and poured the coffee onto the parking lot. The passenger door opened and Ross got in.

"Had enough coffee?"

"Enough of that coffee. Buckle up; we have a lot to do." Jack put the car in drive and drove out of the lot while Junior struggled with the seat belt with his one good arm.

"You sure you're OK, Jack?" Junior asked.

"Patty's been shot. I'm OK, but I'm pissed." Jack turned left through a yellow light, and then made a quick right into the drive of the Marriott Hotel at the downtown Depot, a refurbished train station that now housed a hotel, water park, and indoor ice-skating rink.

"What're we doing here?" Ross asked the empty driver's seat. Jack was already out of the car and walking back to the trunk. Ross fumbled with the seat belt and opened the door. "You want me to come with you, Jack?"

"Yep, let's go. This is the first stop." Jack didn't stop to check on Ross. Instead, he walked straight up to the front desk.

"Can I help you, sir?" The college-aged woman with blonde, shoulder length hair smiled at Jack.

Jack returned her smile. "Hi...," Jack searched for her name tag, and Ross joined him at the counter. "Hailey. I need two rooms, preferably across from each other. One with two beds for a woman with two children, the other room can have one or two beds."

Hailey directed her attention to her computer. "Let me see what we have available." She guided the mouse as she searched. Her manicured nails clicked on the computer keys.

"Above the ground floor," Ross added.

Jack looked at Ross, nodded, and turned to Hailey. "Right, above the ground floor." Jack was glad Ross was along. He may be beat up, but he was thinking straight and had figured out what was going on.

"I have two rooms on the second floor, across the hall from each other. Both have two queen-size beds." Hailey looked at Jack, then quickly glanced at Ross, his face, and then the arm in its sling and she smiled again at Jack.

"Sounds great, I'll take them."

"Did you want the water park package too?"

"For the room with the mom and her two kids."

"What credit card did you want to put this on?"

Jack took out his wallet. "I'll be paying in cash."

"That's fine, sir, but I still need a card in case there are other charges."

Jack laid his FBI credentials on the counter in front of the young woman. She looked down and then back and forth from Ross to Jack. Jack leaned forward and spoke in a husky whisper. "I need to pay in cash and I can't have anybody be able to track these rooms right now." Hailey nodded, the smile gone from her face, and Jack continued. "I'll put one room under Julie Jacobson." He spelled the last name and looked at Ross. "That's her maiden name."

"The second room?" Hailey asked.

"Just a minute. Are you working the check-in desk for a while?"

"I'll be here all day."

"I'll have her ask for you. She may be looking for a room under Miller, but please don't put that in the computer." Jack smiled, still leaning forward on the counter.

"Not a problem, sir. And the second room?"

"Hailey Fruen." Jack pocketed his credentials. "And Ms. Jacobson isn't to know about the second room. Check them in, give them their water park passes and let them enjoy the evening. If they want anything else, keep the bill and I'll cover it when they check out."

"You can just pay later, sir." Hailey slid card keys to both rooms across the counter to Jack. "The elevator to the second floor is down the hall on your left."

"Thank you, Hailey. I'll put their bags in their room and return the key to you in a few minutes. Remember, this is to be kept quiet and no word of the second room to Ms. Jacobson."

38

Jack drove the Mercury Cougar through the curves of River Road. The windows were down and the hot air blew through the compartment as the car approached a speed bump. Jack accelerated and the car smoothly but loudly passed over the bump as the suspension absorbed the shock.

"Geez, Jack. Where's the fire?" Ross asked as he braced himself and hung on with his one good arm.

"We have a lot to do and not a lot of time." Jack accelerated again. "Hold on." The car slammed over another speed bump. "That's it for the bumps. Get out your phone. Call Sure Thing." Jack kept up the speed down the hill into the lowest part of River Road that ran parallel to the Mississippi, honked his horn, and passed an older Volvo Wagon, its driver honking back at Jack for passing on the two-lane road. An Asian couple standing at the retaining wall fishing looked back from the river to see what was happening behind them on the road while their lines hung in the water eight feet below. The car's transmission shifted as Jack pushed the car up the hill from the river flats.

"I'm getting his voice mail," Ross said loudly to get Jack to hear him over the sound of the car and the wind. Ross held the phone to his ear with his good hand. "Can you roll up this window, Jack, so he can hear me?"

Jack rolled up Ross' window and answered, "Give him the room numbers and tell him I need some tools for surveillance to keep them safe through the night. We'll meet him there in a few hours to see what he has for us." The turn-off of River Road was just ahead. Jack didn't brake, but took his foot from the accelerator as he steered the car through the curve up and around to Franklin Avenue.

Ross leaned to the right to counter-act the force as he spoke into the phone to leave the message for Sure Thing.

There was a stop sign at Franklin Avenue. Jack looked back, accelerated onto the road, and drove across the bridge to the other side of the river. He honked his horn in a staccato pattern, swerved around the cars waiting at the stop light on the east end of the bridge, and headed south.

"Watch out for the St. Paul cops, Mario."

"We're still in Minneapolis, Junior." Jack sped down East River Road. "The St. Paul border is a little farther south. After we go under the train tracks. We need to get you out so you know the city." Jack pushed the button on his door and lowered Ross' window again. "Hey, you know what Sure Thing drives?"

Ross raised his voice again to battle the hot wind blowing through the car. "Something with air-conditioning?"

"I think it has air-conditioning, but it doesn't need much. It's smaller than this car. It's one of those Mini-Coopers." Jack said.

Jack continued to push the Cougar south down East River Road while he and Ross yelled at each other over the sound of the winds that buffeted their hair, debating the benefits of air-conditioning and power controls versus open windows with manual cranks to raise and lower them.

Jack braked and drastically slowed the car down to a stop. Cars were lined up ahead of them on the road and not moving. "Junior, get out and see how long the line is."

"You get out. I'm injured." Ross flapped his elbow, his arm in the sling.

"My car, I'm driving. I have to move up with the traffic."

Ross looked at Jack. Jack looked to the left at the large houses that faced the river. Along this part of the river the houses and yards on the St. Paul side were larger than their Minneapolis counterparts on the other side.

"What do you think these people do?" Ross asked.

"Doctors, lawyers, bank robbers, drug dealers."

"And they say crime doesn't pay."

Jack looked ahead through the windshield. "We're not moving. Hang on." He cranked the steering wheel to the right and slowly drove the car to the curb. The front wheel hit the curb and the car stopped and rocked back. He accelerated the car again and the front wheels climbed up the curb with a lurch, first the right, then the left.

"Ow! What are you doing?" Ross' head bounced off of the door frame. He braced himself in his seat, his good arm on the dashboard of the car.

"Anybody on the bike path?" Jack asked.

"What? No."

Jack pushed the car ahead, the rear wheels bouncing up the curb, before he raced down the paved bike path. He tapped the horn, warning walkers to get out of his way.

"Watch out, Jack!"

Two coeds stepped aside and gave him the finger. Jack

waved out the window in return. "This is much better. Don't you think, Junior? We're moving now."

A St. Paul traffic cop stepped onto the path ahead of them and held out her hand, palm out. Street traffic was turning left at this point. Barricades placed across River Road and the biking path kept automobiles and pedestrians from continuing south from this point. Jack stopped the car on the path ten feet from the officer.

"Sir, what do you think you're doing?" The St. Paul officer approached and stared at Jack through the window of his car, her eyes hidden behind her Oakley sunglasses. "The road and bike path are off limits right now. Do you live up here?"

"Special Agents Miller and Fruen with the FBI. We're going to the site by the river to check it out."

"Couldn't wait in line, gentlemen?"

"We're kind of in a hurry. Lots to do today. First thing is to try and catch the guy that shot at me from up here."

The officer leaned over and looked through the window at Ross. "And you're the guy that got hurt in the car accident."

Ross nodded and Jack answered, "You should be a detective instead of pulling traffic duty."

"You guys be careful. I'll move the barricade for you. The road's clear from here to the site. You'll see where it is. Lots of cars parked in the road." She stood up and yelled at a bike rider starting to ride around the barricade. She moved it out of the way and Jack bounced the car down the curb and accelerated down River Road.

JACK AND ROSS stood in the shade under the mature trees at

the edge of a scenic overlook above the gorge and looked across the river. "You were running over there?" Ross pointed to the riverbank on the other side of the river.

"Yep. And he shot at us from down there." Jack nodded down the bank to the area of sand where a dozen people were milling about. "Think you can make it down there with that bad arm? You could stay here."

"Lead the way. I'll be fine."

There was a path worn through the vegetation that clung to the side of the gorge. Jack and Ross followed it down toward the river, carefully testing their footing so they wouldn't lose their grip and slide to the bottom. By the time they reached the sand beach along the river, they were both sweating.

"It's different down here, Jack. Like a nature reserve in the city."

"That's why I like to run down along the river in the morning."

"And you can smell the river." Ross wrinkled his nose.

"Part of nature, Junior."

They slowly walked over to the group of people clustered around a dead tree lying in the sand. Their shoes sank into the fine silt and sand deposited when the river was at a higher level in the spring, filled with winter snow run-off. Jack addressed one of the men in white Tyvek coveralls. The man was short and overweight. He looked like the Stay Puft Marshmallow Man wearing a blue baseball hat on his head with FBI across the crown in gold letters. Sweat streaked the man's cheeks and ran down his neck.

"Hey, Pete? Hot out here, isn't it? You know Junior?"

Ross stepped forward and shook Pete's hand. "Agent Fruen." He discreetly wiped his hand on his pants to dry it.

Jack stood with his hands in his pockets, looking over the site. "What've we got, Pete?"

"This is ground zero, Jack." Pete squatted down a few feet away from the tree so as not to disturb the area around it where the shooter had laid waiting. "You ran along the opposite bank, right to left, north to south. You can see the shooter was laying in the sand here, the rifle propped on the tree." There was a large depression in the sand the length of a body, deeper depressions where the knees and elbows rested in the sand. The dead tree, half-buried in the sand, showed lighter marks on top where something had scratched its weathered wood. The scratches presumably came from the stock of the rifle resting on the tree for support. "We found a couple of slugs across the river. It was a hell of a shot to hit a moving target."

Ross followed what Pete said and looked back across the river. "Jack, you know he was waiting for you. He wasn't just taking shots at whoever happened to be running by this morning."

"Yeah, he's been watching me, that's how he knew I'd be out for a run. He was waiting here in the shadows. The sun lit us up on the bank over there. He was trying to scare me off. Must've surprised him seeing two of us running." Jack turned around in the sand and looked up the hill, then up and down the shore. "So where did he go?"

Wires with colored plastic flags were stuck in the sand, a different color running off in three directions.

"Guess."

"Pete, come on. Where did he go?"

Pete grunted and stood up, pushing his body up by placing his hands on his knees. "You guys are detectives."

"OK, we'll play." Jack looked at Ross. "Junior? Your case. What do you think?"

Ross stood back and studied the area.

"And don't take too long," Jack added.

"OK. My bet is he didn't go downstream. The bank gets really steep and further downstream is the dam. He couldn't go past there."

"I didn't ask where he didn't go. Where did he go?" Jack asked.

Ross shook his head, smiled, and looked out to the river. A silver powerboat from the Sheriff's department idled twenty feet out from the riverbank. Two deputies in life jackets were in the boat; one driving it and keeping it in place against the current, the second was manipulating something over the side, hanging from a rope.

"What's up with these guys?" Jack asked.

"They're looking for the gun," Pete said. "It's not here. He either tossed it or took it with him. Me, I think he threw it in the river and took off."

"Good luck," Jack said. "Junior, where did he go?"

Ross started walking along the flags and followed the blue ones to the storm sewer. "If he followed the other path up stream, he ran the risk of somebody seeing him. If people up above on the paths heard shots from the gorge, they would have been more alert to strangers. I think he disappeared into this storm sewer and came out a distance from here."

"How'd he do, Pete?"

"Not bad for a new agent. That's what we think happened." Pete stepped up next to Ross and shined a flashlight into the dark sewer. "These things run all over under the city. Farther in there, we found tracks that look like they match. Looks like he came up in a church parking lot about three or four blocks from here. Abandoned his vehicle up in the lot up here. Just walked away. Maybe had another car."

"Or a bike," Ross added.

Pete thought for a second. "Yeah, maybe a bike. That would blend in here."

"You couldn't have told us that sooner, Pete?" Jack asked.

"If you just wanted me to tell you how he got away, you wouldn't have walked down that hill through the brush dragging your injured partner along with you. You wouldn't be standing here looking around to make sure we did the job right. You wanted to be here, see where he was when he shot at you. You wanted to get in his head." Pete reflexively reached for a breast pocket and then the back pocket of his pants. "You guys don't smoke, do you?"

Jack yelled out to the group of investigators standing at the edge of the river watching the sheriff's deputies fish for a gun. "Who has a cigarette for my friend, Pete?" Jack caught the pack of cigarettes that one of the men tossed to him. He stepped forward and offered the pack to Pete. "Thanks, Pete. We'll look for your report later. Figure out how tall he was from the impression. I want to make sure it was the Governor."

Ross and Jack worked their way back up along the rocky path and through the trees to get back to Jack's car. At the top, they stopped to catch their breath, sweat running freely down their faces. "Think Pete will make it up this hill?" Ross asked.

"If he's lucky, the sheriffs will give him a ride back to the boat ramp. Otherwise it'll take more than one of those guys down there to get him back up the hill alive." Jack looked across the river where he'd ran that morning. The image of his morning run with Patty replayed in his mind. The path, the light from the rising sun, the smell of the river, the realization that somebody was shooting at them, that Patty had been shot. Patty was OK. He made it out of the situation a little wet and smelly. He couldn't think of a thing he would've done differently. He didn't know he was in the sights of a shooter. He needed to change up his routine. Somebody was waiting for him this morning. "Come on, Junior. Let's go check on Patty."

39

The hallway was cooler than the outside, but the unique hospital smell struck Jack as he and Ross stepped off the elevator. "This is like déjà vu all over again, Junior. Second time at the hospital this week. Not good."

"At least this time, I'm not a patient," Ross said.

At the counter were a few nurses talking and filling out forms. Jack knew about paperwork. The FBI had more than its share. Jack stood at the counter and waited for somebody to notice him. He cleared his throat to get some attention.

"Excuse me, can you tell us where we can find Patty Lopez?" The nurse closest to them turned and opened her mouth to answer, but she paused when she saw Ross.

"You'll have to excuse him," Jack said. "He usually looks better than this, but he was in a little car accident. Miss Lopez's room?"

The nurse smiled, and looked down at her list. "I'm sorry. I just came on shift. Let's see. She's in room three oh five, just down the hall here."

"Thanks." Jack and Ross walked down the hall in the

direction the nurse had pointed. "Junior, you really have an impact on women. Have you thought about dating a nurse?"

Ross didn't answer, but paused outside of the door to Patty's room and motioned for Jack to enter first. Jack hesitated, thinking of what he was going to say to Patty. Responsibility, guilt, he should have been shot if anybody was. He took a deep breath, slowly pushed the door open, and stepped into the room. Ross quietly followed and stood with his back against the wall at the foot of the bed. Patty was lying in the bed reading a magazine; the shoulders of her hospital gown showed above the edge of the sheet.

Jack walked over and leaned on the bars on the side of the hospital bed that were there to keep the patient from rolling out. "Patty, how're you doing? You're not mad at me, are you?"

"Hey guys." Patty pushed herself up in bed and ran her hands back through her hair. "I'm not mad at you, but I'm mad. Mad that I got shot, and my leg hurts and I won't be able to run for a while. If I don't run, I'm going to get fat. I can't get fat. Can you believe I got shot?" Patty said a few more words in Spanish.

Jack smiled at Patty going on like this. "Hey, I recognize some of those words and I don't think they're nice. You look good and it sounds like you'll be OK."

"Are you OK, Jack?"

"I'm fine."

"You catch the *pendejo* that did this?"

"Not yet. That's what Junior and I are working on. We were just down at the river. It was a freak shot to hit you from across the river with us running. He was probably aiming at me. Or shooting towards me. Trying to scare me."

"My luck."

The room got quiet as they all took a break from the nervous talking.

"Find anything at the river?"

Jack shook his head. "No, nothing obvious. Have you thought of anything that you saw or heard this morning that might help us?"

Patty shifted herself in bed and grimaced. "I peeked after you ran and he was shooting at you. I couldn't really see anything. I wanted to get out of there, but the leg hurt too much. I think he was shooting from a sandy spot across the river."

"That's where we just came from. That was the spot."

"Do you have some info for me?" Jack asked.

"Just shoot me again, Jack." Patty stuck out her lower lip and pouted. "The video we shot at the press conference showed nothing. I was hoping I could learn some more from you. I'm sorry."

"Getting shot once is enough. We'll see you later, Patty."

JACK WAS EXHAUSTED. The mental strain of the investigation, lack of sleep, and the excitement of the morning built up. He sat in the car waiting for Junior to call him and let him know the coast was clear to the room so that his family wouldn't see him going into the room across from theirs. He needed some sack time for both his body and brain to get reinvigorated. He was still disappointed by how little they knew and bothered by the attacks on Ross, Patty, and him. The Governor knew who they were, where they were, and had shown he would go to great lengths and personal risk to get at them. They needed to catch up. Jack closed his eyes and tried to unfocus, to let his subconscious work on the details while he physically rested.

Settling into the seat finding a position that was some-what comfortable, Jack remembered back to when Lynn was born. He was a young agent in his first field office, new at his job and new at fatherhood. He woke often in the night, alert to sounds that he normally would have slept through. He also got the duty of getting up and bringing Lynn to bed so Julie could feed her. There were many days he drove to a quiet spot during lunch, parked the car, and tried to catch a nap, like he was now, propped in his seat. His old FBI car had a lot more room than this car did. His legs were bent, and the steering wheel pressed into his thigh.

The cell phone on his belt vibrated and Jack reflexively twisted to grab the phone. His thigh jammed into the steering wheel, jarring him back into reality. The phone slipped from his hand and fell to the floor on the passenger side of the car. It continued to ring and Jack stretched, his fingers probing the floor for the phone, trying to locate and answer it before it went to voice mail. He found the phone, grabbed it, and answered the phone while he raised it to his ear.

"Hello." Nobody responded and Jack looked at the small window on the phone. There was not a connection. "Damn it." Too impatient to wait to see if the caller left a voicemail message, Jack poked buttons to get to the list of who called and called back. With the phone at his ear he shifted to a more comfortable position in the seat.

"Sleeping, Jack?" Junior asked.

"Dropped the phone. Can I come up?"

"Come on in. Julie and the kids are swimming. The geeks are here. You'll like what they've done."

40

Jack cautiously walked through the halls of the hotel, listening for the tell tale voices of his kids to let him know if the coast was clear or not. At the door to his room, he lightly knocked and the door opened. Sure Thing and one of the other geeks sat on the end of the bed playing a video game. Junior sat in a chair and watched the contest.

"Hey, Jack," Sure Thing said.

"Hey yourself, ST. You guys enjoying yourself?" Jack couldn't keep the frustration from showing in his voice. These guys were playing games? "Junior says you've got stuff set up for me to keep track of my family?"

Sure Thing turned off the game.

"What're you doing? I had you," his video game opponent said.

"Rematch later. Time to get to work and show Jack what we've done for him." Sure Thing stood up and asked Jack to take his spot sitting on the foot of the bed. He handed Jack a larger remote that required Jack to use both hands to hold it.

"I'm not playing," Jack said.

"Don't worry, Jack. The family is safe. We have one of our crew down at the water park reading a magazine and watching them." Sure Thing reached down and pushed a button on the remote. "And you can watch them too." The television screen lit up into split screens with views from four cameras showing on the television at the same time. Two of the screens showed video from the water park. One of the other two showed a hallway in the hotel and the last showed an empty hotel room.

Jack was looking at the water park views. He was able to pick out the kids sitting in the hot tub.

"We're patched in to the hotel's video system as well as a number of our own cameras to pick out views we need," Sure Thing said. He walked in front of Jack to block his view. "Jack, pay attention."

"What?" Jack tuned into what Sure Thing was saying. "Right."

"Push the right arrow and you can cycle through the views."

Jack followed Sure Thing's instructions and went from the water park to reception area of the hotel. Next, he was in a hotel hallway.

"Hold it there, Jack." Sure thing turned to his video game opponent. "Go stand in front of the door across the hall. Then go on in and walk around."

Jack watched the screen and saw the man in front of Julie's hotel room open the door and enter the suite. A quiet beeping sounded from a speaker on top of the television.

"That tells you their room door has opened. Scroll over a couple, Jack."

Jack pushed some buttons on the controller and two of

the views showed the inside of a hotel room. On the television, one view showed the man entering through the door. The other view was from the corner and showed the beds. The man waved at the cameras. "This is great. I can't believe what you guys have set up."

"There are a couple of other things to show you." Sure Thing pulled his cell phone from his pocket, dialed, and walked into the bathroom. A few seconds later, the sound of a ringing telephone erupted from the speaker on the television and Jack watched as he answered the phone across the hall and listened to the conversation. "Time for a rematch. Get your skinny ass back to the office and I'll educate you on the finer points of the game."

"Cool," Ross said, leaning forward in his chair.

Jack used the controller to flip back through the screens. The beep from the speaker told him he had left the room. Jack stopped at the view of the hot tub. The kids weren't there. He scrolled through a couple of other views and found them in the arcade playing skee ball.

"Not as good as being there with them, but pretty cool," Jack said.

Sure Thing rejoined Jack and Ross in the room. "I hope this gives you a little better sense of security."

"Beyond what I expected," Jack answered.

Sure Thing shook Jack's hand. "I'm glad you're OK and glad we could help. Just let us know what else we can do. We want to keep your family safe and catch the bastard."

"What the hell you doing, Junior?" Jack stood over Ross, who had stretched out on the bed with his shoes off.

"I thought I'd get a nap in so I could give you a break later."

"Get out of here. I've got the screens, I'm across the hall."

"Jack, listen. You need to sleep. I know you've taken precautions. Paid cash, changed cell phones, you've got the command center. But, you need to man it and you need to sleep. You can't afford to miss anything or to not be sharp." Junior tried to struggle to a sitting position and stuck out his good hand to Jack. "Give me a hand?"

Jack pulled Ross up to a sitting position.

"Thanks. Let's hang out, order a pizza, give each other a break.

"All right." Jack sat on the foot of the bed and searched the screens for his family at the water park. "Get what you want, I'll eat whatever. Get a couple liters of soda too. It's going to be a long night."

"And a long day too. Aren't you spending tomorrow with the family at the Fourth of July celebration?" Ross asked.

Jack kept his focus on the television. "Yeah, so get that pizza ordered and come take watch so I can get a nap."

"Jack, wake up. Look."

Jack jumped out of bed and stared at the screen that Ross was watching.

"What's up?"

A man stood facing the doorway across the hall from them. He was wearing shorts and a polo shirt. His back was to them so Jack couldn't see what he looked like, but he saw that he was digging in his pocket for something.

"He stopped in front of the door and just stood there," Ross said.

"Tell me what you see him doing." Jack crossed the room to the door, looked out the peephole, and put his hand on the knob. His other hand held his gun. He watched the man remove the card key from his pocket.

Jack turned the knob to unlatch the door.

The man looked at the door, turned, and walked down the hallway.

"He's leaving, Jack. The way he's walking, looks like he may be a little drunk. Stopped at the wrong door."

"Keep watching him." Jack stood at the door and watched the closed door across the hall through the peephole. Two doors between him and his family. He should be in their room watching them, but he couldn't worry them with the truth and Julie wouldn't let him otherwise.

"He went to the stairs, Jack. I bet he was at the right room, but wrong floor."

"What time is it?"

"Have something to eat. It's probably still warm."

Jack sat at the table by the window, helped himself to some pizza, and looked at the scene on the television. His family was sound asleep. Lynn and Willy shared a bed and Julie was sleeping on her stomach on the right side of the bed, her side. His side was empty. The images on the TV next to the bedroom scene scrolled as Ross conducted surveillance.

"Hey, Junior. Did you watch them get ready for bed?"

"No, it's your wife."

"It's OK, I trust you," Jack said quietly.

Ross focused on the screen while he answered. "I checked in on them when I thought they should be done. I tried to scan the perimeter outside and the hallways while they were getting ready."

Jack sat on the foot of the bed next to Ross and put out his hand for the remote.

Ross handed it to him and took his turn lying on the bed for a rest. "It's pretty busy, weekend and all. If you need some help watching the screens, let me know."

"Get some sleep, Junior."

Ross grabbed a second pillow and used his good arm to fluff it up and place it behind his neck so he could see Jack and the TV. "The kids are wound up. Probably excited to see you tomorrow."

"I'm excited to see them too. Get some sleep."

41

"Willy's up. The others are stirring," Ross said.

Jack stretched, grabbed his glasses, sat up, and looked at the television.

"Willy's always been an early riser. Call room service and get us some breakfast? I'll take eggs, hashbrowns, and a pot of coffee. I'm going to shave and take a shower."

"Let me run in there first?"

"Sure." Jack turned on the radio to get some news while he watched his family wake up.

Jack walked out of the bathroom with a towel wrapped around his waist. His hair was slicked back. The air smelled like soap. "Looks like they're having fun." Willy waved a small American flag as they walked down the hall towards their room. "Happy Fourth of July, Junior."

"Today's a holiday, right?"

"A holiday? What's that? Didn't they cover that at Quantico in new agent training? We don't get government holidays off." Jack dressed in shorts, polo shirt, and running shoes. The shirt was untucked to cover the handgun at his waist. "But I'm spending today with my family." The coffee

Jack drank down was lukewarm and he grimaced as he swallowed it. "What are you going to do today for your investigation?"

"It is a bank holiday, so I'm not talking to any bankers or employees." Ross yawned. "What time is check out? Maybe I'll hang here and take a nap." He lay back on the bed, his good arm propped behind his head, the other arm in the sling across his chest. "Then this afternoon hit the office to look through the files again and tonight I'll walk down to Nicollet Island and see the fireworks you've told me so much about."

Jack tossed his duffle bag onto the bed. "Only call me if you really need to. And if you aren't out of here by eleven you pay the extra day."

AFTER STASHING his duffle in his car parked down the street from the hotel, Jack made his way back to Julie's room, waved at the camera for Ross, and knocked on the door. He heard a commotion as the kids ran to the door and argued over who got to open it. Julie told the kids to let her get it. Jack wasn't sure if it was for safety or if she was looking forward to seeing him too.

"Who is it?" Julie asked though the door.

Your lover, your hero, the man of your dreams, your husband, the father of your children, all flashed through his mind. He settled on, "It's me, Jack."

Julie opened the door. Jack didn't know what to say. His wife stood there with her hair pulled back, just the way he liked it, sunglasses poked into her hair above her forehead, a golden tan, no makeup except a light coating of lipstick, khaki shorts, and a sleeveless, off-white top.

"Hi," he said and stepped forward to give her a kiss. Julie

turned her head and Jack kissed her lightly on the cheek. "You look great," he whispered in her ear.

"Thanks. You should have called to make sure we were ready." Julie stepped to the side to let Jack into the room. "Kids, Dad's here."

Both kids charged and grabbed on, one hugging around his waist from each side. "Hey, guys. Did you have fun spending the night here? Did you go down the water slide?"

"It was so cool, Dad," Lynn said.

"Part of the tunnel goes outside," Willy added. "And we went in the hot tub too."

Jack looked around the room. "Smells like sun screen in here. It looks like you're packed. Let's get you checked out, haul your stuff to the car, and walk over to Nicollet Island."

"Yeah!" the kids yelled in unison and ran to get their bags.

42

"On the news it said a woman was shot."

Jack walked next to Julie across the Hennepin Avenue Bridge. His hands were in his pockets, and he looked straight ahead, watching Willy and Lynn who had run on ahead of them. "I'm sure he was shooting at me. He was waiting for me, targeted me just like he went after Ross, Agent Fruen, with the car crash."

"But who was she?"

"Her name's Patty Lopez. She's a TV news reporter. You've probably seen her."

"And, what was she doing there?"

"She told me she had some information for me and would only tell me in person. I told her I was busy, but that I was going for a run in the morning. I never thought she'd go for that, but she was outside waiting for me. We were running along the trail down by the river and she got shot." Jack kept looking straight ahead, telling the story while they walked.

"Is she OK?"

"She's got a hole in her leg. She'll be OK."

Julie reached over and touched Jack's arm to get his attention and to get him to stop. "How about you?"

Jack stopped. The kids were up ahead peering through the cement railing of the bridge, looking at the boats on the river. He turned, took off his sunglasses, and looked at Julie.

"I'm OK." He thought about telling her about the swim in the river, being shot at while he treaded water by the lock doors. "All I could think about was that if he knew me and where I was he might go after you and the kids too. I couldn't let that happen." Jack slid his sunglasses back on, turned, and walked towards the kids.

JACK STARED at Julie's profile. He wanted to hold her hand, but he didn't know if he should try to or not. He rubbed his palms together and then wiped them on the front of his shirt. Not yet. Not with sweaty, clammy hands. He felt like a teenager on his first date. Was she jealous of Patty?

Things seemed to be getting back to normal, whatever normal was, but he didn't want to push it. The trip to the Minneapolis Fourth of July celebration on Nicollet Island was one of their traditions since coming to the Twin Cities, so he was glad they were there together as a family again. Leaning on the fence next to Julie, Jack relaxed and looked around. Training and years of experience had driven the habit into his DNA. Wherever he was, he looked around at the people and the surroundings, searching for what didn't belong, his self-conscious logging anomalies, escape routes, numbers of people. This sometimes caused an itch, a feeling that something wasn't right, but his conscious couldn't see what it was. This feeling was constant lately as his brain worked to process clues, details, and feelings as he tried to catch the Governor.

Jack refocused and watched the kids ride the ponies. Lynn had a look of resignation and a forced smile on her face as they slowly walked by. She had let them know she was too big for pony rides. She stuck her tongue out at Jack as they passed. He feigned he was shot in the heart, bringing his hands up to his chest and lowering his head. Then he stuck his tongue out at her. Willy had a death grip on the saddle horn and a beaming smile on his face as he rode by. Jack gave him a thumbs-up, which Willy couldn't return without loosening his grip.

Jack snuck another glance at Julie. She had a smile on her face, a look of comfort. She looked at him with the smile still on her face, winked, and then reached over and squeezed his hand and released the grip before her gaze returned to the kids and the ponies.

The smile on Jack's face broadened as he turned from Julie to the kids. He wanted more than a hand squeeze, but that would do for now. Things were getting better. It wasn't his imagination. Everybody was smiling. This was a great day.

When the ride was over, the kids ran over to where Jack and Julie were standing by the fence. "Can we go do face painting next?" asked Lynn. "I want a unicorn on one cheek and FBI on the other."

"Me too. I want FBI painted on my cheek," Willy said.

Jack picked up Willy and looked him in the eye. "They can't paint that on just anybody, can they?"

Willy frowned. "Can you show them your badge?"

Jack gave him a quick hug and laughed. "I'll show them my badge just to make sure they copy it and get it right. Maybe I'll get one too. Let's go. You guys lead the way."

Jack put Willy down and the kids took off running. Julie took off after them. "Last one there's paying, Jack." He looked up at the sky hoping that the great day would continue and end with the fireworks before they went their separate ways.

"Please don't rain," he pleaded skyward before he ran after his family.

After face painting, cotton candy, hot dogs, lemonade, and balloon animals, they sat in the shade of the old oak trees and looked across the Mississippi River at the skyline of downtown Minneapolis. An old blues tune wafted through the air as a band played on the patio of one of the restaurants behind them.

Jack rubbed his belly and lay back in the grass. "I don't know about you guys, but I couldn't eat another bite. Where do you guys put it?"

The kids each lay next to him and looked at the sky. "I'm saving room for popcorn," Lynn said.

"I'm looking for animals in the clouds," Julie said. "I see a cow's head."

Jack joined in and gazed up at the sky. Another thing the family used to do on picnics on sunny afternoons. "I think it might be the other end of the cow."

"Jack."

The kids giggled.

Lynn pointed to the west. "Those big white clouds are called Thunder Heads."

Jack looked where she was pointing, past the skyscrapers downtown. "Really? How did you get so smart, Junior Agent Miller?"

"We learned it at the Science Museum this week." Lynn rolled over and looked at Jack. "They're really called cumulonimbus. It means they're big cumulus clouds with rain in them. Maybe hail."

"Forget the FBI." Jack looked at Julie. "This one could be

a meteorologist on The Weather Channel." He looked at
Lynn. "Let's hope you're wrong because I want a clear, dry
night for the fireworks."

"I think it's going to rain, Dad," she said.

"Well, Junior Weatherperson, I guess we'll find out later.
I'd be more worried if you predicted a nice evening since the
weather people always seem to predict the opposite of what
happens." Jack propped himself up on one elbow. "How
about we take the trolley ride next?

"Can't we get some ice cream cones first?" Lynn asked.

"Me too," Willy added. "Then we'll go ride the trolley
with you."

Jack looked at Julie and she shrugged. He dug in his
pocket and handed four ones to Lynn. "Hold hands. One
scoop each and come right back. Mom and I will wait here
for you."

Lynn grabbed the money. "Thanks, Dad. Let's go, Willy."
They both took off running for the ice cream stand.

"Hold hands!" Jack yelled after them. He watched as
they grabbed each other's hand and slowed to a fast walk to
their destination. Julie reached over and covered his hand in
the grass. He pulled it away at first, not sure what was
touching his hand, but when he saw it was her, he smiled
and put it back where it was. "I didn't mean you had to hold
my hand, but you can if you want to." Jack said.

"Thanks for arranging this today. We needed this. All
of us."

Jack snuck a glimpse at the kids waiting their turn in
line. "How are they doing?"

"They're doing fine. And I'm doing better." Julie
squeezed his hand again. "You and I need to talk about us.
What happens after today."

43

The Governor walked among the crowd on Nicollet Island. He wore a Twins baseball hat, sunglasses, and a grey tank top, smiling and nodding at the curious children who approached him and asked if they could pet Vince. While Vince absorbed the affection, the Governor scanned the crowd and kept an eye on Jack and his family.

The atmosphere of music, food, and games was intoxicating. Agent Miller seemed to be relaxed. He smiled and laughed as he played with his kids. The Governor also caught him staring at his wife when she wasn't looking. His family was keeping him busy as they explored the activities so the Governor felt a little safer and confident that his plans would move forward. He still wanted to create a distraction for Agent Miller, to show him that he was still in control of events.

Two Minneapolis police officers were walking towards the Governor, scanning the crowd. The Governor felt exposed, standing in the open alone except for his dog. He turned and walked forty feet to the end of the concessions line without looking back. Vince stood patiently at his side, panting in the afternoon heat. The Governor gently scratched the top of Vince's head as he plotted the path of the officers in his mind, trying to figure out when they would pass and he could feel comfortable to turn around and watch Agent Miller and his family again. He counted down five, four, three...

"Hey, mister. What's your dog's name?"

The Governor's back and arm muscles twitched at the surprise. A burst of adrenaline shot into his system as it responded to the fight or flight reaction. He looked back into the eyes of a young boy. In an instant, he recognized him, Agent Miller's son. He quickly looked around, his eyes hidden behind the sunglasses, to make sure that Jack wasn't standing next to him. He calmed himself as he saw Jack sitting in the grass talking to his wife.

"This is Vince. Would you like to pet him? He loves kids."

"Yes, thanks." Willy squatted in front of Vince and held his big head between his hands, digging his small fingers behind the ears. Vince leaned into Willy and groaned.

Lynn leaned over and scratched Vince's back. "We really like dogs. We're trying to talk our parents into letting us have one."

The concession line moved towards the window as the next person in line was helped. The Governor took a step towards the window, a hand on Vince's leash, leaving him to the kids' petting. "Are you two going to get something to eat here?"

"We're each getting an ice cream cone," Willy answered.

"Well, Vince seems to like you. Could I ask you to do me a favor? Could you hold him while you wait in line and keep my place while I run to the bathroom? I'll be back before you get up to the window."

"Sure," Lynn answered.

The Governor stole a look towards Jack, who remained sitting on the grass with his wife. He handed the end of the leash to Lynn with instruction to keep a hold of it until he got back. Then the Governor kneeled next to Willy and patted Vince. "Be a good boy, Vince. I'll be right back." He turned to Willy, "Keep an eye on him for me. He likes you."

The Governor got up and walked around the corner of the building towards the restrooms without looking back.

"WHERE ARE THE KIDS?" Jack looked over at the concession line where they had been standing in line. He couldn't see them. He jumped up and ran towards the concession booth without waiting for an answer to his question.

"What?" Julie asked, her voice trailing off behind him.

Jack looked left and right. He didn't see them. He pushed through the line, mumbling "excuse me." They weren't in line. Could the Governor have found them here, taken his kids? God help me, he thought. He stood in front of the concession stand where he had last seen them. "Lynn, Willy?" he yelled.

"Hey, Dad." Willy rounded the corner of the building, his face covered with blue ice cream from his nose to his chin. Lynn rounded the corner next.

Relieved, Jack walked to them while he scanned the area behind them and then looked to his left and right. "Where did you go? I got worried." Then he noticed the dog that Lynn was leading on a leash. "And who's this?"

"Can we keep him?" Willy asked. "He's a great dog."

Lynn started to explain to Jack what happened. "This

guy asked us to watch his dog while he went to the bath-room and he didn't come back, so we went looking for him."

Jack looked down at the dog and then at the kids. Vince looked up at him with his tongue hanging out. He reached down and patted Vince on the top of the head. Then he checked the collar for tags. There weren't any there. "Willy knows what this guy looks like?"

"I do, Dad."

"OK. Lynn, you and the dog..."

"His name's Vince, Dad," Willy interrupted.

"Lynn, walk Vince over and introduce him to your mom and see if the owner shows up. Willy and I will go check out the bathroom to see if he's in there. Maybe there was a line."

"Or maybe he had a big job to do, Dad."

"Right, Willy. Get going, Lynn. Tell Mom we'll be right back." Jack watched Lynn and Vince as they made it over to Julie. Vince trotted easily next to Lynn without pulling on the leash.

WILLY RAN up and grabbed Vince around the neck. "He wasn't there. Can we keep him, Mom?" Julie looked at Jack as he walked up to the group and shook his head.

"We'll see, Willy," Julie said.

Willy sat on the grass, his lower lip sticking out. "We'll see means no." Lynn sat next to Vince and stroked his back, listening to her mother and brother.

"No, it means we'll see. You talked to the owner."

"But it's finders, keepers."

"But you didn't find him. The man asked you to watch him."

"But then he left him with us. He said Vince likes kids.

We told him we wanted a dog. He thought we'd be a good match so he left him with us."

"But he said he was coming back."

Jack interrupted the argument knowing there was no winning this one right now. "Ok, ok, let's make a deal." Julie and Willy quit talking. All eyes were on him. "We'll hold onto Vince for now, keep a look out for his owner, and we'll decide later what the next step is. Maybe we'll run into the owner while we hang out here today." Jack put his hand in the center of the circle. "Deal?" One by one, the others put their hands on top of his with Jack topping off the stack with his other hand. "Deal."

44

"How about we rest up and give me some time to digest what we've eaten before we eat anymore. We'll do the loop on the trolley, learn some things, and come back to find a nice place in the grass where the trees aren't in the way so we can see the action and go Ooh, Aaah, for the show." He looked at the kids. "And we'll find a place to buy some popcorn."

"Do we have to, Dad?" Lynn asked.

Jack got up and put a hand out to help Julie up. "Yep, let's go. I'd race you there, but I think I'd puke if I ran."

The kids got up from the grass. Vince stood up wagging his tail. Julie let Jack pull her up and she didn't pull her hand from his. Jack started walking back towards the Nicollet Island Inn holding Julie's hand. The kids each took one of their parent's free hands, Lynn held Vince's leash, and they walked to the trolley.

The trolley, or bus made to look like an old-time trolley, waited for riders in front of the Nicollet Island Inn. Jack and Julie sat in one seat together and the kids sat in front of them with Vince in the aisle. The kids fought for the window seat before agreeing to take turns. Once they were settled into their seats, the driver of the trolley started off the tour explaining that they were going to do a loop of the Mississippi Mile. Along the way, she planned to point out some things and give highlights of the history and development along the river. When she reminded them they needed to remain seated during the tour, Jack gave the kids a little tap on the shoulder to reinforce the announcement.

The trolley left the parking lot of the Nicollet Island Inn, turned right, and bounced along the old brick streets in front of St. Anthony Main. The driver pointed out the entrance to the Historical Society's door where walking tours of the area were offered, talked a little about the buildings, and continued on. Next, they drove by the old Pillsbury flour mill buildings with the bulging walls and the windows white from years of flour dust caked on them. Just a few minutes into the tour and the kids were getting antsy already.

The next landmark was the one the kids liked. The trolley was the only motorized vehicle allowed on the Stone Arch Bridge, which snaked its way across the river. The rest of the traffic on the bridge was people on bike or foot. Midway across the bridge, the driver stopped and told them about the building of the bridge by James J. Hill and the importance the river and the falls played in the development of Minneapolis along the Mississippi at this point. This was where the falls were. Outside of the trolley, people were lined up along the railing at the edge of the bridge, looking out at the falls and the lock and dam on the west side of the river to watch the boats and barges be lowered as they traveled past the falls and continued down the river. Jack and the kids had visited the bridge many times on bike rides and had stood at the railing trying to guess what was in the barges or where the boats were going.

At the far end of the bridge, the driver stopped and told them about the restoration of the area mill buildings into upscale condos and the creation of the Mill City Museum. She pointed out the millraces and tunnels below the end of the bridge. Jack looked up at the condos and noted the people on the balconies partying and waiting for the pyrotechnic displays to begin. He thought his view would be better in the grass; the price was right and the company was better. He gave Julie's hand a squeeze.

"Dad, can you believe there are tunnels under here?"

Lynn tapped Jack's arm to get his attention. He looked at her. "What, sweetie?"

"The driver said there were old tunnels under the ground here from when they used water power to do work at the mills that used to be here. It would be so cool to go down in them."

"I don't think that's part of the tour today."

"They used to give tours in boats, a long time ago. That's what she said."

"We'll stick to the trolley." Jack's mind drifted as the trolley continued on its route up the hill past the new condo development. The driver talked about the restoration of the Milwaukee Depot and the development of the hotel and indoor ice-skating rink that was open year round.

Jack thought again about his family, being with them, holding Julie's hand. He looked over at Julie and studied her profile until she looked over at him. He smiled and leaned over. "Are you having a good time, Jules?" Before she could answer, Willy interrupted.

"Dad, Dad, I told you it was going to rain. Look." The

windshield wipers squeaked back and forth to remove a few drops from the trolley windshield.

"Well, I hope it's just a sprinkle." Jack turned back to Julie to get her response. The trolley started over the Hennepin Avenue Bridge to return them to Nicollet Island.

Lynn spun in her seat. "Dad, did you hear that?"

"Yeah, I know, it's raining."

"No, she said the Federal Reserve has never been robbed. Is that right?"

"What's the Federal Reserve?" Willy asked.

"It's that building back there at the end of the bridge. It's like the bank for banks." Jack looked back at Lynn. "What did you say?"

"The driver said that building was the Ninth District Federal Reserve and that the Federal Reserve had never been robbed."

Jack looked back through the windows at the Federal Reserve; the color from the lights blurred by the rain running down the glass. That had to be it.

"You guys are so smart." He cupped Lynn's face in his hands and kissed her on the forehead. He pulled his cell phone from his pocket and called Ross.

"Junior, I think I know what he's after."

"Jack, I was just going to call you. We figured who Sandy was with at Sheiks and on the boat. He's a ..."

Lightning flashed and thunder drowned out Ross' voice. Sheets of rain pounded the windows and roof of the trolley like a snare drum. "Can you repeat that?" Jack asked. "It's storming out here and I couldn't hear you."

"We figured out who Sandy was with at Sheiks and out on Lake Minnetonka. It was a developer who lives in The Riverview condos by St. Anthony Main."

"I'm right there." Jack thought about the developer who

had been complaining about the dead body found in the river when he was out on his run and ran into Patty.

"I know. That's why I was going to call you. Even though you said not to call. I'm heading over there now."

"I'll meet you at the street entrance. Hurry up."

The trolley pulled to a stop in front of the Nicollet Island Inn, completing its loop. The driver spoke over the loud speaker. "Well folks, I hope you enjoyed the tour. Happy Fourth of July. Sorry about the weather. If you want to wait on the bus for a while, feel free."

Jack jumped up. "I have to get off."

"Jack, what are you doing?" Julie asked.

"I have to go, Jules." Jack sat back down and leaned over to speak quietly so others on the trolley wouldn't hear him. "That was Ross. The agent I'm working with. They're going to search a condo near here that they think belongs to the Governor. I have to be there."

Julie turned away and looked out the window of the trolley.

"Come on, Julie. I have to go. This guy's killed a couple of people and I think he tried to kill me."

"I know. Just go, Jack."

"Julie, look at me." Julie turned and looked at him out of the corner of her eye. "You don't know how much I've been looking forward to spending the day with you guys." Jack took a deep breath and braced himself. "But I have to go."

"I know."

"I'm sorry." Jack slid out of the seat and bent down by the kids. "Guys, I have to go catch a bad guy so I can't spend the rest of the day with you. I feel real bad about it. I hope it stops raining so you can see the fireworks." He kissed his right hand, then his left and put one on each of their heads.

"I had a great day. I'll see you later. Watch your mom for me. And take care of the dog."

Jack got off the trolley, the rain immediately attacking him. He saw a police officer sitting in a cruiser and asked him to keep an eye on his family until somebody from the FBI office came. Jack took off at a jog to meet Ross at the apartment building.

Puddles were forming in depressions in the streets and sidewalks. Water ran down the gutters into the sewers on its way to the Mississippi River. People were huddled in the buildings and under eaves waiting for the storm to pass. Jack splashed through the puddles, his feet squishing in his waterlogged shoes.

45

Rain pushed the people from the balcony back into the condominium. The Governor made sure the servers kept moving about the rooms serving the hors d'oeuvres and that the bartenders poured the drinks.

"It's a great view." The Governor handed two glasses of wine to a couple standing at the window. "If the rain stops we'll have a great view of the fireworks in a few hours." He pointed out some of the landmarks to the couple and talked about the development of restaurants and stores that made the location more desirable. "No, questions on the property? Enjoy the evening."

The couple left the Governor to his view. He looked over the river and Nicollet Island where people were soaked and looking for shelter from the rain. He thought about his crew underground and looked towards the Federal Reserve. He was excited. He felt like a young boy at Christmas waiting for Santa. A few hours and he would be at the end of his journey. A caravan of cars, and a panel truck with a police escort crossing the Hennepin Avenue bridge caught his attention.

"Sir, could we see a couple of the other units that aren't quite so expensive?"

The Governor tried to watch where the cars were going, but was pulled back into the party and the sale of the condos. He smiled and answered their questions while he sat with them in the living room where he showed them condo layouts, pictures, and price ranges.

As he was talking with them about financing options, his mobile phone rang. The Governor's pulse quickened and he excused himself to take the call when the caller identified herself as an employee of the security system for his condo and said that the alarm had been triggered. The Governor stepped to the window and looked across the river. The rain-streaked glass obscured his view. He opened the patio door and stepped outside. He looked and saw that the lights were on in his home.

He didn't know how they had found him, but he knew he needed to leave. It wouldn't take them long to search for him at the party. They may already be coming for him. He checked his watch. There was still time to execute the plan. He was so close to the end. The Governor hurried to the elevator and took it to the basement parking garage.

JACK AND ROSS hung back while the team went to work executing the warrant. Neighbors had been moved from the adjacent quarters on either side, above, and below. They'd used the key from the landlord so they didn't have to break down the door. The security alarm was blaring and team members were calling out directions to each other as they checked out the condo.

When it was determined that the condo was secure and empty, Jack and Ross entered. "Can somebody shut off the alarm?" Jack yelled over the din. He tapped Ross on the shoulder and leaned into him. "This noise is giving me a headache. What do you want to do?"

Ross spoke into Jack's ear. "You check out the living room and kitchen, I'll take the other rooms."

The living room drew Jack's attention first. He looked around with his fingers stuck in his ears to muffle the alarm. The room was neat and orderly. Nothing personal was visible. The room felt more like a furniture store display area than a home. The décor was tasteful, with a touch of class. After checking a couple of drawers in the side tables and looking behind the paintings on the wall, Jack ventured into the kitchen. "Who's taking care of the alarm?" he yelled as he passed the alarm panel.

The refrigerator was modestly stocked with green bottles of water and a couple bottles of wine. Two Chinese food take-out containers were on the second shelf. A few apples were in the proper storage compartment. He looked under the sink and found a garbage can, but it was empty. Everything was too neat.

The alarm continued blaring. He couldn't think. He stood and leaned against the counter while he massaged his temples. Now they know who the Governor is, they just have to find him. "Would somebody stop this alarm? I'm trying to think here." Jack closed his eyes, thinking back over the past few days. He and Patty had watched a real estate developer, the Governor, walk across the bridge with a dog. Silence pressed on Jack when the alarm abruptly ended. He opened his eyes and pulled his fingers from his ears. "Finally."

Jack decided to finish looking through the kitchen. The cupboards held some crackers, cereal, and cans of soup along with plates, bowls, and glasses. Everything was clean and stacked neatly. Labels all faced forward. Around the corner by the stove, Jack found dog bowls on the floor, one empty, one filled with water. An empty hook on the wall would have held a leash. He looked down at the black rubber matt that the food and water bowls sat on. White letters across the matt spelled out

VINCE

JACK PICTURED Willy looking up into his face. His name's Vince, Dad. Panic gripped him. It was hard to breathe. His vision was a blur as he pictured his kids with the dog just thirty minutes ago on Nicollet Island. Jack found himself at the living room window looking down on the bridge and the island. People were huddled under the eaves of the buildings. The sky was still dark with storm clouds. He grabbed his phone and dialed, looking down, hoping to spot them.

"Nice view, isn't it?" Ross asked. Jack turned and found Ross unrolling plans on the coffee table.

"I have to find my family." Jack walked over to Ross. "Some guy left a dog with my kids. I think it was the Governor. He left his dog with my kids!"

"What? Well take a look at this." The top-half of the top page was an overhead view of the area of the Mississippi River they were at from Boom Island to the north to locks south of the Stone Arch Bridge. There were notes written in pen and pencil at various locations. The bottom half of the page had some elevation views, cross-sections of what was below ground.

"What is this?" Jack asked as he dialed another number.

"Hold down this side." Ross peeled back the first page like a giant book to show the second page. "He's got sewers marked and named. It shows their depths, routes, etc."

"Just a second, Junior. Jules. That dog, Vince, he's the Governor's dog. The Governor gave him to the kids. Tell the officer to take you all to the FBI office and stay there until I get you. Bye."

"OK, Junior. Sewers, depths, and?"

Ross turned back the second page. The third page was a cover page for the rest of the documents. The seal for the Ninth District Federal Reserve covered the center of the page. "These are the plans for the Minneapolis Federal Reserve from when it was built in 1994."

Jack leaned forward, then back to bring the drawing into focus. He used his free hand to smooth out the page. "Guess what I learned today from my daughter?"

"What?"

"The Federal Reserve has never been robbed."

46

"**D**amn it." The Governor stood next to his car in the parking ramp underneath the condos. The cellular phone in his hand showed he had no connectivity to the tower network. He couldn't get a call through. He stared at the screen and walked towards the garage door to see if he could pick up a signal. One bar flickered, there then gone again. "Come on." He walked out the door to escape the reinforced concrete and earth that kept him from getting a signal. Drops of rain flung through the air by the wind, peppering his face and arms. Finally the signal was strong enough. He dialed and waited.

"Yes."

"Vadim, it's me. I'm just calling to check in, see if there's anything you need. What do we have, seven hours to go?"

"Six hours and thirty-three minutes. Is something wrong, my friend? You sound funny, not yourself."

The Governor took a deep breath and cleared his throat. "No, everything is fine. I'm standing outside in this beautiful Minnesota summer weather and I'm a little nervous or anxious, I guess. I just wanted to make sure everything was still on track."

"There's nothing to be nervous about. This rain won't bother anything. Everything is in place. Soon you and I will be very rich men."

The Governor closed his eyes. Soon he would be a rich man. It was something he had dreamed of all of his life. No more dealing with architects, coordinating builders' schedules, or dealing with the worries of homebuyers spending beyond what they could afford. Soon he would be a rich man. "You're right, Vadim. But still, I'll be nervous until it is done."

"My friend, you do your part and my men and I will do ours. Do not call me again, until tomorrow."

The Governor closed his cell phone and put it in his pocket. He knew what he had to do next. Time was counting down and he and Vadim had scripted the job down to the end. He put on his caving gear and entered the tunnels.

JACK AND ROSS burst out of the condo tower doors onto the street. Ross had the roll of plans tucked under his good arm. Lightning flashed across the sky, followed immediately by thunder which reverberated through the air. Strong winds swept the rain through the air. "Better stick those under your jacket, Junior. Don't want them getting all wet."

Ross struggled getting the plans inside his windbreaker with his good arm. He grimaced as the end of the roll bumped his hand sticking out of the sling, which forced his arm back in a direction that hurt.

"Let me help you." Jack grabbed the roll, pulled back the jacket, and pushed them against Ross' right side. "Clamp down on that." Jack snapped up the jacket, sealing the plans inside.

"Where's your car?" Ross asked.

"I ran over here from Nicollet Island. I'm parked back by the hotel still. Where's yours?"

"This way." Ross ran across the street like an escapee in a straight jacket. His right arm held the plans against his chest under his windbreaker while his left arm, still in a sling, moved with his body. The loose sleeve of his windbreaker flew forward and back against the rhythm of his run.

Jack followed, splashing through the puddles in the street as they were too wide to avoid. His shoes and socks were still wet and were getting wetter. He followed Ross to a beat up Chevy pick-up where Ross stopped and waited for him.

"I forgot La Reina is out of commission," Jack said.

"The keys are in my pocket. You drive." Ross turned to offer the right pocket of his jacket to Jack.

"You sure?"

"Come on, let's go. I need to keep the plans dry."

Jack got the keys, unlocked the door, and got in. He reached across the seat, pulled up the lock, and opened the passenger door for Ross.

"Where's your family?"

"They're safe at the office across the river. I told them to get a vet ASAP to check out the dog, who's quarantined for now in the SAC's office. The kids aren't too happy about being separated from the dog." Jack shifted the truck into drive. "Hold on."

The Federal Reserve was straight ahead of them, across the river. Jack pulled out from behind the SWAT team's van and headed for the Hennepin Avenue Bridge. "Where are the wipers?" They could barely see where they were going.

"Turn the second knob on the right."

The wipers cleared some of the water off the windshield, but left streaks of water across much of their field of view. "Remind me to get you some new wiper blades."

"You think this is it?" Ross asked. "You think he's got a plan to rob the Federal Reserve?"

"Why else would he have plans for the building?"

At the Federal Reserve, Jack pulled the truck up over the curb onto the sidewalk and parked near the covered walkway leading up to the door. "Go," was all he said to Ross.

"What do you mean?"

"Go talk to these guys and get them ready to save themselves from being robbed."

"What about you?" Ross asked.

"I gotta' go see a guy about a condo."

Ross just looked at him with a question on his face.

Jack reached across Ross' chest and opened the truck's passenger door for him. "Go."

THE VALET PARKING sign was on the sidewalk in front of the building between giant searchlights parked at the curb that swept the sky. Raindrops sparkled in the bright lights and sizzled when they hit the giant lenses pointed above the city. Jack pulled the rusted truck into position, got out, and handed the keys to a young man holding a large umbrella, wearing khaki shorts and a blue polo shirt with the development company's logo over his heart. "I won't be long. Be careful with her, she's not mine."

He walked past the elevator doors and the sign that announced the Independence Day party on the fourth floor and opened the door into the stairwell. It was empty. He went up taking two stairs at a time, leaving wet footprints on the stair treads.

The image of the Governor and his dog walking across the Stone Arch Bridge a few days ago as a dead man floated in the river played through his mind. Patty said he was a prick. More worried about the police and their tape around the crime scene than anything else. He had a party going on tonight. What was he worried about, the party being disrupted, or the police being so close to the Fed just up the river while he was making plans to rob it?

Jack reached the fourth floor and exited the stairwell. He stopped to catch his breath and get a look at what he'd be facing. He double-checked that his gun was still tucked in place against his lower back.

He was definitely underdressed. Couples strolled around the room. The men were in tuxes, the women in cocktail dresses. It was summer and everyone was showing off their tans. Waiters and waitresses in black outfits were working the room, handing out food and drinks. A hostess at the door spied him and watched him without trying to be obvious. She was twenty-something, beautiful, tan, and dressed in a low cut outfit that was slightly elegant without overshadowing the people attending the party. Jack smiled and approached her directly and spoke quickly.

"Hello, miss. I'm looking for Mr. Tyler. I hope I'm not too late. We really had our hearts set on one of the units here. My wife said, I don't care what you look like. You get up there and get that unit for us." Jack leaned forward on the podium the hostess was posted behind and looked into the room. "Is he here? If I don't close the deal my wife will kill me."

"I think he's here. But, he might have run home. He said

something about getting a call from his security company that his alarm was going off."

Jack looked around the room some more. "The lightning probably set it off."

"That's what he said. I can call him for you. He'd be happy to talk to you about the units here. There are some great ones."

Jack scooted around her. "Thanks. I'll look around and track him down. If I can't find him I'll be back."

After a quick walk through the suite to confirm that the Governor wasn't there, Jack found a position where he could keep an eye on the door into the suite and most of the living room. He called the FBI dispatch on his mobile phone.

"Hi, Jack. Heard you guys are getting close to the Governor tonight."

"We're on his trail, but haven't found him yet. Sorry you have to work the holiday."

"Over forty, not married, nothing better to do tonight. All's quiet, maybe I'll do some knitting."

"Put the knitting needles down. I've got some work for you to do." Jack listed out the things he needed. First, she was to check with the security company and find out what number they had called. Then she would call the cell phone company and find out if the Governor was currently on the network. If he was, they had to pinpoint where he was. If not, they needed to monitor and let them know when he came on. She needed to get an agent to stake out the condos, and last, she needed to call Sure Thing and his crew in. They could help if the Governor was using his phone. "Give me a call when you hear back from the cell phone carrier."

"Thanks, Jack. Just so you know, I might not get your sweater knitted by Christmas now."

Jack laughed. "Talk to you soon." He put the phone back

in his pocket and looked around the room. The Governor wasn't here and he probably wasn't coming back after the warning he got from the security company. Jack left his phone number with the hostess and headed back to the Federal Reserve to join Ross.

47

Jack closed his eyes and breathed through his nose as he walked through the revolving door into the Federal Reserve. Ross and two guards were waiting for him in the lobby when he exited the revolving closet. An older man with grey hair and a bit of a paunch stood to Ross' left. His hands were on his hips. He had a hint of a smile on his lips. A younger man with a shaved head stood to Ross' right. His feet were set slightly wider than his shoulders, hands clasped behind his back. His spine was straight and his chest thrust out. Ex-marine, Jack thought.

Ross looked over Jack's shoulder, through the glass doors at his truck that Jack had parked on the sidewalk.

"Did you lock it?" Ross asked.

"I think so. Does it matter?"

"Did you at least take the keys?"

Jack held them up in the air to show him and then stuffed them in the pocket of his shorts.

"Don't lose them."

"Don't worry, Junior."

"Gentlemen, this is Special Agent Jack Miller. One of our best," Ross said.

Jack smiled in surprise. The younger guard barely nodded. The older man stepped forward and shook Jack's hand. He had a catcher's mitt of a hand. Jack's fingers barely wrapped around the palm.

"Welcome to the Federal Reserve. I'm Mark Granowski. My loud partner here is Jerome Stone." Mark hung on to Jack's hand and lowered his voice. "Don't like our doors, huh?"

"Not a fan."

"They don't bother most people, but there are a few that would rather just skip 'em if you let them."

"Well, I'm in. Let's get to it."

Granowski set two cups of coffee on the table. "Black?"

Ross nodded. He and Jack sat on one side of the rectangular table.

"As long as it's hot," Jack said. "Catch me up?"

Mark slid a chair out across from Jack and lowered himself to a point and then let himself plop into it. He clasped his hands and rested them on his belly. "So, somebody wants to rob us."

"You don't seem too worried."

"We're the Fed. Any dreamer thinks about robbing us, but it's not like we're a bank. You can't walk in, show a teller a note, and expect to get some money." Mark pushed his chair back further and crossed his ankle over his knee. Most of our focus is inside the walls to make sure employees don't take anything. I'd send you on your way, but you're with the FBI so you must have something worth listening to or you wouldn't be here."

Jack blew on the coffee and took a sip. "Not bad."

"The coffee's OK, but the food sucks."

"This is about the Governor. You've seen the news?"

"I thought he was robbing banks."

Jack looked at Ross, raised his eyebrows, and nodded for him to answer.

"Go ahead, Jack. You're on a roll."

"All right," Jack said. He looked at Granowski. "He was robbing banks, but we don't think it was the money he was after." Jack unrolled the plans on the table. The stack of plans was about an inch thick. The off-white sheets were three feet by four feet and covered a majority of the table. "We found these in his condo and can't think of a reason why he would have them."

"Unless he was planning to rob the Fed," Granowski answered.

"Right."

Granowski got up and pulled his chair around to sit on the same side of the table as Jack and Ross.

"Here's what I was showing Agent Fruen before you got here," Granowski said. He paged through the first few pages which included the cover sheet and the index pages and ruffled through the plans, examining page numbers.

"Looks like he has an entire set of building blueprints. HVAC and electrical schematics, plan and elevation drawings and plans for the vault."

"Would these do him any good?" Ross asked.

"I don't know. I don't think so. It's not like he's coming in the door, going to the vaults, and hauling money out. And he's not digging his way in. The vault's forty feet underground with walls a couple of feet thick made of reinforced concrete. We have sensors underground around the perimeter of the vault also."

"All the money's in one vault?"

Mark looked at Ross. "One vault, inaccessible."

"So how would you rob it?" Jack asked.

"We're running scenarios and simulations all of the time." Mark looked up at the ceiling and closed his eyes. "The money's most exposed when we're moving it in and out of the building. But, we've got that covered; random schedules, unmarked trucks, multiple trucks with some being empty, some not, decoys. We were at the most risk when we were moving the money from the old Fed building to this one when this one was built in ninety-four. Fifteen million dollars moved five blocks. Nothing happened."

Jack got up and refilled his coffee cup. "There has to be something to this. He's got the plans. Why was he robbing the banks?"

"We move a lot of money electronically between our partners, clear checks, stuff like that. But, we have our own arsenal of people and tools to keep that secure. Passwords, tokens, dedicated networks, monitoring of networks. Stuff I don't know much about. We find people snooping around, but nobody's ever been successful."

"That's what my daughter told me," Jack said.

Mark looked at Jack questioningly.

"We were on the trolley tour today over on Nicollet Island. Part of the Fourth of July celebration. My daughter heard the driver say that the Federal Reserve has never been robbed."

Mark sat forward and nodded. "Well, she's right. Never has been and never will be. I can't imagine the havoc that would be caused world-wide in the markets if it ever was."

THE GOVERNOR HAD SCRAPED and squeezed his way through the tunnels to find his crew. They had been so close before and hadn't been discovered yet. The time was approaching for the grand finale of his plan.

"Look who's here, guys!" Steve yelled over the sound of the jets of water which were cutting their way through the limestone like beavers on a tree. He shut down the sprayer so the team could talk. "We're right on schedule, boss. No surprises."

The Governor's headlamp speared through the mist that clouded the cave. A layer of water covered everything.

"You guys are doing great." He clapped them each on the shoulder, his enthusiasm showing. A toothy grin on his face. "Dreams gentlemen. They will soon come true." He stepped forward to see the current work.

"This is just like cutting through butter with a hot knife. The rock just disappears. It's amazing. You want to try it?"

The Governor stepped back. "No, I'll leave it to the professionals. You guys have done an amazing job." He used his thumb to wipe the grime and water off the face of his watch. "By midnight you need to be in position by the vault door. I'll let you get back to work."

48

"This is it, gentlemen, command central. From here we watch the grounds, the vault, and the people running the machines counting the money." Granowski put a hand on each of their shoulders and guided Jack and Ross across the room. "And over here we have the crew watching the FedWire." A dozen people sat in front of computer screens. On the wall in front of them were larger screens and an electronic depiction of the United States with lines and numbers between cities.

"And FedWire is?" Ross asked.

"It's the electronic network used to wire funds between Federal Reserves and the member banks. There's real money out there, but now it's all just numbers, record keeping." Mark looked up at the screen. "The instantaneous movement of money."

Ross looked up at the screens. "And nobody can hack this?"

"Nope. Not that they haven't tried. I've been doing this a long time and I've seen lots of different schemes." Mark started walking across the room. "Greed is a strong motivator. People on the outside want to get in here at the money. But, we have lots of people already inside. I spend most of my time watching those already inside the doors." He stopped in front of a bank of monitors. "We have a lot of safeguards, lots of smart people, lots of redundancy. We're just the network and center point or clearing house. If you want money, rob a bank."

"Which brings us back to why we're here." Jack stood with his hands in the pockets of his shorts, looking at the screens, talking to the air. "Junior, who does this room remind you of?"

"Who does it remind me of?"

"Look around. Who would feel at home here?"

Ross looked around the room and smiled at Jack. "Sure Thing would love this room."

"Exactly." Jack pulled his cell phone out of his pocket. "Mark, could I invite another person from our office to join us here? He's a little more technical than we are."

"A little?" Ross asked.

"OK, a lot. But, he'd be a good addition while we're here. He's seen what the Governor and his friends can do with technology."

Granowski pointed at the phone in Jack's hand. "You can call him, but not with that. You probably couldn't get a signal in this room, and just to make sure, we've got jammers in place. No calls out of this room unless they're on a land line."

"OK, get me to a phone. We'll get him over here and we'll see if we can figure out what's going on."

JEROME STONE WALKED into the room and looked at Granowski, showing the first emotion Jack had seen him exhibit. He rolled his eyes up, closed them, quickly shook his head, and frowned. Sure Thing and Squeaky followed Jerome into the room.

"Sorry we had to drag you in on a holiday." Jack handed Sure Thing a large bottle of Mountain Dew. "Maybe this will make it up to you."

Sure Thing sat across the table from Jack. His jacket was soaked and he was using some napkins to wipe the water from his shaved head. "Can somebody get a Coke for my friend?"

"Regular, not Diet," Squeaky added.

Granowski and Jerome looked at each other at the sound of her voice. Granowski nodded, giving Jerome permission to fulfill her request.

Sure Thing opened the bottle and took a long drink. "Damn, that's good. I had a couple of beers at a barbeque this afternoon, before the rain started." He struggled out of his wet jacket and draped it over the back of a chair. "I need something to get me going." He stood by the table wearing flip flops, cargo shorts, and a Hawaiian shirt.

Granowski and Ross sat at the ends of the table, the same one they had been at earlier, with the plans for the building laid out in the middle. The fluorescent lighting buzzed in the ceiling above them.

"We'll catch you up." Jack leaned forward against the edge of the table. "Our suspect has been robbing banks, but it appears he has a bigger target than the bank and its money. He's tried to harm both Ross and myself." He pointed at the plan on the table. "The Fed seems to be what he has his sights set on. We found these at his apartment."

"So you know who he is?" Sure Thing asked.

"We do now. And he's not stupid. We would have caught

him by now if he was, so we need to figure out what he's really up to. Or we need to find him."

"Maybe I can help there," Sure Thing said.

"Maybe you can. In a little while we'll show you a room that's got all sorts of techno stuff that will get you drooling." Jack sat back and looked at Ross to give him a chance to speak.

"Are there any shipments of money in or out of the bank scheduled?" Ross asked.

"Not for a couple of weeks," Mark answered. "Maybe you're early?"

"Maybe we're not," Jack said.

"Right, maybe you're not."

"And the Fed Wire is secure?" Ross asked.

"One, it's secure," Granowski said.

"Nothing's secure," Squeaky said.

Mark looked at Squeaky. "It's not," she said.

"It's secure." Granowski looked back at Ross and continued. "Lots of monitoring, redundancy, and security controls."

"So you know when you've been robbed."

"Let him finish, Squeaky," Ross said.

"And two, it's not even operating right now. We're down for the holiday. We come back online at one o'clock."

"Well, then you're secure until one o'clock."

Granowski looked at Squeaky and then at Jack. "We've never been robbed."

"What time is it now?" Jack asked, wiping his hands over his face.

Jerome walked back into the room and handed Squeaky a plastic bottle of Coke. "Eleven o'clock."

"Squeaky said it. We're secure at least until one o'clock."

Jack looked around the room. "If he's after the Fed. Let's split into groups and figure out what's up."

Ross brought a Styrofoam cup of coffee to Jack and set it on the table. "How many times do we need to look through these plans?"

The blueprints were turned to the page depicting the drawings for the vault. Jack supported his head with both hands, his elbows resting on the table. "Nobody's breaking in here. Look at this. The vault's what, thirty or more feet underground and the concrete walls are at least two feet thick, filled with steel bars."

"Jack, look." Ross pointed to the cup of coffee sitting on the table in front of them. Small circles radiated out from the center as if something had been dropped in the center of the cup.

"Something's vibrating." Jack picked up the cup and took a drink. "They have all kind of big equipment in here to count the money. It could be that." He set the cup back down and put his palms flat on the table to see if he could feel anything.

Alarms started blaring and strobe lights in the ceiling blinked. Jack stood up, put his hands over his ears, and thought, not again.

Granowski stuck his head in the door. "Stay here, don't go anywhere!" he yelled over the alarms.

Jack leaned towards Ross until his mouth was near Ross' ear. "Or it could be something else. Let's go see what's going on." He looked at Sure Thing and yelled, "you two get to the control room and see what's going on there!"

Emergency lights were blinking in the hallway. The alarm

continued to sound. It grew fainter as Ross and Jack walked down a hallway, away from a speaker, only to grow loud again when they rounded a corner to face a different alarm blaring from the ceiling. Men and women hustled through the halls. Jack and Ross went with the flow, following the people who had donned helmets and protective vests, the people exuding a strange calmness who seemed to have a destination in mind.

They followed the jump-suited group of six dressed in black down the narrow, fluorescent-lit stairwell one flight and out into another hallway. The hallway was quiet except for the murmur of voices as twelve uniformed, heavily armed Federal Reserve guards stood in a group.

"OK, listen up." Granowski stood on a chair at the end of the hall. Jack waved from the back of the group. When Granowski saw him, he squeezed his eyes shut before he continued. "There's been an explosion underground in quadrant E4. We don't know what it was, but it wasn't fireworks. This was big. It's not a drill. The vault's secure, but we need to find out what this was." Mark pointed at the group on his left. "Team one, you're going underground from down here." The group of four nodded as one. "Team two, get outside and come in underground from the east side." Mark looked to his right. "Team three, you're above ground patrolling the grounds." He pointed to the back of the groups. "Back there we have two visitors from the FBI. Don't shoot them unless I tell you to." He paused one beat, then another. "Go."

The teams dispersed as ordered. "Agents Miller and Fruen," Granowski yelled out. "Please wait."

Jack spoke out of the side of his mouth as they waited for Granowski to make his way back to them. "Looks serious to me, Junior."

"What do you think is going on in our office?" Ross asked.

"We're probably the only ones with the FBI that know anything is going on." Jack turned to Ross. "Let's listen more than we talk and see what we can learn."

Granowski approached them and walked on past. "Didn't I ask you to stay put?" He didn't wait for an answer. "Follow me, gentlemen."

49

Granowski stopped in front of a plain, steel door. The room was simply labeled with a number next to the doorframe. He held a plastic key card in front of a sensor; there was a soft, short beep and he entered a number in the keypad on the wall left of the door.

"Double security?" Jack asked.

"You get five seconds to enter your number once you've scanned your card." Granowski pushed on the door. "Follow me."

Jack and Ross followed him into the room.

Faint lighting lit work areas where it was needed. There were groups of people in twos and threes focused on the task at hand. Nobody looked up when they entered. Sure Thing and Squeaky were already working with people in the room.

Granowski led Jack and Ross over to a bank of monitors. "We'll be able to monitor the teams and what's going on from here. The teams will be in place shortly." He pointed up at the monitors to the left that showed video feeds from outside of the building. "The police are blocking off the streets around the Fed. Nobody will be driving past until we're clear about what's going on." They could see the flashing lights from the patrol cars and the absence of traffic on Hennepin Avenue.

"What do you think happened?" Jack asked.

"There was some sort of underground explosion. It was big."

"We felt something," Jack said.

Granowski nodded. "Our sensors picked it up immediately and set off our alarms. There are a series of old tunnels under the city and sometimes the tunnel rats set off our alarms."

"Rats?" Jack asked.

"Well, they're not rats, but people that like to explore underground. They're a little..."

"Different?" Ross finished for him.

"I was going to say friggin' weird or crazy, but different will cover it." Granowski sat at a workstation, scanned the monitors, and started checking in with the teams on the radio. "Team three, report." He pointed on the screen to show Jack and Ross where team three was.

A voice filled the room from speakers around the area. "Team three leader. Nothing unusual to report."

"Team two?"

"Team two leader. We've entered the tunnels. There's definitely been a disturbance. There's a lot of dust in the air. Our lights can't penetrate very far. We're proceeding slowly ahead."

Jack noticed Granowski tense up and focus on the monitors. "Ten-four, team two. Slowly but surely ahead. Stay in contact."

"How can you talk to the teams underground?" Ross

asked. "I wouldn't think their radios would work through the rock."

"They run a hard line back to a transmitter station they leave behind by the entrance," Granowski answered without looking back. "Team three. Report."

"Definitely evidence of a detonation. We can smell it in the air. We're going on respirators and moving in deeper."

"Now what?" Jack asked.

Granowski stayed glued to the monitors. He was leaning forward with both elbows on the surface. Jack watched as his eyes moved across the monitor bank in front of him. Granowski held a pen in his right hand and fiddled with it; he stuck the end in his mouth, pulled it back out, and scribbled something on the pad in front of him. He used his thumb to click the plunger on the pen like Morse code. "Now we wait." He put the end of the pen in his mouth, and then spit it out. "I wish I had a friggin' cigarette."

THE EXPLOSION PUSHED air through the tunnel, followed by a muffled roar. The Governor crouched down and leaned against the wall as he waited for the pressure from the blast to move past. It was right on schedule. Once the main blast dissipated, he got up and hustled ahead through the dust-filled air. He held his right hand out and kept in contact with the wall. His headlamp reflected off of the particles flowing on the air waves through the tunnel, filling the shaft with a glow and making it impossible to see ahead. He had to make it to where the controller was set up to carry out the rest of his plan.

The Governor had a smile on his face and felt like a giddy kid on Christmas morning. He thought about the money that would become his in just a short time. The air cleared and he checked his bearings. A few more tunnels to work his way through and he'd be ready for the real treasure he was after.

JACK LOOKED at his watch and paced around the room. It had only been five minutes since the last team checked in, but it seemed like hours. "Ross, we have to do something."

"They're doing it, Jack. There are two teams down underground and they'll have news for us soon."

"I can't wait."

"You're worse than your kids." Ross grabbed a chair and wheeled it over to Jack. "Sit down and relax. We'll know as soon as they know something."

"You sit, Junior. I have to move." Jack walked across the room and watched the monitors, standing behind Granowski. "It's still raining out?"

Granowski answered without looking back. "It's raining." He tapped his pen on the desktop. "The good thing is that the weather is keeping people away. There's hardly anybody out there."

"No media trucks yet?" Jack asked.

"Not yet, but if they show up they'll have to stay back. We'll put out a story about a missing puppy in the sewer or something." Granowski turned and winked at Jack.

Jack continued to stare at the monitors. The roads were shiny from the reflection of the streetlights and the lights from the buildings reflected off of the wet surface. A monitor above broadcasted the local news. Everything seemed normal there, with the focus on the weather and the impact to Fourth of July celebrations. Jack drummed his fingers on the work surface and asked without turning from the multiple views laid out before him, "Is there a schedule for the teams to check in or do we just wait?"

"We're on ten minute intervals unless something of interest comes up sooner. The teams are working in close quarters so they can communicate without radios, but they'll check in."

Jack pushed back from the console. "How much longer?"

"Three minutes."

"Three minutes, three days, it's forever sitting here waiting." Jack started walking towards the door.

"Jack," Ross started after him. "Jack, where are you going?"

"I can't wait around in here, Junior." Jack grabbed the handle and pulled the door open.

Jack stood in the tiled hallway and looked left, and then right, trying to remember which direction he came from, or which way looked like it would get him outside. He was going crazy sitting in the room not knowing what was going on underground. He needed to get closer to the action.

The door hissed behind him as it slowly closed, pulled shut by the piston designed to keep it shut. The right looked familiar. Jack turned to head down the hallway. "Team two to base," he heard from inside the room, causing him to stop and lean back into the doorway. The closing door bumped into his shoulder as he held it open a few inches.

"Base here," Granowski answered.

Jack stayed still and listened to Granowski and the team.

"We need an ambulance where we came in. We've got two bodies and one survivor."

"Get the survivor out. Leave the bodies until you've assessed and secured the scene. I want to know what happened down there."

"I need to get Jack," Ross said to Granowski.

Jack pushed the door open. "I'm here, Junior. Let's go."

The sky was black with water pouring from it, splashing as it hit the ground already saturated with pooled water. "It's still raining."

"Thanks for the update, Junior."

Jack and Ross ran across the grass and down the hill to where the team would be coming out of the ground. Ross, with one arm in a sling, wobbled as he ran. Jack slipped twice on the wet, grassy slope. The first time he saved himself. The second time he fell on his butt with a splash.

"You all right?" Ross asked.

Jack rolled over in the soaked turf and pushed himself up. "I'm OK. Let's get down there and see what this guy has to say."

They made it to the entrance cut into the side of the hill and stood by the black, wrought iron gate that hung open on its hinges. One of the Federal Reserve's incident team stood inside the opening out of the weather. He swung his assault rifle up when he saw Jack and Ross. "Halt!"

Jack put his hands up, palms facing the guard. "Hold it, buddy. We're with the FBI."

The guard kept his weapon pointed at Jack while he looked him up and down. Jack could see a look of doubt on the guard's face as he took in Jack's shorts and polo shirt.

"Listen. Granowski knows we're here. Didn't he tell you we were coming? We wanted to see the survivor the team is bringing out." The guard relaxed a little at the mention of Granowski and the tip of the gun dropped a little lower and to the left so it wasn't pointed directly at Jack.

"ID?" the guard asked.

Jack slowly reached into his pocket and pulled out his credential. He held on to one side and let it flip open to reveal his ID and FBI shield.

The guard swung the weapon back and away from Jack and Ross. "Sorry, I'm a little jumpy."

"You have every reason to be," Ross replied, speaking for the first time since they had seen the guard.

"Any news on the survivor or how long it will be until they get him out?" Jack asked.

"Sounds like he's mobile. His hearing's shot from the explosion." The guard put his hand to the side of his head and adjusted his earpiece. "They should be out in about ten minutes."

Jack looked at Ross. "Guess we didn't need to hurry down here."

The rain continued to fall on Jack and Ross as they stood outside the entrance. Water dripped off of their noses and chins. Their wet hair stuck to their heads and blades of grass clung to Jack's legs from his fall.

"Can we come in out of the rain?" Ross asked.

The guard stepped over a half step and made room for Jack and Ross to enter. "Sure, just be careful of the wires and equipment." He motioned to the box and black cables that ran along the ground into the tunnel to maintain contact with the teams inside.

"Thanks. We're drenched." Ross stepped forward and squeezed past the guard.

Jack stood in the rain, not moving inside to the protection from the weather.

"Come on in, Jack. It's not raining in here."

Jack stepped forward enough to get a little protection and turned around to look back outside the cave. "I'm fine here. It'll be crowded in there and they'll be bringing the prisoner out soon."

Ross tried again. "Come on, Jack. He said it would be ten minutes. No reason to keep getting wet."

"I'm fine, Junior," Jack replied back over his shoulder.

"Jack, you claustrophobic?"

Jack didn't reply.

"I'm fine where I'm at, Junior." Jack turned and looked into the cave. "We didn't introduce ourselves," he said to the guard. "I'm Jack and he's Ross. Agents Miller and Fruen."

"I'm Alex," the guard answered with a nod of his head. He turned back towards Ross. "Officer Butler." Then he returned his gaze to Jack and whispered, "I don't like the tunnels either. That's why I'm guarding the entrance."

Lightning flashed across the sky, followed almost immediately by claps of thunder. Jack jumped and looked back into the cave. The rain refreshed its intensity, pouring out of the sky, splashing on the saturated grass. Alex took a half step back into the cave to get out of the rain, but kept facing outside.

"Jack, come on!" Ross yelled from inside the entrance. His voice was muffled, echoing off of the concrete walls, and was almost drowned out by the rain splashing on the ground. "Get in here before you get hit by lightning."

"Alex, how much longer?" Jack asked, ignoring Ross.

"They'll be out soon."

50

J ack walked down the slope towards the river. If he was going to get wet, he wanted to move around. He couldn't just stand and wait. When he reached River Road, he turned around and looked back up the hill at the Federal Reserve. What the hell was going on? The Governor had been robbing banks and killing people. There was an explosion in the tunnels under the Federal Reserve and he was standing here in the rain hoping he wouldn't be hit by lightning. He looked across the river, barely able to see the other side through the sheets of rain. Nobody could be watching him in this weather from over there. They had to be closer. He looked back up at Alex. Somebody on the inside?

Alex stepped out of the tunnel and waved. "They're coming. They'll be here any minute."

Jack waved back and started up the hill.

The team put the stretcher down inside the tunnel out of the rain. "Call it in, Alex," the team lead commanded. "We're all back. We found two dead and one survivor who needs attention."

"Can he talk?" Jack yelled in from the entrance. "Do we know what happened?"

The lead looked at Jack and then at Ross. "You're with the FBI?"

Ross nodded.

"These three had some sophisticated digging equipment. They knew what they were doing."

"They hit a gas main or something?" Ross asked.

"No, somebody else detonated the explosion. It looks like they wanted to collapse the tunnel and kill or trap these guys underground."

"A diversion," Jack said.

"Maybe." The team lead looked down at the man lying on the stretcher. "This guy's going to make it. Hasn't said a word once he found out the other guys were dead."

The man looked up at them from the stretcher, his unfocused eyes darting back and forth between them as they spoke. The whites of his eyes floated across his face black with dirt.

"They knew how to dig, but I don't know how smart they were. They were digging a long ways from the vault."

"We were so close," the man said, struggling to sit up. "Thirty more minutes and we would've been at the door into the vault."

Jack took another step into the tunnel. "Did you say a door into the vault?" He glanced at the team lead who shook his head.

"Sure. I'll tell you who's not smart." The man patted the thigh pocket of his cargo pants. "Where's my drawing?"

The lead held out a folded piece of paper. "You mean this?"

The man grabbed it from his hand. "Who's the dummy?" He unfolded the paper and held it out so he and the others could see it. "Shine a light down here." He moved the paper around until the beam from a flashlight illuminated the paper. "Who'd put a door in a vault you can get to from the outside?" Then he laid his head back down, exhausted.

Jack took another half of a step into the tunnel. "Can I see that?"

The team lead handed Jack the piece of paper. Alex handed him a flashlight. After looking it over, Jack looked at Ross and then the team lead. "Let's go. Bring him along. I need to compare this to something else. He might not be so smart, but somebody is."

Jack led Ross and the team carrying the stretcher back into the Federal Reserve building, where their wet shoes and boots squeaked on the tile floor. They paraded into the cafeteria where Jack and Ross had left the drawings they had recovered from the Governor's condo. "Put him down there next to the table," Jack directed the two guards carrying the stretcher.

"Junior, come here." Jack leaned over the drawings on the table and spread flat the sheet that the man had shown them. "Look at this." He pointed to the sheet and then the blue line drawings of the Federal Reserve that Ross had carried through the rain. "What do you see?"

"His drawing is the same as ours. Links them to the Governor."

"Come on, Junior. What else?"

Ross looked back and forth between the drawings and sat back. "There's some kind of door or hatch in the corner, underground. It's not in the originals." He looked at Granowski who had joined them. "There's no hatch in the vault, is there?"

"No," Granowski laughed and shook his head.

Ross walked over to the prisoner still lying on the stretcher and squatted down next to him.

"Did you hear that, buddy? There's no hatch underground through the vault. Who's the dummy?"

The man just stared at Ross and then closed his eyes.

"Come on, man. Talk to us. Somebody took you guys for fools and then tried to kill you. He had you go to all that work for what?"

The man opened his eyes. "No hatch?"

Ross looked into the man's eyes and shook his head.

"Can I sit up? Maybe have a Coke and a smoke?"

They got the man situated at the table with a plastic bottle of Coke, an empty coffee cup for ashes, and a pack of cigarettes. He guzzled half of the bottle of soda, burped, tapped a cigarette out of the pack, put it to his lips, and asked for a light. After inhaling heavily and blowing a cloud of smoke towards the ceiling, he leaned forward on the table and spoke. "That bastard. There's no hatch?" He looked at Ross.

"One way in. And it's from inside the building. Look here." Ross took his turn pointing out the differences between the drawings. "Here's your drawing, given to you by your boss? And these drawings are the original engineering drawings we got from his condo today. Yours were modified to show the hatch you thought you were digging to. And when you got close, he tried to kill you. All the Federal Reserve guards would have found were the dead bodies of some idiots trying to dig their way into the vault."

The man stared at the drawings and shook his head. "Am I the only one that survived?"

"How many were down there? The team found you and two bodies."

The man closed his eyes. Tears slowly formed at the edges and dribbled down his cheeks. He was trembling. Ross started to reach out for the man. Jack grabbed his arm and shook his head. "Wait," he mouthed.

The man inhaled deeply and blew out a long breath through pursed lips. Then he opened his eyes. He looked at Ross. "They're both dead?"

Ross nodded.

"Shit. One was my brother." The man leaned forward and looked down at the table, his shoulders slumped. "What do you want to know?"

Twenty minutes later, they knew his name, the names of the deceased, and most of the plan as far as he was aware. It had been an elaborate scheme that was surprisingly successful at penetrating the ground beneath the city, working its way towards the Federal Reserve vault. Up until the explosion.

"Your boss was down there shortly before the explosion?" Ross asked. Jack and Granowski leaned forward to listen.

"He came down to check our progress. Congratulated us and said we had until one o'clock to make it to the vault. Then he left."

"Where did he go?"

"I don't know. He left."

"How did you get in and out of the tunnels?"

"We had three different routes. Each was a hike. An hour or so."

Jack stood up. "He might still be down there." He ripped a page out of the set of drawings, flipped it over, and sketched a crude overhead view of the area showing the Mississippi River, the bridge, and the Federal Reserve building. He held out his pen. "Show us where the entrances are that you used."

The man sketched them in outside of the boundaries Jack had drawn and described where each one was.

"Can you get some of your team to check these out?" Jack asked Granowski.

"We'll get them covered, plus some of the others we know about."

"What others?"

"These are more out of the way, but there are lots of ways down into the sewers. Some that are farther away. There are some that are closer. Especially the sewer manholes in the streets."

"Junior, get somebody from the Minneapolis sewer department that knows what's down here and tell them we might need some equipment for going down there."

Ross started dialing the phone. "How about some maps?"

"Good thinking, Junior. I knew I brought you along for something." Jack flashed Ross a quick smile and then returned to his conversation with Granowski.

Jack tried to focus the group while they waited for the sewer crew and tried to decide what to do next. "Come on, guys." He looked at Granowski. "The Governor created this whole thing to distract you from something else. The Fed is still the target. He staged the attempt on the vault, created an explosion, expected everyone to be killed." Jack looked over the drawings on the table. "If it's not the vault, what is it?"

Granowski had a worried look on his face. "Could he be hitting something somewhere else after bringing the focus here?

"Good question, but I doubt it. We can work that angle while we continue looking here." Jack looked at Ross. "Why don't you have a couple of guys in the office work that one?" Ross started to leave. "Wait a second, Junior."

Jack looked back at Granowski. "If it's not the vault, any plans to move money?"

"No trucks are scheduled for another day."

"Anything other than money?"

"Check clearing, funds transfer, it's all money," Granowski said. "It's what we do."

"And you've never been robbed?"

"Never."

"What happens if you are?"

"The shit hits the fan." Granowski looked worried. "It would have a world-wide impact. Confidence in our money system could plummet. Banks wouldn't know what to do. We'd stop moving money for a while until things got sorted out. That would cause a shortage in areas."

"No trucks scheduled to move anything, but you'll wire transfer?" Jack asked.

"That's how most of the money is moved today. Lots of security, passwords, tokens, special secured computer network."

"Is the network up now?"

"It was down for the holiday." Granowski looked at the clock on the wall. "Like I said, it will be back up and running at one o'clock."

"That's what he's after," Jack said.

"Impossible. I told you about all of the security. It's the safest, most monitored network in the world."

"Can you delay restarting it?"

"Yes, if we really need to, but they aren't breaking in there."

"Maybe they don't need to." Jack stood up. "Junior, now go make the call. Have a couple of people at the office work the angle that something away from here is the target. Get Sure Thing, Squeaky, and anybody else he needs down here to help with the computer network stuff."

51

The round circle of light from the headlamp cut through the darkness and lit up the black plastic bag that was hanging from the large conduit that ran through the tunnel. The Governor removed the leather gloves and tucked them in his pocket before grabbing the dust-covered bag.

They had been planning this for over a year and placed the controller here almost six months ago in preparation for this moment. The Governor wasn't even sure that the equipment was still in place. He had kept himself from checking on it until a month ago. He couldn't believe he was standing in front of it now ready to end the wait. He tore open the bag and carefully removed the controller. Made up of a small computer screen with a thicker, plastic shell behind it, everything appeared intact. He pulled a small, flexible computer keyboard from his pocket, unrolled it, plugged it into the port on the side, and said a small prayer. Then he flipped a switch and watched the screen come to life. He was ready to make himself rich.

~

THEY PULLED another table over next to the one that had the Federal Reserve blueprints laid out on it. Two men wearing stained overalls and worn leather work boots stood among the group, looking out of place among the clean tile floors and cafeteria tables and chairs.

"I'm Jack, Special Agent Miller." Jack stuck out his hand and looked into the eyes of the man closer to him, the man with his hands in his pockets. "With the FBI," he finished, grabbing the wide, strong hand of the man and shaking it. The hand felt rough and calloused. Jack glanced down and saw that splotches of dirt and rust colored the skin on the knuckles. The fingernails were uneven and dirty underneath and around the cuticles. The first two fingers had tobacco stains mixed in among the dirt and rust. "The other two here are Special Agent Fruen and Officer Granowski with the Federal Reserve."

The man finished the handshake and put his hand back in his pocket. He was in his fifties, with a shaved head and a short, grey goatee. He had a cigarette tucked behind his right ear. "I'm Mike. This here's Jimmy." He tipped his head back at his partner standing behind him. "No titles, just Mike and Jimmy."

Jimmy was mid-twenties, a little over six feet tall, and lean. He smiled and squinted his blue eyes quickly at Mike's comment. He had a faded Minnesota Wild baseball hat on his head. It looked like it had fallen in the sewer more than once. He stood behind Mike and held rolls of yellowed paper in his arms.

"What's going on?" Mike asked.

"Those are maps of the sewers?" Jack asked in response.

Jimmy nodded.

"Put them on this table and we'll tell you what we need."

They stood around the table looking down at the maps of the sewers that Mike and Jimmy had brought. The corners of the paper were held down with salt and pepper shakers to keep the map from curling closed. "This one covers most of the area around here on this side of the river," Mike said.

"So we found them somewhere around here." Jack pointed to a spot on the map where the three diggers had been working their way towards the vault when the explosion happened. "It wasn't a sewer, but more of a tunnel. Those aren't on the maps?"

Mike placed his palms down on the maps and leaned in with his unlit cigarette held in his right hand between his pointer and middle fingers. "No, but we've got notes or know about most of the tunnels under the city here. The sewers and tunnels are all tied together one way or another." He flipped his thumb at his partner. "Jimmy is the one that knows what it's like down there. I used to go down, but now I'm senior so I stay up and operate the truck and equipment and Jimmy goes down for inspections."

"If a guy was down there and knew his way around, where could he come out?" Jack asked.

"And he doesn't want to be noticed," Ross added.

Mike leaned over the drawings. He put the cigarette between his lips and put on a pair of reading glasses. "I've got a couple of ideas."

Jimmy spun the baseball hat around backwards on his head. "Here, here," he stabbed at the map. "Maybe here."

"Fuck, Jimmy." Mike looked at Jimmy with a look of frustration. Then he looked at Jack. "Pardon my French. I don't know what Jimmy's thinking." He stabbed the cigarette at the paper. "He started here. He could go three ways from there."

"He'd go one of two ways," Jimmy interrupted.

"Like I was saying, he could go three ways."

"But he wouldn't head towards downtown, would he?"

Mike inhaled deeply. "Jimmy, just shut up. We'll work through this."

"You just need a smoke."

Mike looked at Jack. "He's young."

Jack nodded towards Ross. "I know how it goes. Do you want a smoke while we talk through this?"

Granowski interjected. "He can't smoke in here."

"Just one," Jack answered.

"Everybody smokes now?"

"Light 'er up, Mike," Jack said while he looked at Granowski. Then he leaned back over the map. "We need to hurry, guys. If the man we're after is still down there, where should we look? Give me your three best guesses on his route and where he could get to in, what?" Jack looked at his watch. "Ninety minutes."

Mike inhaled deeply and blew the smoke towards the ceiling. "OK, I'm thinking here by the Stone Arch Bridge," his stubby finger jabbed at the map, "or north of the train bridge here, there's a sewer that empties into the river."

"That's it?" Jack asked.

"Where else do you think?" Mike asked, looking at Jimmy.

"Those two are the easiest, most direct paths." Jimmy put his dirty finger on the map at the point they'd found the tunnelers. "If they said he went this way, he came to here." He traced the path on the map. "From here he could go three ways to start with and then depending on which way he went it branches out multiple ways from there. Your guess would be as good as mine."

"So it sounds like we need to start there," Jack said.

"Maybe if we get down there we can tell which way he went," Ross said.

"Junior, you're in no shape to go down there with one arm in a sling."

"Who's going? You?" Ross asked.

"There's nobody else," Jack said.

52

"Here, put these on." Jimmy stood at the back of the panel truck and set a pair of faded, blue coveralls on the bumper along with a pair of knee-high, green rubber boots and a yellow hard hat with a light attached to the front. Everything was filthy.

The rain was still coming down, but not as hard. Mike was setting up a barricade around the open manhole. His raincoat was wet and shiny. Jack sat on the bumper of the truck and pulled the coveralls on. He stood up, pulled the bottoms up past his waist, and struggled to get one arm in, then the other. He pulled the zipper up to his chin and swung his arms around to get the coveralls to sit right on his frame. They fit, but they smelled; a combination of sweat, long-wet cloth, and whatever was in the sewer.

"You'll get used to the smell," Jimmy said. "They look like they fit. The main thing is to keep you dry and warm. It's damp down there and always cool. The boots are the most important part. They'll keep your feet dry, as long as you don't fall down."

Jack pulled the boots on and fastened the chin strap for the hard hat. The rain drops echoed off of the shell like rim shots on a drum. He sat on the bumper and waited for Jimmy and tried not to think about what they were going to do. He told himself that he could do it. He had to do it. The Governor had to still be down below ground and they were going to find him. If they could find a clue at the tee that Jimmy described, they would catch him. He was trying not to think about going in the sewer, but that wasn't working.

"You don't look so good," Jimmy said.

Jack just peered up at him.

"There's nothing to be nervous about. It's actually kind of neat. There's all sorts of history down there and if we go outside of the sewers into some of the caves there's flow-stone and stuff. It's pretty."

Jack stood up and faced Jimmy. "I'll be all right. One thing I'm worried about is you." Jack tugged at the seam on the shoulder of the coveralls to adjust them a bit. "I don't want to put you in any danger. But this guy we're after? I have to catch him and he's dangerous. And I can't go down there alone. I don't know my way around."

"Hey, you're not forcing me to go down there. I know my way around better than anybody. Once we get down there he won't be able to hear us and if we go with low lights he shouldn't see us coming either."

Hearing "low lights," Jack's chest tightened and his throat constricted, making it hard to breathe. He closed his eyes and tried to force a deep breath into his lungs. He got a small amount of air in. He tilted his head back and looked at the sky in attempt to open his airway further. He still couldn't breathe.

"Hey, you OK?"

Jack looked at Jimmy, almost panting to get a small

amount of air in and out of his lungs.

"Here, sit down and try to relax." Jimmy lightly grabbed Jack's upper arm and guided him back a couple of steps to the bumper of the truck. "You need to relax."

Jack leaned forward and rested his elbows on his knees. He focused on a spot on the ground between his feet and slowed his breathing. He felt his chest start to relax and he worked on taking larger breaths.

"You sure you want to do this?" Jimmy asked.

"I have to get this guy." Jack took another deep breath. "I'll be OK in a minute. Then we have to go."

"All right. Don't hyperventilate. Just sit here and relax. Long, deep breaths." Jimmy climbed into the truck. "We'll give her a shot in a second!" he called from inside the truck.

Jack sat on the bumper and closed his eyes. His chest was still tight, like a belt cinched around it keeping him from breathing. He concentrated on taking shallower breaths and tried to slow his breathing. He cupped his hands over his mouth, remembering that people who were hyperventilating sometimes breathed into a paper sack.

Jimmy was banging around in the truck. Above the sound of the rain hammering the top of the truck, it sounded like Jimmy was opening drawers, poking around through tools. Jack caught movement out of the corner of his eye and tensed. His right hand instinctively reached for his gun, which was at his waist under the coveralls.

One of the Federal Reserve guards dressed in black, a hood protecting his head from the rain, and a short machine gun slung across his shoulder and hanging below his chest, approached Jack. "Are you Agent Miller?"

"Yeah," Jack answered without getting up, working at slowing his heart again.

"Granowski sent me over." He handed Jack a couple of

bundles. "The other agent, the guy with his arm in a sling, thought you needed these."

"Thanks. No other developments?"

"I haven't heard anything," the guard answered and walked away through the rain.

Jack looked at Mike standing at the manhole smoking a cigarette in the rain. The guy was used to waiting; Jack wasn't. He turned around and yelled over his shoulder. "Jimmy, let's go!"

Two nylon belts landed on the ground and Jimmy jumped out of the truck. "So, you're ready to go through with this?"

"Yeah," was all Jack said.

Jimmy held out a closed right fist and a bottle of water in his left hand. "Take this?"

"What is it?"

"Something to help you relax, take the edge off. I can't afford to have you freak out down there."

Jack just looked at him.

"It's not illegal."

"What is it?" Jack asked.

"It's Xanax. As long as you aren't pregnant, plan to become pregnant, you'll be fine. It'll calm you down."

Jack laughed and held out his left hand, palm up.

"Take one now and save one for later, just in case." Jimmy dropped the pills into his hand and handed him the bottle of water. He waited for Jack to take the one, then he handed him one of the nylon belts. "Now put this on. The tag goes in back."

Jack handed Jimmy one of the Kevlar vests the guard had brought him. "And this is for you."

"Is this what I think it is?" Jimmy asked.

"It is if you think it's a bullet-proof vest. I told you, this guy's dangerous."

53

Rain splashed by the round, black hole. The drops that fell over it continued to fall down it into the ground. Jack leaned over and looked down into the manhole. Raindrops reflected light from his headlamp and looked like streaks of light zooming down into the darkness below. It gave him a slight case of vertigo and he leaned back and focused on the truck to regain his feeling of balance. He hoped the pills were going to help.

Mike put a hand on Jack's shoulder. "You'll be fine. Just listen to Jimmy. He'll tell you what to do."

Jack swallowed. His tongue felt swollen and his mouth was dry. "Let's go. I gotta' go catch this guy."

Jimmy took a first step down the ladder into the manhole. "Jack, there's a ladder bolted to the wall. Don't come down until I'm at the bottom." He started climbing down and disappeared into the ground.

Jack looked at Mike. "How deep is it?"

Mike looked down into the hole. "At this point, it's probably thirty feet or so. You're attached to a cable on the way down so you'll be fine." He looked at Jack. "But once you're down in the sewer you never know how far underground you are. It's all the same. You'll be able to walk through most of the sewers. Might have to crouch once in a while. They're old brick sewers that have been there a long time." He peeked back down. "You're up." Mike raised the safety cable and clipped it onto the metal loop at Jack's back.

Jack stepped slowly over to the manhole. He was starting to sweat. He told himself it was from all of the gear he was wearing. He grabbed on to the round, metal barricade and turned around. Then he stepped down into the manhole and tried to feel the metal rung of the ladder with his foot. The rubber boot was a little big and he poked around with his toe to find the rung.

"A couple more inches, Jack. Once you get on the ladder, you'll be fine."

Jack lowered himself a little further and felt his foot rest on the metal bar. He looked at Mike. "I'll be fine," he said to Mike as well as to himself.

"Yep, just listen to Jimmy. Good luck."

Jack put his weight on the foot on the ladder and lifted his other foot off of the ground. He lowered himself until that foot found the next rung. He repeated the process and started climbing down the ladder. He stopped when his head was still above the ground and took a deep breath.

"You'll be fine, Jack."

"Yeah," Jack whispered. He looked around at the ground. Water splashed his face when the rain hit the puddles. The staccato sound continued as the rain hit his hard hat. He looked down into the manhole again. Thirty feet, he could do it. He took a deep breath to try to loosen the tightness that squeezed his chest.

"Jack, Jimmy's waiting." Mike walked over and crouched next to the hole. "You can do this, Jack." The red ember on the end of his cigarette glowed as he sucked in. He flipped the glowing butt down into the darkness and exhaled a cloud of smoke. "You gotta' go down to get this guy."

"Yeah." Jack looked down and then at Mike. "Gotta' go," he said and climbed down into the ground.

The ladder felt cool and rough under his gloves. From the light of his hard hat, Jack could see the dark walls. They were damp with bits of dirt and broken mortar hanging between the bricks. Jack tried to control his breathing, keeping it steady, concentrating on inhaling and exhaling in rhythm to his climb down. Sounds from above disappeared as he went lower into the ground. They were replaced with a muffled sound as well as dripping and the sound of his boots and gloves scraping the rungs with his descent.

"You're doing fine. Almost down!" Jimmy yelled up to him.

Jack stopped and looked down between his body and the ladder. His hands were tired from holding so tightly onto the rungs. Jimmy was standing off to the side in water that was about mid-shin deep. Jack saw his feet were still above Jimmy's head so he figured he had about ten or twelve feet to go. He took a calming breath, flexed the fingers on one hand, then the other, and continued his climb down.

When he reached the bottom, he carefully stepped into the water with one foot and then the other before he let go of the ladder.

"How you doing?" Jimmy asked.

"Fine, I think. Better than I thought I'd be doing. Those pills seemed to help." Jack looked around where they were standing.

"Well, you made it. Now that you're here, the rest should be easy. Just a couple of quick tips and we'll be off." Jimmy unclipped the cable and shined his headlamp at Jack's feet.

"Most of the sewer is like this. It's a storm sewer so it's not too nasty. Watch your step. Put a hand on the wall to steady yourself if you feel like it. We'll head downstream towards the river. There's more water than usual since we've had all of this rain." Jimmy took a step downstream and shined his headlamp into the dark ahead of them. "Everything runs in straight lines down here. We'll go down here about forty yards and then turn left and go upstream into a sewer from the north to the point we were talking about."

"I'm ready. We better try and stay quiet," Jack said. "If anything appears strange or out of place to you, let me know. We need to figure if he was down here, where he went, and if he's still here." Jack tapped his hand to his vest to make sure his gun was still there. "Let's go."

"WHAT DO YOU MEAN, there's a delay?" The Governor stood over the controller. A headset was attached and he was speaking with Vadim over a phone line to coordinate the timing of his entry of codes to reroute the Fedwire transmissions and cover their tracks. The time on his watch showed that that should happen in six minutes.

"We've been monitoring communications and traffic. They haven't said anything about the explosion or an attempt at the vault, but they're communicating that they want to send some test messages and that Fedwire coming back online will be delayed."

"I guess we should have anticipated this might happen," the Governor said.

"It is nothing," Vadim answered. "Just some time. We'll keep monitoring and we'll execute the plan when they come back up. You can wait?"

"I'm fine here. We don't know how long?

"No."

"If I'm not online, I'll check back in every quarter hour, every fifteen minutes of the hour," the Governor said.

"Ten four," Vadim answered.

The Governor shook his head. Ten four? Vadim must have been watching some American TV or movies. He looked at his watch, an hour delay. He thought that after the explosion and the probable discovery of the bodies that the Fed would have believed that the attempt was over and regular operations would resume.

They were just being careful, weren't they? Could they know about him underground? The Governor thought about it. There was no way. That's what he believed, but there was no way to check. His team was dead, all except Vadim, snuggled safe away in some hotel room in downtown Minneapolis. The Governor turned and placed his back against the wall and then slid down into a sitting position on the ground. He might as well get comfortable. He looked at his watch and then turned off his headlamp to conserve the batteries and hide in the dark.

"This is it." Jimmy stopped and Jack took a few more steps and joined him at his side. Their headlamps lit the sewer walls and ceiling. Water, about a foot deep, ran past them as it made its way to the Mississippi River. The walls were approximately eight feet across and the ceiling was eight feet high plus or minus. "You still doing OK?"

"Yeah," was all Jack said. His answer sounded muffled and seemed to disappear down the sewer along with the storm water. Out of the corner of his eye, he saw Jimmy look at him. He turned and met his stare. "I'm fine." Jack turned forward again, and took a deep breath to calm his nerves.

Ahead of them were three openings. Water ran in from two of the others and the forth carried all of the water farther along towards the river. "This is it." Jimmy walked ahead and stood at the junction. "He didn't come up the tunnel we were in, so he's probably either up here," Jimmy pointed at the first tunnel on the left. "Or down this one." He shined his light down the sewer where all of the water was flowing.

"Why not that one?" Jack asked, nodding at the last one, which was straight ahead of him.

"It's short and drains River Road. There's nothing there."

"What should I be looking for?" Jack looked around the tunnel at the walls, the ceiling and the water, anxious to find a sign of where the Governor went.

"Look for something new, out of place. Dirt rubbed off of the walls, a fresh scratch." He shined his light down at the water. "Look to see if there's a fresh disturbance on the bottom. If he walked through here, we should see something."

Jack followed his flashlight beam around the interior and focused on the walls, the area where the walls met the water, and then looked down into the water at his feet. The water was clear. He could see the toes of his boot below the surface. Cigarette butts and plastic straws floated by in the water, the current carrying them away from him and down into the tunnel ahead of them. His focus on finding a clue distracted him from his surroundings. He pulled up the sleeve of his coveralls and looked at his watch. "We've been down here a while. Find anything?"

"Nope."

"Where do you think we should go?"

Jimmy nodded to his left. "This way. Downstream." He adjusted his helmet and the belt around his waist. "More options down this way. Side tunnels, utility tunnels. Let's look around as we go to see if we see anything that might give us a clue. I vote we go this way."

"Well, you're the expert. Lead the way. I'll be right behind you," Jack said.

"Is it always this clear?" Jack asked. The water he was walking through was so clear his headlamp cut through it and illuminated the bottom so he could easily pick out rocks and sand at the bottom.

Jimmy continued to wade through the water ahead of him. "It's usually pretty clear. It's just storm water and we've had so much rain lately that it washed the muck through already. The only stuff you'll see down here is garbage that washed off the streets and down the sewers. Plastic straws, cigarette butts, stuff like that."

"Have you seen anything that makes it look like somebody else has been down here recently?" Jack asked.

"Not yet. But I'm looking."

Jack wondered if they were wasting their time. But if they weren't down here, what would they be doing? They didn't have any other leads to follow.

Ahead, a small circular sewer pipe, about a head high, stuck out of the wall and a stream of water poured out of it into the water in which they were walking. Jimmy ducked under the water, letting it arc over his head. Jack followed him, moving to the left and bending over as he walked under the fountain. He felt the cool spray hit his neck. He told himself it was just rainwater.

They passed another larger sewer and continued walking downstream. "We don't want to check that one out?" Jack asked.

Jimmy stopped and looked back. "Nothing there. It's just a short feeder. Collects run-off from a bunch of shorter sewer lines, like that one we walked under, and feeds it in here."

Jack fell back in line behind Jimmy and they continued on. The pressure on his booted feet changed. Jack looked down and then swung his headlamp to Jimmy's back and looked at his legs. "Jimmy?"

"Yeah," Jimmy called back over his shoulder.

"Is the water getting deeper?"

"Yeah, and a little faster. Can you feel it pushing your feet forward when you walk?"

Jack didn't answer. He looked at the back of Jimmy's legs where the water was now almost up to his knees. With each step he took, the water pushed the free foot ahead.

"Watch your step," Jimmy yelled back. "You don't want to fall here. It's deep enough that it will start to wash you downstream. It can be tough to find footing to stop yourself."

"Thanks for the tip," Jack said only loud enough for himself to hear.

54

Jack looked ahead to see what was in front of them. His light illuminated Jimmy's back and more wet, dirty, brick walls and things hanging from the ceiling. The water pushed harder on his feet, making him take bigger steps than he had before. Farther up the tunnel, he illuminated a ladder running up the left wall leading to a hole about eight feet up.

"What's that?"

Jimmy stopped and Jack bumped into him. "Watch it."

"Sorry. What's that ladder?" Jack shined his light on the wall about fifty feet in front of them.

"It leads up to a tunnel with electrical conduit and stuff like that in it."

"We have to check it out. Electrical, communications, it's a great place for him to be."

Jimmy took a step downstream towards the ladder when a horn sounded from behind them. Jimmy stopped in his tracks and Jack bumped into him again.

"Did you hear something?"

"Quiet," Jimmy said. Two more blasts sounded and

carried down the tunnel. "That's Mike. Get to that ladder. There's a water surge coming."

"What do you mean?" Jack asked.

"Remember the stuff on the ceiling?" Jimmy unclipped one end of the safety rope from the back of Jack's belt. "It probably started raining harder and all that rain made it to the sewer and it's filling up and coming this way towards the river," Jimmy said. "Go get up that ladder. I'll be right behind you."

THE GOVERNOR HEARD A MUFFLED horn echo through the tunnel and walked to the opening above the ladder to investigate. He cocked his head one way and then the other to try to pick up any sounds besides the water passing by below. He heard voices and peeked around the corner. To his right he saw two people in coveralls with hard hats and head-lamps, talking. He ducked back behind the corner and listened. He pulled his gun out of his pocket and held it in his right hand, his back against the wall. To his right he could see the reflections of the headlamps dancing on the walls as the two men continued to walk towards him. The gun felt cold in his hand and he gently rubbed the trigger with his finger as he tried to decide what to do.

How could this be happening now? How many minutes left? He was so close. Were these men looking for him or exploring? He could hear voices now above the sound of the water. They were getting too close. Would they simply walk by? He couldn't take the chance.

The Governor realized he couldn't aim down the tunnel to his right with his right arm. The wall was in the way. He switched the gun to his left hand and turned right to face the wall, standing just inside the opening so he wouldn't expose himself to the men. He strained to hear what they were saying. He saw them point and heard them say something about the ladder. He had to stop them. The wall was a dark, gray blur in front of his face, the only light coming from the men's headlamps. He peeked out around the corner, sighted down the barrel of the gun at the closer of the two men, and pulled the trigger.

JACK STUMBLED AND FELL FORWARD. His outstretched arms punctured the water and his face splashed the surface before his arms hit the bottom of the sewer. His hard hat fell off and floated away. A loud sound filled the tunnel, hurting his ears. The current tugged at his legs, threatening to pull him through the sewer towards the river. He dragged his hands on the bottom over the bricks to slow himself, but his legs swung to the left and started to float past his body. Jack clawed at the bottom, trying to stop, his fingertips just reaching the bottom. His body screamed for a breath as he continued to try to halt his trip down the sewer. He thought of the ladder on the side of the wall. If he hadn't floated past yet, he needed to grab it. He rolled onto his back and ran his left hand over the rough bricks, searching for the ladder or something to grab on to.

ONE MAN FELL. The Governor shifted his aim to the second man, who was standing in the middle of the tunnel, and pulled the trigger again. His target fell back from the force of the shot and splashed into the water. The Governor watched as the body drifted by the ladder and kept watching as one headlamp and then the second disappeared and the tunnel became dark again. He leaned back into the wall to get his bearings in the total darkness. He shivered as much from the cold as from the excitement. The darkness was total. He used his senses to place himself back in the present. His ears rang from the gunshots and the water rushing past. He smelled the water and the mustiness of the sewer. Only his sense of touch was of any use in the dark, dank, noisy tunnel. His hand pushed against the brick wall to help him keep his balance.

He had to get back and check on Vadim's progress. They had minutes until the holiday system maintenance kicked in. It was their only chance to execute their plan.

He shuffled back to the command post, guiding himself by touch along the wall until he found his light and equipment.

JACK SCRAPED his left hand along the wall. There was another bright flash and an explosion above him. His hand bumped into the ladder and he grabbed onto the vertical bar. His arm extended over his head as the water swept his body along. The force of the water threatened to rip him from the ladder. He gritted his teeth and hung on, vowing not to let the water win and carry him through the sewer out to the river. He'd never survive. He raised his other arm over his head and got another grip on the ladder. This relieved some of the stress in his left hand.

Jack struggled to keep his face above the water so he could breathe. Something bumped into him. Jimmy! Jack reflexively reached out and grabbed onto his collar. The force pulling on his one hand gripping the ladder now doubled. "Come on, Jimmy," Jack grunted through gritted teeth as he hung onto the ladder. Jimmy was lifeless, but

Jack wasn't going to let him go. He'd risked his life to bring Jack down here.

The water surge couldn't last much longer, could it? Jack felt his grip on the ladder weakening. He wiggled one finger, then another, to relieve some of the stress, but with the water dragging over both of them, he had to choose, let go of Jimmy or hang on. One finger slipped from the ladder, then another. Two fingers wrapped around the bar. Maybe he and Jimmy could make it together. But, Jack had a family. Jack's hand slipped from the ladder and he grabbed at the wall to find another way to stop them as the water swept them away.

He grabbed onto Jimmy's collar with both hands, determined not to lose him, when he suddenly jerked to a stop. Something yanked at his waist and Jimmy slipped from his grip. Jack stabbed in the dark to find him, but Jimmy was gone. The water pulled at Jack as he hung in place, something pulling at his waist. He twisted his head to get it above the water so he could get a breath. He felt at his waist and found that the rope from his safety belt had snagged on something.

"VADIM, just a second, I can't hear you." The Governor adjusted the headset. "My ears are ringing from gun shots and water's roaring through the sewer." He put his hands on either side of his head and pushed the ear muffs from the headset tightly against his head. "Say again, please."

"We have three minutes," Vadim said. "You are ready and OK?"

"Yeah, I'm ready. The equipment is set and the tunnel appears to be high enough to stay dry."

"You don't need to hear me. When you see the green light, enter the code and hit enter. Be ready."

"Vadim, I'm ready." The Governor looked at his left forearm under the light. He'd written the coded string of letters and numbers in permanent marker on his skin from his wrist to his elbow. He was ready. His ears still rang. He pulled the headset free. Three minutes couldn't go fast enough.

JACK FELT his heels hit the bottom of the sewer. The water surge was past and the tunnel was draining. He saw a light coming from the utility tunnel at the top of the ladder.

He stood up and noticed that his boots were gone. They must've been ripped from his feet by the water. He felt for the gun and found that it was gone. He pulled at the rope secured to his safety belt and found the other end attached to the ladder. Jimmy must've clipped it to the ladder as he drifted by and saved his life.

Jimmy was dead. The Governor had tried to kill Ross and Jack. He'd had enough. Jack grabbed onto the ladder and put one sock-covered foot onto the first rung. His arms were tired. He started to climb. It was time to end this and stop the Governor. Jack peered over the lip into the utility tunnel. Twenty-five feet ahead, the Governor sat on the floor of the tunnel with his hands on a keyboard.

Jack was trying to decide what to do when he heard the sound of the horn echoing through the sewer again. He ducked down so the Governor wouldn't see him and hung onto the ladder. Another surge? Jack felt the air move as it was pushed ahead by the water and he heard the roar approaching. He risked a peek over the edge and saw the

Governor getting up. He felt the water pushing on his legs as he stood on the ladder.

THE GOVERNOR HEARD the horn and the sound of water rushing through the sewer. He had to take a quick look to make sure he was going to stay dry. He grabbed his flashlight, walked towards the end of the tunnel, and pointed the beam upstream where he saw the water churning through the sewer. He looked back at his controller. He'd be OK. The water wasn't getting any higher. Two minutes to go. He took a step back towards his outpost when something grabbed his leg.

JACK USED his legs to push himself off of the ladder into the utility tunnel and grab onto the Governor's leg. He locked an elbow around his ankle and held on. The Governor swung the flashlight and hit Jack in the head. Jack twisted and pulled. The Governor fell on top of him and Jack turned over and twisted again to try and gain the advantage. The Governor hit him again with the flashlight. Jack leaned back and they both fell over the edge into the roiling water.

55

"Hey, Jack. You OK?"

Bright lights shined in his eyes. Jack turned his head and threw up. First, a gush of water and then dry heaves as his body tried to rid itself of the water and grime of the sewers.

"Are you OK, Jack?" Ross asked.

Jack spit and looked around. He was lying on the floor of the sewer, soaking wet. His shoes were missing. Ross and Mike, the sewer crew foreman, knelt by him with lights on their helmets and flashlights in their hands.

"Where's Jimmy?" Mike asked.

Jack struggled to sit up. He looked at Mike, then down the dark length of the sewer. It was just the three of them. "Have any water?" he whispered.

Ross handed him a bottle of water. Jack took a swig, sloshed the water around in his mouth and spit it out.

"Where's Jimmy?" Mike asked again.

Jack took a long drink of water, looked at Mike and then back down the tunnel. "I don't know. I think the Governor shot him." Jack paused and looked back at Mike. "The first water surge got us. Somehow he tied me off on this ladder. Saved my life. But he got swept away."

"How about the Governor?" Ross asked.

"Yeah. He's down there too." Jack nodded in the direction the water flowed. "The second surge took him."

"We have to get you out of here. Can you walk?" Ross asked. He reached down with his good arm and helped Jack stand up.

Jack pointed to the utility tunnel above them. "Can you get up that ladder with one good arm and see what the Governor left behind? He had a keyboard or something. Make sure it isn't on."

"We talked the Fed into staying offline. I'll bring Sure Thing back down here and he can check it out." Ross put his arm around Jack's waist. "We need to get you out of here."

"I can make it, Junior. Just go kind of slow. I don't have any shoes on." Jack lifted his sock-covered foot to show Ross.

"The rain's stopped, so we can go back to where you came in without a worry of any more water surging through," Mike said.

"We need to get a crew down here to look for Jimmy and the Governor. Think you can lead them, Mike?" Jack asked.

"No problem."

"OK, get me out of here. I'm kind of claustrophobic."

THE WINCH PULLED Jack up through the manhole. Ross pulled the cable to move Jack over the pavement so he could stand on solid ground and unclip himself. Jack looked around and took a deep breath. It was dark out. "What time is it?"

"A little after two," Ross answered.

"I missed the fireworks," Jack said.

"Jack!" Julie appeared out of the dark, ran up, and threw her arms around him. Jack winced. "Are you OK?" she asked.

Jack returned the hug and buried his face in her hair. "I'm OK. Just a little beat up. Glad to be out of that hole." He gave her a squeeze to make sure she was real. "Sorry we missed the fireworks."

"There's always next year," she said.

Jack pulled back, looked her in the face and smiled. "I'd like you to meet Special Agent Ross Fruen."

Julie turned, an arm around Jack. "It's nice to meet you, Agent Fruen. If you don't mind, I'll be taking Jack home now to make sure he's OK."

"Yes, ma'am. Nice to meet you too."

Jack took hold of Julie's hand and they started to walk away.

"I'll take care of things here, Jack."

Jack looked back over his shoulder. "You better, Junior. It's your case."

EPILOGUE

A kid ran by. He was maybe fourteen years old. Jack didn't even think about giving chase. Instead, he just yelled, "The tortoise and the hare, kid, the tortoise and the hare!" The man running next to Jack laughed.

Plodding along, Jack looked ahead. Once they ran across the Hennepin Avenue Bridge they'd have one mile left to reach the finish line in the center of downtown. He couldn't believe a week ago he'd been down below these streets chasing the Governor.

Jack looked to his left, the same guy was still there. "Should we go see if we can catch the kid?" The guy nodded and they picked up the pace.

JACK CROSSED the finish line behind a guy wearing a Speedo and a lei. His own costume was his standard dark blue t-shirt with the gold FBI across the chest. They couldn't catch the kid. He grabbed a bottle of ice-cold water and looked for his family among the throngs of people on the sidewalks. He knew about where they would be and finally found them in the crowd in front of the Pantages Theater. The kids were sitting on the curb eating pink and blue shaved ice. Julie and Ross stood behind them on the sidewalk.

"Hey, Dad! Did you win?" Willy asked.

Jack laughed. "Not quite. I didn't even see my time. I finished behind a Hawaiian wearing a lei." He looked at the crowd standing on the sidewalks filling the block on both sides of the street. "Did all of these people come just to watch me run a 10K?"

"Funny Dad." Lynn said. "We're here for the Torchlight Parade."

Jack squeezed in between Ross and Julie and gave Julie a kiss.

"How was the run?" she asked. She handed him a dry shirt to put on.

"It was OK. I'm old and slow. But, it felt good." He took another drink of water and changed shirts. He leaned over to Ross. "Sorry you couldn't do your triathlon. How's the arm?"

Ross flapped and flexed his arm. "It's getting better."

"No body yet?"

"Not yet. I think the Governor's floating his way to The Gulf Of Mexico. Maybe they'll find his dead, bloated body in New Orleans."

"Yeah, maybe. I'll believe it when they've found the body." Jack looked up the street. The parade was finally approaching. "Get ready kids."

A group dressed in red t-shirts with the Target logo on the chest pushed red shopping carts past in a synchronized dance. They stopped in front of the kids and started tossing candy to the crowd. Jack watched his kids reach out and try to grab their share of candy from the street. He looked at Julie, who was smiling. Things were good.

The Shriners came next in their little go-carts driving in circles down the street. Ross punched Jack in the arm. "Shouldn't you be out there in your bureau car?" he asked.

"Funny for a guy with no car," Jack answered. He leaned over to Ross. "So, what's next for you? The SAC give you any options?"

Ross smiled. "He said now was the time to ask. I asked for HRT."

"Hmm, Hostage Rescue Team. So, you're ready to give up small-time bank criminals and go after terrorists? Sounds exciting." Jack stuck out his hand, "Congratulations."

"I figured now's the time to do it. And this case was exciting, bigger then a onetime bank heist. I'm young, in shape, unattached. The SAC said to report to Quantico after Labor Day, so I have about a month to get my shoulder ready. He's giving me the shot, but I need to earn the spot."

"You'll do fine," Jack said. "OK, kids. Time to share some of that loot with Mom, me and Ross." He put his hand down. "Daddy tax time."

The last float of the parade with the Aquatennial royalty passed in front of them. The Commodore, dressed in his whites looking like a boat captain, the Queen of the Lakes and the princesses in their white dresses and tiaras, all waved the parade wave. Willy stood up and saluted. A princess blew him a kiss and he turned his head, scrunched up his shoulders, embarrassed, and sat back down. "I think you have an admirer Willy, or was that kiss for Ross?"

Ross answered, "Wasn't mine."

"Willy has a girlfriend," Lynn teased her brother.

As the final float passed, the people on the sidewalk started to move away from their stations on the curb. Many started heading towards the river. This was the last day of the summer celebration and a large fireworks display marked the end.

"OK, gang." Jack said. "What's say we all wander down to the river and watch the fireworks."

Julie squeezed Jack's hand. "That would be nice since we missed them last week."

The kids stood up. "You joining us, Ross?" Jack asked.

"Wouldn't miss it."

<<<<< >>>>>

THANKS FOR READING

Thank you for reading THE NINTH DISTRICT.

I'd appreciate it you'd write a review. It's a simple way to pay back an author and is important in getting other readers to think about reading it too.

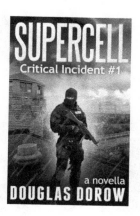

Join the Dorow Thriller Reader list.

> get the spinoff novella SUPERCELL featuring Special Agent Ross Fruen- aka Junior, as the joins the FBI's Hostage Rescue Team

> stay up to date on new releases, exclusive promotions and other info.

FREQUENTLY ASKED READER
QUESTIONS

Q: Are the tunnels below the city real?

A: I haven't been in them, but I've seen pictures on websites from the Urban Explorers who have been down in them and on television stories on the local news. Minneapolis got its start harnessing the power of the Mississippi to transport goods and to use in the grain mills built along it.

Q: Where did the idea for the book come from?

A: I've always been a big reader of fiction; spy & espionage, mysteries, thrillers and suspense. They say to write what you know. I decided to write what I would like to read. I also have a friend who is an FBI agent today and wanted to write a story showing the FBI differently than the bumbling law enforcement branch as they are sometimes portrayed in movies.

I was writing the story after taking a writing class, rewriting parts of it and trying to decide what story I was going to tell. Then I read a story in a local weekly paper about an urban explorer talking about what was underground. He also talked about how they were leery to explore across the river from The Federal Reserve because of heightened security after 9/11. That was all it took. I knew the story I was going to write and it took off from there.

Q: Why do you have the pregnant woman get killed in the first scene?

A: Because I really wanted you to hate the antagonist, from the very beginning.

Q: What does your family think about your writing?

A: My wife doesn't usually read this genre, but she's trying to read it. Sometimes, when she's reading it, she just looks at me and asks "Who are you?"

I really am a nice guy. She can't understand how I can come up with some of the things in the story.

Q: What's next?

A: I've got the sequel started. It shows Jack a few months later, on vacation in the Minnesota lake country with his family. He just wants to relax, fish and have fun. But, he gets pulled into a local problem and the vacation goes out the window.

In addition, I've decided to try my hand at a couple of

novellas focused on Ross, aka Junior, showing him and his FBI Hostage Rescue Team on some adventures.

I have an Action / Adventure series planned as well. More along the lines of James Rollins, but with a domestic bent.

ABOUT THE AUTHOR

Douglas "Doug" Dorow, lives in Minneapolis, Minnesota with his wife, two children and their dogs. The Ninth District is his first book.

If you enjoyed the book, I'd appreciate a review on your favorite ebook site and/or Goodreads.

If you have friends who you think would enjoy the book, but they're not ebook readers, THE NINTH DISTRICT is also available in paper and as an audiobook. And it's in Spanish too!

Sign up for the Dorow Thriller Reader list and be the first to know about new releases, sign-up for book giveaways and other thrilling reader news.

Sign up now and get the spin-off novella SuperCell - Critical Incident #1.

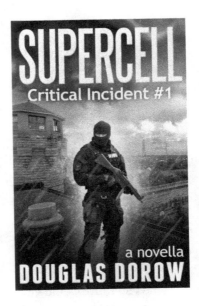

Keep reading for the THRILL of it!

For more info about my writing:
www.douglasdorow.com
doug@douglasdorow.com

ALSO BY DOUGLAS DOROW

The Ninth District - FBI thriller #1

SuperCell - Critical Incident #1 (novella)

www.douglasdorow.com for more info.

DEDICATION

For Debra, Olivia and Elliot. Thanks for waiting and supporting me during this long journey. And for my mom, who taught me how to read.

I am indebted to the members of Writers Quest, my critique group I have been a part of for so long. The various members, my friends, have been instrumental in helping me learn about the writing process through their support, example, and tough reviews. Thank you to all of you.

As a fund raiser for an auction at my kids' school, I donated a kindle and the naming of a character in this book. A big thank you to Mr. Kelly Griffin for the winning bid for this item and supporting the school and naming a character after his good friend, Ross Fruen.

In addition, I solicited authors for books to load onto the kindle for the auction. I was amazed at the response. 26 authors donated 35 books.

Check these authors out:

Ryne Douglas Pearson
Confessions
All For One
The Donzerly Light
Dark and Darker

Lee Goldberg
Dead Man
The Walk

John L. Betcher

A Higher Court: One Man's Search for the Truth of God's
Existence
(Winner of Gold medal eLit Awards)

Melissa Miller
Dark Blooms: Two Crime Fiction shorts
Irreparable Harm

Blake Crouch
Run

Glenn Skinner
The Keya Quests: Three Soulds Destiny

Audrey Mckay
No Weapon (Good News Series)

Debora Geary
Matchmakers 2.0

Scott Nicholson
Flowers
Duncan the Punkin

Heather Wardell
Go Small or go Home
Life, Love and a Polar Bear Tattoo
Planning to Live
Seven Exes Are Eight Too Many
Stir Until Thoroughly Confused

Shawn Hopkins
Progeny

L.K. Ellwood
Saints Preserve Us

C.C. Jackson
Stay

MJ Grothoff
EverWing

J.T. O'Connell
Justice Aside

J.C. Pheleps
Color Me Grey

Steve Glossin
Death Mask

Eric Kobb Miller
Spit Toon's Saloon

Paul Mansfield Keefe
Digger's Bones

Guido Henkel
Demon's Night

Jeff Bennington
Reunion

Autumn Rosen
My Four Fathers & Eleanor